The Widow's Savior

Ian Griffin

Acknowledgements

Book Cover
100Covers

Back Photo
Skylar Fondren

Editing
Kayla Wilkinson

Writing Advisor
Wibke Griffin and Deborah Wooten

Dedication

For those who have lost loved ones in war.

Epigraph

There are times when karma is delivered in its rawest form. On those rare occasions, it is always seem to be the most satisfying.

Contents

Chapter 1 Message Delivered

H enry looks down at the brown bag through his corn-flower-blue eyes. His sweaty hand opens the bag, slightly revealing the liquor bottle. He licks his lips, bringing the liquor to his mouth, and takes a swig. The warm liquor soothes his palette, and a fire roars in his chest as the liquor goes down his throat. A grin of satisfaction emerges on his scruffy face. Henry looks at Will and says in a deep East Texas accent. "Now that will put hair on your chest right there."

Will smirks, revealing that his youthful face is beginning to lose its innocent appearance. He looks at his Uncle Henry and then glances back at the axle. He wipes sweat from his brow with his forearm. The unbearable East Texas humidity weighs down on them as if they are stuck in a sauna.

"Uncle Henry, do you think Paw will get back soon?"

Henry screws the lid back on the bottle and then slides it into the back pocket of his overalls. He looks at the young man and places his arm across his shoulders. "Will, I sure hope so. I miss my brother. Texas is a lot better with Joseph in it, that is for sure."

Henry walks over to the John Deere tractor. His overalls move loosely over his tall and lanky frame. He grabs the grease gun off the ground. "Okay, have you ever used one of these before?"

"No Sir."

"Well, today is a day for learning, I guess. I remember the first time I learned to use a grease gun, your Paw taught me."

A smile comes over Will's face. "Really?"

"Yes Sir. Your Paw was good for those things." Henry smiles. "He also would get me in trouble from time to time."

"Paw? He would get you in trouble?"

"Yep, your Paw is a jokester. To you, he is Paw, but to me, he is a prankster, always crackin' wise on me."

Henry places the grease gun tip on the zerk fitting and waves for Will to come and grab it. Henry pumps it twice, then points. "When you see the grease come out at the joint, it is good. You can stop then."

Will nods his head.

"So, your Paw, Mr. Joseph Wood himself, knew I liked this one girl, Betty. In my eyes, she was the best thing to Rita Hayworth, a boy could find around here. At least, that is what I thought. Your

Paw figured he would set me up with her. When I say set me up with her, that doesn't mean arranging a date or something. Nope, your Paw wouldn't have any fun with that, would he? He knew she didn't like me. So, he told me otherwise and convinced me to go up and kiss her." Henry rolls his eyes, "You know that is just too forward, but when you're thinking about a girl, all common sense goes out the window." He points to his head, leans to Will, and winks. "All those thoughts of a girl cloud your thinking. A man is lost once a girl gets in his head. He is doll dizzy."

Will hangs on to every word.

"So, I go up and kiss her. Needless to say, I got more banged up from her beating me than I did in the war."

Will laughs while holding his stomach.

"And your Paw just laughed like you are doing right now." Henry shakes his head. Then he gazes at Will. "So, a fifteen-year-old boy like yourself, got you one of them dames as a girlfriend?"

With his cornflower-blue eyes gleaming, Will smiles. "I do, Uncle Henry. Her name is Helen Bennett."

Henry steps back with amazement. "Oh, I see. That wouldn't be Bennett from the name of Bennett Town, would it?"

Will nods.

"Be careful around her Paw. He is a ruthless man. He plays chess while everyone else plays checkers if you know what I mean. But that isn't your concern. Is she pretty?"

"She is. She has curly blonde hair above her shoulders and the prettiest brown eyes I have ever seen. She is very pretty."

Henry tries not to chuckle. "Hmm, look here, Romeo. It seems I am looking at someone who is doll dizzy."

Will face turns red.

"Well, there is nothing wrong with a young man being infatuated with a young lady. Your Paw would be proud. You know you told me about your Helen but let me tell you this. You look so much like your Paw when he was younger. You have his wavy blond hair. I can see his blue eyes in you, and you're about the same size as he was at your age. What are you around now?"

"Oh, I am about five foot ten now and tip the scales at 160 pounds. What about you, Uncle Henry? Did you lose weight in the war?"

Henry smirks. "Yep, sure did. I am five foot eleven, but when I went into the army I weighed 190 pounds. I think I am lucky to squeeze out a good 170 now." He points to Will. "But I still can fight with the best of 'em."

"Uncle Henry, was war tough?"

"Oh, that is a fact. It was rough." Henry pulls out a harmonica from his front pocket. The chrome Mississippi saxophone shines brilliantly in his hand. He looks it over for a second. "When I got shot, I thought it was the end of me." Henry blows the dust out of the harmonica. "Didn't realize that would give me a ticket home. Got a few buddies that weren't so lucky." He pulls the bottle from his back pocket, unscrews the lid while holding the harmonica, and takes a swig. His visible Adam's apple gulps as he swallows, and he slowly screws the lid back on and looks at Will.

Will looks on in understanding. "Is that why you drink?"

"You know that is an adult question you got right there, Will." He licks his lips for a moment. "I guess part of me is still over there. The sauce numbs the soul, I do say." Henry places the bottle in his back pocket and then moves the harmonica to his mouth. He closes his eyes and slides the harmonica to one side of his mouth, gracefully belting out the old, familiar tune ♪*Danny Boy*♪. His hands skillfully overlap the harmonica, guiding the soft sounds from the chrome piece. Henry plays the Mississippi saxophone so passionately that the beautiful tunes soothe the ears as Henry's movements mesmerize Will.

Will watches on in amazement.

Henry stops after the first verse, points the harmonica to Will, and speaks with his best Irish accent. "That's for me, lads. Not all made it back home."

Will respectively watches and nods. He looks down for a moment, then back to his uncle. "Uncle Henry, what do you think happens when someone dies in a place like that? Do you think they feel anything anymore?"

Henry takes a deep breath and looks away for a moment. "You know, Will, I truly don't know. I know everyone misses them and wishes they were still around. But after they die, I am not sure what happens to them. I don't think they feel anything, only the ones who loved them feel emptiness or regret. I don't have an answer, Will. Just some guesses, is all. I think that is something each man has to settle for himself."

Will takes it in and ponders for a moment.

"So, where were we on this tractor?"

Will looks at the axle and points. "There is another grease fitting."

Henry nods. "Well, those grease fittings aren't gonna grease themselves, Mr. William Wood."

Henry walks over to a wooden table in the barn, grabs an old rag, and hands it to Will. "Now, just wipe the excess grease that comes out of the joint so it doesn't collect dirt."

Will quickly cleans around the joint, then places the rag into the back pocket of his overalls.

"I got to hand it to your Maw. She has done a great job with your Paw and me gone. Life on a farm is hard work, and some ladies would have let it go to the wayside, but not your Maw."

"Oh, that would never happen with Maw. She would do men's chores out here wearing one of her dresses, that's for sure. I think it also kept her from always thinking of Paw. You know her staying busy and all."

Henry shrivels his face briefly, "Kinda lonely out here on the farm, just you two, isn't it?"

"Yes Sir. Not much for fun. Maw stays busy working as a clerk for Drum's Department Store. She also sews for the dress orders that the ladies in town make with the store." Will smiles. "Paw always said Maw was a classy dame because she was always decked out from Drum's in the nicest dresses."

Henry shakes his head. "That sounds like Joseph."

"I have been going to school. Mom likes to dance to ole records from when Maw and Paw first met. She likes ♪*Cheek to Cheek*♪ playing over and over. I have to reset the arm and crank the hand crank on the record player a lot. Mom says, 'Paw loved that song.' Other than that, the chores keep us both busy. I play football or smear the man with the ball with the fellas."

"So, are you any good at football?"

"I can hold my own," Will says confidently.

"When was the last time someone changed the oil on the tractor?"

"Oh, it has been some time. It was probably right before Paw left. The rationing makes it hard to get certain things."

Henry nods, acknowledging.

"Uncle Henry, it is good having you back home."

"Well, thank you, Will. Trust me, it is good being home." He looks around. "Maybe it is time to head back to the house. We don't need your Maw worrying."

Will takes his rag, wipes the grease gun clean, and places it on the wooden table in the barn. As Henry and Will walk out, Will looks at the sides of the barn as they step away.

"Hmm, maybe in the fall, you and I paint this ole barn. It is way too hot for June to do that. What do you say?"

"Sounds good, Uncle Henry."

They walk through a trail in a thicket of pine trees to the house. The towering pines block out the sun from above, casting a cooling shadow over the trail on a hot summer day in Texas. As they approach the house, Henry notices a Western Union vehicle parked in front of it. He stops in his tracks abruptly. He swallows hard as shivers run down his back. His face loses its color as he turns pale. Will looks at him in bewilderment.

Henry's head tilts as he tries to speak, but the words don't come out. He coughs and speaks in a quivering and respectful voice, "Will, Sir, let's go see what this is."

They walk faster to the house, and a man steps back into the car, cranks it, and drives away. Margaret Wood is on the front porch. A thin, beautiful, red-headed woman in a yellow pinafore dress crying uncontrollably as she clings to a telegram.

Will darts to her. "Maw, Maw!"

Henry falls to his knees and starts crying. "No, Lord. No!"

Margaret looks up and hugs Will. She tries to make out the words as tears pour down her cheeks. "Your Paw, son. He, he didn't make it. He died in France."

"No! Maw, it has to be some mistake," Will says in denial.

She shakes her head and speaks softly, almost angelically, "I wish it were, William."

Henry walks over and hugs Will and Margaret. She hands him the telegram. Henry takes a deep breath and reads it aloud.

THE SECRETARY OF WAR DESIRES ME TO EXPRESS HIS DEEP REGRET THAT YOUR HUSBAND SERGEANT JOSEPH W. WOOD WAS KILLED IN ACTION ON SIX JUNE IN FRANCE.

Margaret clings to Will. "I don't know what to say, William." She looks at Henry. "It is just us from now on."

Henry nods, pulls out his bottle, and unscrews the top. Margaret watches cautiously, grabs the bottle from him, and takes a big drink. The liquor slides down her throat and burns in her lungs. She moves the bottle from her lips and coughs as her face turns to disgust. "Oh, Henry, that is just too rough." She wipes her cheeks and then looks at Will, sobbing. Gently, she places a hand on his cheek, as only a mother can, then speaks softly in a soothing manner. "William, dear." He looks up with tears streaming out of his eyes. "Let it all out. It's okay to do that." He wraps his arms around her waist and unintentionally pushes her back on the porch as he sobs.

Margaret pats the place next to her for Henry as she cries, cradling Will's head in her lap. Henry sits down as he is sobbing. She looks out along the driveway, barely able to see with her tear-filled eyes. "We are going to make it. It just won't be the same or as good."

Henry nods his head and takes another drink from his liquor bottle.

Chapter 2 Pastor Visit

Margaret sluggishly opens her gemstone-green eyes. Clinging to her pillow, she takes a deep breath and methodically exhales. Her eyes fixate on the wall, which has light green wallpaper with thin trees and a few leaves blended into the background.

A painting on the wall with a thick golden frame depicts two children crossing a worn-out, dangerous bridge that crosses a roaring river and waterfall. Behind them is a guardian angel protecting them. Margaret thinks for a moment, *Where was Joseph's guardian angel? I don't understand this.* She slowly sits up and looks at herself, then shakes her head. *I must have fallen asleep in my dress.* As she gets up, she pulls her blanket up neatly to make the bed. She then walks over to the window and opens it for some fresh air.

The morning birds sing in the distance. Margaret leans through the window and watches the birds for a moment. A bluebird flies up on the green railing along the porch and lands on it. Margaret smiles. *It is Joseph's favorite bird. He loved the bluebirds.* The bluebird turns to her, tilts its head as if communicating in some strange way, then flies off. Tears fill her eyes as her chin quivers. She places her hand over her mouth, and sobs.

Shaking her head as she cries, Margaret clinches her fist. *Why?* She takes a deep breath, regains her composure, leaves the bedroom, and walks through the corner of the living room down the small hall to the bathroom. Along the wall is a photo of Joseph and Will standing next to each other, with Will in a baseball uniform. Before entering the bathroom, she peeps into Will's room. He is lying on his bed in the fetal position. Next to his wooden headboard are two small nightstands—one on each side of his bed. The nightstand beside his window has a baseball glove and some wooden jacks. The opposite nightstand has a photo of Joseph in his military uniform with a slingshot lying on the stand.

Henry is lying on the floor asleep at the foot of Will's bed, on a small makeshift pallet. An army-green wool blanket covers him. Margaret takes a deep breath and steps into the bathroom.

Knock! Knock!

Margaret looks down at her watch. It is 7:30 a.m. *Who would be out here at this time?* "Just a second." She looks in the mirror and adjusts her hair. As she approaches the front door, she looks out the living room window to see if she can notice a vehicle.

As the door opens, a couple in their fifties is standing outside. The man is short and stocky, fitting snuggly in a grey suit with a vest. His collared shirt under the suit is light blue, and his dark blue tie matches the neckerchief in his left suit pocket. His grey hair is parted on the side and his eyes are brown. Standing next to him is a woman who is tall and slender, wearing a classy light pink peplum dress with a pink and white checkered tie-neck. Her blonde hair is made up in a Victory Roll, and her eyes are baby blue. With both hands she is holding a casserole dish.

"Mr. and Mrs. Drum, please come in."

Mrs. Drum hands the dish to Mr. Drum and then hugs Margaret. As they embrace. "Margaret, I am truly sorry to hear about Joseph. Now, I will be by this evening to see if you need anything. If you need something, let Robert or me know."

Margaret nods.

The gentleman hands her the casserole dish. "Margaret, Lucy made this for you. Now, you don't worry about coming to work this week. Lucy will step in and help out."

Will steps behind Margaret, she turns and hands him the dish. "Please go set this in the kitchen."

"Yes Ma'am."

Mr. Drum looks around momentarily. "Margaret, I mean this when I say it. If any one in Bennett Town doesn't treat you right, you come and let me know. I will handle it personally. That is a Drum guarantee."

Margaret forces a slight smile. "I bet you say that at least ten times a day."

Mr. Drum smiles, then gets serious. "Margaret, is there anything you need?"

Margaret shakes her head. "No, no, Sir. We are fine."

"How is the boy holding up?" Mr. Drum asks.

"He is in a bit of shock, but that is to be expected," Margaret says. "Henry is taking it tough."

Lucy looks at her. "How are you taking it?"

"I am staying busy."

Lucy nods. "Margaret, you have worked for Robert for almost a decade now. You are like family, so don't forget that." Lucy hugs Margaret again. After they embrace, Lucy steps to the side.

Robert steps forward and hugs Margaret. He pulls out an envelope and hands it to her. "Consider that money that I owe you for your dedication. If you need more, don't hesitate to let me know."

Margaret's eyes water. "Yes, Sir. Thank you."

Robert steps down the porch steps and sticks his hand out to guide Lucy. They walk back to their car, and he opens the door for Lucy, as she gets in. He swiftly walks around to the driver's side. As he cranks the dark maroon car, Margaret walks back into the house.

Margaret steps into the kitchen and notices Will there. She puts her hand on his head and rubs it. "How are you doing, William?"

"Maw, I'm hanging in there."

"Good, do we know what they brought?"

"I didn't look, Maw."

Margaret slowly opens the lid, "Awe, good ole meatloaf." She leans down to smell the aroma of the dish. "Oh my, it smells delicious. I can smell the brown sugar on it."

Will sits down at the small dining table in the kitchen. Margaret pulls out the envelope that Mr. Drum gave her. She looks inside and notices two twenty-dollar bills in it. She gasps, placing her hand over her mouth. "My goodness, that is more than I make in a week." She looks around, then places the money in a jar in the cupboard. She looks at Will. "Never know when we will need this, but it will come in handy."

Will nods.

Knock! Knock!

Will looks at Margaret. "I'll get it, Maw."

"Only if you want to. I guess it will be like this most of the day."

A familiar gentleman in a black suit is standing outside. He is tall and slim, in his late forties, and has black hair parted to one side. In his right hand he is holding a Bible.

Will turns to the inside of the house. "Maw, it is Pastor Phillips."

Margaret tidies herself and walks towards the door.

"William, how are you holding up?" Pastor Phillips asks.

William looks down at the porch. "I am holding up, Sir."

Pastor Phillips places his hand on Will's head. "We don't know the answers here on earth, but God does have the answer."

"Pastor," Margaret says.

Will walks back into the house.

"Why don't you come in," Margaret suggests.

"Thank you, Margaret."

Margaret guides the Pastor into the living room and points to one of the cushioned chairs on each side of the window. A small coffee table is in the center, and a fireplace is along the exterior wall. Pastor Phillips sits in the chair beside the fireplace, and Margaret sits closer to the door.

"Margaret, I came over to offer my condolences and to pray for you and Will."

"Thank you, Pastor."

"Is there anything you need?"

"No, nothing I can think of."

Henry walks into the living room, still in his overalls. He reaches into his back pocket and pulls out his liquor bottle.

Pastor Phillips looks at Henry in a disapproving manner. "That there is the devil's sauce."

Henry licks his lips. "Me drinking is really between me, the bottle, and God, I would think. From my understanding, no one has been given the power on this earth to judge, not even you, Clyde Phillips."

Pastor Phillips's cheeks turn red with anger.

Henry points to Pastor Phillips's bible. "That book you brought in has a lot to say about judging and God's children. Perhaps you should read it from time to time. I sure have. What you cling to is amazing when you think your days are numbered. There is a lot of talk about judging and sitting down with those that sin, not just the ones that are righteous in your eyes." Henry points to Pastor Phillips. "I do believe we are all God's children." Henry snarks, "Even us sinners."

"Henry!" Margaret scolds as she stands up.

"I know. Margaret, I will go out to the back." Henry turns, takes a drink, and heads to the back of the house.

Pastor Phillips quickly changes the subject. "Margaret, now we will have a lot of ladies bringing things over the next week. We would love to see you at church on Sunday if you can."

"We will be there," Margaret affirms.

"Good. I will return to check on you in a few days. Don't hesitate to reach out to us." Pastor Phillips stands up.

Margaret gestures to him to sit back down. "When should we expect Joseph to return home? So, he can be laid to rest properly."

Pastor Phillips looks down at the ground for a second, takes a deep breath, and replies. "Right now, Margaret, the men are laid to rest in a cemetery overseas. There are plans to return them if that is something you would like once the war is over. I know a few families have thought about it and have decided to let them rest where they are buried so as not to disturb their peace. That will be a decision for you and Will to make."

Margaret looks away to gain her composure, then nods. She stands up, and Pastor Phillips follows her lead. "Thank you, Pastor. We will see you on Sunday."

"Good. I will see you then," Pastor Phillips replies as he walks to the door. He steps out, and Margaret closes the door. She turns and beelines down the hall to Will's room.

"Henry," Margaret says in a sharp tone. "I know you are my husband's brother, but I will ask you kindly not to butt in again. Do you understand me?"

Henry stares at the floor, nods, then lifts his head and looks Margaret in the eyes. "Margaret, I will not do it again. That I swear but listen to me. I know I have my vices, but I have always been able to sum someone up rather quickly. I have been around many people. I will tell you Clyde Phillips is not one I trust. This goes way back. There I said it." He lifts his hands over his shoulders, then grins. "But I would be honored to sit with you and Will in church on Sunday."

Margaret smiles. "Good, Henry. I would like that."

Chapter 3 Reminiscence

Margaret sways back and forth on the front porch swing with Will lying in her lap. She gently runs her fingers through his hair, while she looks down at Will and forces a smile.

Henry steps onto the porch and plops down as the sun fades for the evening. His overalls and white shirt fit loosely. Margaret glances over and acknowledges Henry's arrival.

A large willow tree stands tall in the front yard towards the left side of the house. The summer breeze causes the drooping branches to shift with the drift of the air, swaying an enchanted dance. The birds catch the wind as they take flight.

Margaret continues to run her fingers through Will's hair. Softly, she says, "William, your Paw used to love it when I ran my fingers through his hair. He would lay in my lap just like you are."

Will's chin quivers as his eyes water.

"You miss him, Maw?"

"I have since the moment he left over two years ago."

"It's been a long time, Maw, and now we will never see him again."

Margaret takes a deep breath, "No, we won't, but we can have his treasured memories in our hearts. That is about all we can do."

Will sits up as Henry pulls out the harmonica. "Maw, do you mind if I go see the boys tonight? I need to get out of the house if that makes sense."

Margaret gives an approving nod.

The summer breeze shifts slightly, causing the limbs from the willow to change their dance routine.

Henry takes a sip from his bottle and brings his harmonica to his mouth. He looks up at Margaret and Will, nods, and then blows into the harmonica, calmly blowing out a melody close to ♪Greensleeves♪.

Margaret quietly says, "Oh, how peaceful."

Henry nods as he continues his rendition of the song. As he gets to the second verse, Margaret's angelic voice pierces the summer night with beautiful lyrics to the song. Her charming voice compliments Henry as he continues to play.

Will lays back down on Margaret's lap as she sings. Margaret's voice is intoxicating. Will grins, and his mind drifts. *The last time I saw my Paw was on this porch. I was shorter then. He told me I was the man of the house and always to treat any woman with respect.*

Keep my manners and act like an adult but most of all, take care of Maw. Paw was so confident.

Margaret stops singing, and Henry winds down on the harmonica. He looks out in the distance. "You know, Margaret. I don't understand things. I don't understand God."

"Neither do I."

"As you know, I have read much about him in his book, but I don't know. Why would God spare me and take my brother? It makes no sense. Joseph was always a better man than me. He has a family that needs him, but he took him. Why would he do that?"

Margaret swallows and says, "Henry, I don't know. I don't have the answers. I have similar questions for God. I don't understand it. I plan to attend church on Sunday, hoping it will provide us peace."

Henry nods while still looking off in the distance. He raises his bottle. "To peace."

Margaret looks down at Will, "William, you still going out?"

"I think so, Maw."

"I don't want you out too late. I would like you back in a couple of hours."

Will sits up and nods.

Margaret forces a smile. "Well, you better get going."

Will steps off the porch swing and walks into the house.

"What are your plans tonight, Henry?"

"Well, I might head downtown to Rosie's tonight. Who knows, maybe there will be some dame that will bat her eyes at me. Then I can forget about things for a bit."

Margaret stands up, walks over to Henry, and pulls him to his feet. Henry stands up, and Margaret steps to the door. She stops and turns around. "Henry, go have fun. Please listen to me; I need you to be William's uncle. He is going to need a steady man in his life."

Henry looks at her in bewilderment. "Do you need me to marry you, Margaret? I mean, if that is needed, I will do it."

Margaret chuckles and places her hand over her heart. "Oh, heaven's no, Henry. I have no room in my life right now for another man. Joseph is my husband; even though he is gone, he is still my husband. That might change one day, but that is too far down the road for me to worry about. I need you to be the best Uncle Henry you can be."

Henry nods. "I understand."

"Good, but thank you for asking, and thank you for being here, Henry." Margaret walks into the house.

"Margaret, I think I am going to get cleaned up so I can head into town."

"Well, when you change, drop me off your coveralls. I will fix the seam on them. The right leg has an opening."

Henry looks down momentarily and sees the gap by his inner knee. "That helps cool me off on the hot days," Henry jokes.

"Maybe so, but if I don't fix it now, you will have to buy another pair soon."

Will walks into the living room as Henry passes by him. "I am heading out, Maw. I will be back later."

Margaret walks over and kisses Will on the forehead. "You going to be, okay?"

Will nods as he leaves the house.

Margaret grabs her sewing kit from the kitchen, and finds a nice sewing needle that is perfect for the coverall's denim material.

Henry walks back into the kitchen wearing his white shirt and underwear.

Margaret lifts a curious eye as she takes the coveralls. "That will do, Henry. I will have them fixed by the time you get back tonight."

Margaret sits down in her bedroom rocking chair and begins to split the seam on his coveralls, shaking her head as she frees the material from the stitching. "That Henry is too rough on his clothes."

Henry knocks on her door and pokes his head in. He is wearing light tan slacks and a blue button-up casual shirt.

Margaret smiles. "Well, don't you look dapper, Henry."

"I do dust off from time to time. I am going to get out of here. I'm not sure if I will be back tonight. Do I need to bring you anything?"

"No, I think I am fine. Just going to sit here and reminisce for a bit."

Henry nods. "Do I need to leave my bottle?"

Margaret shakes her head. "No, I have my own in the kitchen cabinet. I am sure I will cozy up to it tonight, but thank you."

Henry waves two fingers from his brow in a saluting fashion and leaves.

Margaret can hear the door shut. She gets up and walks into the living room, picks out the record ♪*Cheek to Cheek*♪, and cranks the handle on the phonograph. She walks into the kitchen, reaches into the cupboard, and pulls out a hidden bottle of brandy. The old bottle is dusty from sitting so long. She spins the top off and lets it hit the floor, then takes a sip and closes her eyes as the record player plays. Swaying to the music, holding the bottle—mimicking dancing with a partner as if Joseph were there.

She takes another big drink from the bottle; some brandy runs down her cheek. A tear escapes from her eye and meets the brandy. She takes a deep breath, then walks back into the bedroom. She bends down next to the bed, reaches under the bed, and pulls out a box twice the size of a shoe box. She stands back up, lies belly on the bed, and rummages through the box. Sifting through letters and photos, she slowly pulls out each letter and starts reading each letter word for word.

After indulging in the letters, Margaret wipes her eyes and moves to the rocking chair. She picks up the overalls and cleans the old seams. Then, the pants leg is sewn back up. As she pulls the needle and thread through the seam, she thinks about Joseph. I wish I

24

could dance one more dance with my Joseph. She leans over, takes a sip of brandy, and finishes the coveralls. She folds them neatly and return to the kitchen, returning her sewing supplies and placing the coveralls on the kitchen table.

She pauses for a moment, taking in the silence in the house. Then she walks into the living room and cranks the phonograph again. As the music plays, she returns to the bedroom and plops down on the bed, reviewing every photograph and every letter like an accountant scrutinizing the books for the missing dollar. She takes her last sip of brandy and rolls over on her back, clutching the letters to her chest as her eyes slowly close.

Chapter 4 Helen

Will walks down a dark alley in Bennett Town. A few street-lights sparingly illuminate the town. He notices that the lights at Rosie's, the local bar, and the movie palace are on. He walks down a side street where several prominent Victorian-style houses are standing. Will stops in front of one of the nicest houses with a large wrap-around porch.

The light tan house with a black roof is a spacious three-story structure with many windows. The porch railing is white and matches the window trim and shutters where the massive wooden front door is stained brown. Hanging from the beams the porch has a two-seater swing. To the right of the house is a large, towering Magnolia tree.

Will reluctantly walks up to the front door of the Bennett House, which is known throughout the county as the most awe-inspiring house in Bennett Town. Mrs. Bennett opens the door cautiously. She is of medium height and petite with short blonde hair. A little startled by the sight of her black eye, he swallows. "Hmm, Mrs. Bennett, Helen wouldn't be around by chance, would she?"

"Oh, Will, Helen is here. I am truly sorry to hear about your Paw." She hugs Will. "Let me go get Helen."

Will looks around the house as he's waiting, he hears jazz music playing on the radio in the background.

Helen comes down the staircase wearing a red skirt, which stops just below her knees, bounces with every step, and her white bobby socks are pulled straight up. A white blouse with lace at the top covers her petite frame.

As Helen notices Will, she quickly hugs him. With her honey-brown eyes, Helen gazes into Will's eyes and says softly, "Will, I am really sorry about your Paw." Helen turns over her shoulder. "Mom, do you mind if we go out or outside for a bit?"

"Helen, be back in two hours."

"Yes Ma'am." Helen looks at Will and nods for them to leave. She opens the door, and Will waits for her, then follows her.

They walk down the street holding each other's hands and taking their time without hurrying. Helen is just about an inch shorter than Will. They make their way downtown, walking along the sidewalk and passing houses.

Helen looks up at Will, "Are you okay, Will?"

"I am, it's just weird." Will looks down at her. "I haven't seen my Paw in over two years, and now I will never see him again."

Helen leans on Will's arm. "That is rough, Will."

"Yep, it is hard for me to see his face in my mind anymore; it has been so long. I am just blah right now. I had to get out of the house."

"Well, I am glad you came to me, Will." Helen says, smiling at him.

Will smirks. They walk up to a green street bench and sit down. Will pulls out some Lucky Strikes and offers one to Helen.

She shakes her head. "I'll share yours."

Will pulls one out and lights it. He takes a drag off the cigarette while putting the rest in his pocket. Then he hands the lit cigarette to Helen by holding it with his thumb and forefinger. Helen places it between her forefinger and middle finger and takes a slow puff off the cigarette in a more dignified fashion.

"So, what's up with your Mom's eye?"

Helen looks around for a moment, then back to Will. She hands him the cigarette. "Maw went to bed and didn't have it, but she had it when I saw her in the morning. She claims," Helen pauses and makes quotation marks above her head, "that she ran into the bathroom door. I am not buying it. Dad was drunk again, and they were arguing. You know he likes to hit the sauce."

Will shakes his head, then takes a puff on the cigarette. Slowly, he exhales. "That is a shame."

"Yep, Maw probably won't go to church Sunday until after it heals."

"Will you be at church?"

Helen nods yes. "What about you and your Maw?"

"Oh, I think we are going along with Uncle Henry."

"No, I mean, what will happen to y'all? Will y'all have to move or something?"

"I don't see why we would. Maw is from here. So is Uncle Henry. Not sure where we would go. I will probably need to see if they will give me a job at the lumberyard to help out."

"I can see that." Helen smiles. "Good ole Will, always doing the right thing."

"So, have you ever seen your Paw hit your Mom?"

Helen looks around cautiously, then nods yes.

Will shakes his head in anger, takes a puff on his cigarette, then hands it to Helen. He watches a car pass by on the street. Suddenly, he turns to Helen. "Has he ever hit you?"

Helen nervously nods yes.

Will breathes deeply. "You let me know if he does it again."

Helen forces a smile and nods. Will stands up and pulls Helen to her feet. "You ready to go back home?"

"Wait. Before we go." She gives him a peck on the lips. "That is for my Will."

Will grins ear to ear.

"I figure you needed something to smile about."

"Well, that will do it, I guess."

Will and Helen slowly stroll back to her house. Along the way, he flicks what is left of his cigarette out in the street. They hold hands as they walk back.

"So, will I see you tomorrow, Will?"

"Well, that depends."

Helen tilts her head and looks at Will suspiciously. "Depend on what?"

Will breathes deeply. "That depends on whether you will kiss me again."

Helen smiles and kisses him on the lips. She steps back. "There then. So tomorrow?"

"Yes Ma'am."

"Good." Helen smiles as they walk up to the front door.

They stop by the door. Will turns to Helen and looks into her eyes. She kisses him on the lips one more time, and then hurries back into the house. Will smiles from ear to ear and skips off the porch, barely touching a step as he skips to the ground.

As Will walks to the alley leading out of town, he reflects. *Wow, I have never been kissed before.* He takes a deep breath. *Paw would be so proud right now. Maybe he is weaving some magic from heaven right now. It is hard to believe I will never see his face again or have him pat me on the back and say, "That's my boy."* Tears well up in his eyes as he walks home.

Will can hear the frogs croaking in the distance and the crickets chirping as he wanders home, not thinking of the time. As he approaches their humble home, he notices that the light is still on in his Maw's bedroom.

Will opens the front door and walks in quietly. His Maw's room door is open and he looks in on her. Margaret is passed out sprawled out across the bed, still in her blue dress. She is clinging to a photo In her right hand and a brandy bottle in her left. There are photos and letters laid out all over the bed.

An open letter catches Will's eye. He knows he shouldn't read it and he knows it is private but his curiosity gets the better of him. As he reads the letter, *Paw sure does speak highly of his buddy Tom. They seem to be inseparable.* He picks up another letter. *Paw sure loved my Maw and me. But it is evident that Tom has been by his side for the last two years when we couldn't be.*

Will finally walks over and takes the bottle from her hand without waking her. He places the bottle on the nightstand, then puts the photos and letters in the box. He looks at the photo in Margaret's hand and smiles. The photo shows Margaret sitting on Joseph's lap by the lake being happy.

He closes his eyes as so many memories flood his mind about his Paw. Tears slide down his cheeks and he wipes them off. He patiently retrieves the photo and places it on the nightstand. Will then takes the box, sits down in his Maw's rocking chair, and quietly goes through each photo. He pauses with each photo to reminisce about his Paw.

Chapter 5 Rosie's

H enry steps in front of Rosie's as the music from inside the bar permeates the streets. He opens the wooden door and smirks, he is returning to his comfort zone. As he walks into the bar, the smokey atmosphere lingers in the air, surrounding him while the nightlife immerses him. The thick smell of tobacco from cigars and cigarettes overwhelms most of the cologne and perfume that is worn by the crowd.

He looks to the left and nods to Bruce, the bartender. Bruce is a dark-haired man in his forties with a stout build. He is wearing a black button-up shirt with sleeves rolled up.

Bruce returns a smile as he washes a glass. He looks across the way and back to Henry.

Henry looks over at the tables opposite the bar and notices a jukebox. *Wow! When did that get in town? I wonder.* He points at the jukebox and looks at Bruce with a questioning look.

"I know Henry, we are big time now!" Bruce yells.

Henry nods and looks across the room. Three young women are seated close to the jukebox, smoking cigarettes. Two attempt to look sophisticated by smoking cigarettes with a cigarette holder. He notices a small congregation around a table, in the back of the room.

"What's your poison, Henry?" Bruce asks.

"Make it a French 76."

"I can't do a 76, my friend, but I can do a 75. We are out of vodka, and Norman should be back any minute with vodka. But we got plenty of gin."

"French 75 it is."

"Coming right up."

Henry reaches for a cigarette and slaps his shirt pocket. *Strange, I swear I had some smokes in here. Hmm.* He glances around, surveying the bar's scenery.

As he scans the bar room, Henry thinks. *I still can't believe Joseph is gone. Everyone here is drinking and smoking. They are all having a good time, but my brother is gone. He will never see his wife again. He will never see Will grow up.* His eyes water up as he sits down on the bar stool.

Bruce slides the drink over to Henry. "Your French 75, my friend. This one is on the house. Let's celebrate your homecoming. The next one will be on the house, too, Henry. Sorry about your brother. Joseph was a good man."

Henry nods and takes the drink. He lifts it, savors the flavor, and swallows the tasty beverage. He takes a deep breath. "Bruce, that is good."

Bruce winks at Henry. "I put a little extra kick in there for you."

"Hey Bruce, y'all do gambling here?"

"Oh, the Sheriff only allows it if Earl Bennett is playing. You know he owns the town." Bruce says quietly. "The Sheriff allows anything if Earl plays, he can pretty much do whatever he wants. I provide the table and alcohol. If they get unruly, I either kick them out or call the Sheriff."

"I see," Henry says as he looks around. His eyes lock into a stare with one of the ladies at the table smoking. She is a brunette with brown eyes, and she smiles at Henry, then stubs her cigarette out in the ashtray. The lady who is tall and slender gracefully walks over to the bar next to Henry. Her caramel brown hair falls over her shoulders. She wears a red skirt that ends just below the knees, which compliments her tan skin.

Her mischievous grin catches Henry off guard. "You're Henry Wood."

Henry nods but is unsure who he is talking to. "I am, and you are?"

She smiles and pauses for his reaction.

He looks over at her. "Hmm, you never told me your name." He winks at her. "Some might say angels don't have names." He licks his lips. "But I would venture to say that little devils don't have names either."

She laughs. "So, you're calling me a little devil."

Henry takes a sip of his drink. "Maybe, I think only time will tell."

"Well, Henry, your little devil is Peggy Ward."

Henry gasps. "Nope, I am not buying it. There is no way you're Peggy Ward."

Peggy grabs his drink, finishes it, and returns it to him. She winks at him and says. "Yep, it's me."

"Then I was right. You are a little devil."

"Time will tell, Henry." Peggy then places her hand on his arm. She leans up and gives him a peck on his cheek, leaving some lipstick on it.

Bruce walks over wiping the counter. "Watch out, Henry. You are returning from the war and will find out these dames will flock to you." He looks at Peggy, and she gives him a look of disapproval. "But Peggy here is one to latch onto, unlike the others. I have never seen Peggy put herself out there like some dames." Bruce winks at Peggy, and her demeanor changes back to happy.

"What would you like to drink, Peggy?" Henry asks.

"I will take a Ward Eight, Henry."

Henry nods to Bruce.

"A Ward Eight it is." Bruce quickly starts mixing the drink.

"Peggy Ward wants a Ward Eight. How appropriate," Henry jokes.

Peggy laughs.

"You know, Peggy, it has been probably five years since I have seen you."

"I know. Now, you have gone off to the war and returned. I just stayed here and grew up, that is all."

Bruce slides the drink to Peggy.

"Thank you, Bruce," Peggy politely says as she picks up the drink.

Bruce gives a two-finger salute from his eyebrow.

Peggy taps her glass to Henry's. "To Henry coming home."

She smiles as she enjoys her drink while Henry motions for another.

"NO!"

Bruce, Henry, and Peggy all turn to the back of the bar. A man stands up, slamming his fists down on the table, then points to a chunky man sitting in the back of the table facing the door. "Earl Bennett, you no good son of a bitch!"

With a cigarette hanging from his mouth, Earl Bennett remains calm and says, "No one forced you to play Don. That was your choice. I can't help that you don't know how to play cards or bet more than you have."

Peggy looks at Henry. "The busty brown-haired woman by Don in the red dress is his wife, Judith. She is Earl's secretary at the bank.

Harry Stewart is the guy in grey pants and a white shirt with a mustache. He works at the steel mill in Steel City just down the road from us. The other guy at the table is Leonard Watson, who works for a construction company. Don Ross is the only one who doesn't have the money to gamble there. He works on cars."

"I see. I wonder what all the commotion is about."

Peggy clings to her drink, steps off the bar stool, and nods for Henry to follow. As they make their way to the table, the bar doors open, and the Sheriff walks in.

The Sheriff looks at the back table, and Earl nods to him.

Peggy and Henry stand behind Harry Stewart, opposite Earl. The Sheriff steps over by Leonard. "How is the night going?" The Sheriff asks.

Earl looks around. "Well, all seemed to be going well. But now, Don seems irritated and may be out of money, although he placed bets saying he had money."

Judith who stands behind Don has her arm wrapped around his neck. She looks at Earl and says, "Mr. Bennett, please, give him some time. I will work extra hours at the office. Please, Mr. Bennett."

"What do you think, Sheriff Welch? Should I have him put in jail for reneging on a debt, or should I provide an alternative?"

The Sheriff, a tall, lanky man, ponders momentarily, then smiles. "Mr. Bennett, you should give him an alternative to jail, Sir."

Judith grabs Mr. Bennett's hand. "Please, Sir, just name it and we will do it."

Earl nods, smiles, and then takes a puff from his cigarette.

"I have a resolution that we can all appreciate."

Everyone listens eagerly.

"Don Ross, I will say this. We can play one more hand. It will be just you and me." Earl looks at Harry and Leonard. "You fellas won't mind sitting this one out, do you?"

Harry replies, "No problem, Earl."

"I agree, Earl, we will sit it out and watch," Leonard says.

"Good. I will have, Leonard, be the dealer."

"If you win, you owe me nothing, and you leave. We all go about our business. Are you good with this, Don? "

Don takes a deep breath. "That sounds good, Mr. Bennett. I like that. What happens if I lose?"

"Oh, I am a reasonable man since we are not betting with money, and you owe me more than you will make in four months." Earl pauses and smiles. He looks at Judith. "If you lose, I get a night with Judith. A night with her and me between the sheets."

Silence falls over the table as rage builds in Don's eyes.

Henry gasps and looks at Peggy. She grabs Henry's arm.

Judith looks at Don and takes a deep breath. Then turns to Earl. "And the money?"

"The money slate will be wiped clean," Earl says proudly. "So, if you play this one hand, you owe me nothing."

Don looks at his wife and shakes his head. Judith closes her eyes and places her hand on his cheek.

Bruce swallows hard. "Mr. Bennett, I am not sure that this is something I like going on in my bar."

Earl nods. "Bruce, we can simply shut down your liquor supplier if you don't like it."

Bruce turns red and nods. "Does anyone need a drink?"

"I do," Judith says. "And so does Don."

"What do you want?" Bruce asks.

"The strongest thing you got, Bruce."

Henry leans to Peggy's ear and whispers, "Isn't Earl married to Joan?"

She leans closer to Henry. "I like it when I feel your breath on my neck and ear."

Henry's eyes grow with excitement as his heart flutters.

She whispers, "He is married to her, but many know that marriage hasn't meant much to Earl. For Joan, it means something; for Earl, nothing."

Henry looks at Peggy and acknowledges her comments.

Meanwhile the Sheriff remains quiet.

"So, Don, what's it going to be? You go to jail tonight, or you play me one more hand of five card draw to wipe your slate clean. You might have to give up something close for one night. But it is only one night. You will forget about it in a few days."

Don's anger brews. Judith turns to Don and hugs him. She whispers in his ear, "Don, my love, just win this, and let's be done with this."

Judith kisses Don passionately as everyone watches.

Henry and Peggy look at each other, speechless.

Judith looks at Earl. "Let's get this over with, Mr. Bennett."

"Good, Leonard, can you deal the cards out? One deal and one trade, that's all."

Leonard nods and starts shuffling the cards.

"Oh, one more thing with this. If I win, Judith cannot quit the bank for at least a year. I want to see my prize every day." Earl states.

Leonard starts passing out the cards one by one.

Bruce walks up and sets two drinks in front of Judith and Don. He looks at Don and says, "Whiskey straight, and they are on the house. Good luck."

Everyone in the bar gathers around the table.

Judith hands Don one glass and then picks hers up. They look at each other and then both down the drink.

Don exhales loudly. Judith's hand trembles as she places the empty glass on the table.

The tension around the table is as thick as New England fog. The cards fly across the table from Leonard's hands in slow motion. Bruce stands over by Henry and Peggy. The Sheriff discreetly moves behind Don.

Earl picks up his cards and smiles. He rearranges them to suit him, places one card on the table face down, and then looks at Don. Don moves his cards around as Judith looks on. He places two cards on the table.

Leonard passes two cards to Don and then one card to Earl.

Don and Judith give each other a confident nod. Earl smirks at his hand.

"Well, Don, it is time," Earl says.

Don looks at Judith and then places a Jack of Clubs and a Jack of Hearts down. He then places the King of Diamonds and King of Spades down and an Ace of Hearts.

"WOW!" Harry exclaims as everyone mumbles around the table.

Earl places an Eight of Spades and Eight of Clubs down, then places the Four of Hearts down. He puffs on his cigarette and exhales while looking at Don and Judith. Earl tosses the Ace of Spades and Ace of Clubs on the table. Earl smiles with a huge grin.

"NOOO!" Judith screams, and it echoes in a bone-chilling fashion throughout the bar. Tears stream down her cheeks.

"Well, Don, it looks like your wife will pay your debt tonight." Earl leans to Don. I will make her work for every penny you owe me."

Don jumps up. "You Bastard, one day you will pay. Mark my words. I will spit on your face as you breathe your last breath."

"Don, you lost. Don't make it worse," the Sheriff says as he pushes him down to his chair.

Henry looks on. "I wouldn't celebrate this, Earl."

Earl looks at Henry, a bit confused, "You, ole Henry Wood, right?"

Henry reaches into his pocket and pulls out his Mississippi saxophone. He blows through the harmonica briefly, then looks at Earl. "I am, and that right there is the famous Dead Man's Hand. It is marked. That hand says your days are numbered. You know, one guy that had that hand was shot in the back, and it doesn't seem to me like you're making any friends around here." Henry says with Peggy clinging to his arm. He blows into the harmonica, adding tension to the confrontation.

Bruce looks to Henry with respect.

Earl, a short but sizeable man, pushes the table back, stands up, and looks at Henry. With his fat fingers he reaches for his cigarette in the ashtray.

"It seems to me, soldier boy, that you are intruding. We call it sticking your nose in someone's business. That doesn't bode well for those who stick their nose in other people's business." Earl slams his fists on the table. "You don't know who you are messing with, soldier boy."

Henry moves the harmonica from his mouth and places it in his pocket. He smiles, then audaciously steps to the table's edge. With a menacing pointing finger, he confronts Earl, his voice exuding confidence. "Au contraire, Earl." Placing his drink on the table, Henry boldly moves into Earl's personal space. Earl stands in fright and a bit uneasy, yet in a defiant manner. Henry snatches Earl's cigarette from his grasp and takes a comfortable puff. He nods his head in satisfaction as he feels the nicotine rush. He turns back to Earl with a grin, proclaiming. "We are all walking to our graves. Some are walking faster than others; they just don't know it yet. Others are at full sprint. Utterly oblivious to their destination. It seems to me you are the latter, the sprinting kind." Henry stubs out the cigarette in the ashtray on the table and looks at Earl with a menacing look. "You don't know who you are messing with, Earl. I am not afraid of the likes of you or your puppet Sheriff. Hell, one day, I may be the Sheriff here."

Earl is speechless.

Peggy's chin lifts with pride as she looks on, and Bruce grins from ear to ear. Silence falls over the bar as everyone watches with anticipation.

The Sheriff looks around. "Are you threatening Mr. Bennett?"

Henry looks back at the Sheriff. "I don't see no Mr. around here; I just see Earl. Of everything wrong in this bar tonight, you are worried about some words against your boss? Is that what you're saying?"

"Um, it sounded like a threat." The Sheriff says nervously.

Henry smiles as he looks at the Sheriff. "Oh, you will know when I threaten someone. I won't mince words." He looks back at Earl and leans closer to him. In a soft manner Henry says. "This is where you be the upstanding citizen that you are, Earl, and say, Mrs. Judith, not Judith but Mrs. Judith, your husband's debt has already been paid in full. Then you leave them alone. Once you do that, I will hand your balls back. Do we understand?"

Earl takes a nervous, deep breath.

As Earl tries to speak, Henry places his hand on Earl's chest to stop him. "You know, Earl, when I got shot in the ribs. I thought I was dead." Henry pauses. "I had nothing to lose. I lost it and went through the enemy like no one had seen. My people thought I was a madman. At least that is what they told me at the hospital when I came to. Now I have my wits and just think what I can do with a clear mind." Henry's eyes are laser-focused on Earl's eyes. In a fierce tone, Henry says, "So I say to you, say it where everyone can hear it. Go ahead."

Earl shrivels his lips; they tremble as he looks around, agitated. Then, he lifts his chin slightly as he looks at Judith and Don.

"Judith—

"Mrs. Judith to you. That is Don's wife. She is not Judith to you."

Earl glances back at Henry, nods, then looks back at Judith. "Mrs. Judith, Don's debt has been paid in full. I look forward to seeing you back at work on Monday."

Judith claps her hands in a frenzy. Unable to control her emotions, she jumps up and down enthusiastically. She turns to Don and kisses him rapidly.

The crowd claps. The Sheriff looks at Earl with a worried expression on his face.

"Excuse me," Henry roars.

The crowd simmers down.

"Earl, you have one more thing to do. That is to apologize for insulting Don and for the proposition of his wife."

Peggy's chin drops as she watches on in admiration.

Earl looks at Henry with hatred in his eyes. He turns to Don and says, "Don, I apologize. I was wrong for suggesting that."

Don stands up. "You're a bad man, Mr. Bennett. You better not look at my wife with lustful eyes again, or I will deal with it in a way you won't like."

"Fair enough," Earl says. "Now, if everyone will excuse me, Sheriff." As he walks through the crowd.

"Coming, Mr. Bennett," the Sheriff follows as Earl leaves.

Peggy runs to Henry and plants a kiss squarely on his lips. Henry, caught off guard, embraces the moment.

"Drinks are on the house," Bruce yells.

Henry and Peggy break from the kiss; their eyes lock like no one else is there.

"Henry, Henry," Judith yells as she taps Henry on the arm.

Henry shakes off his gaze into Peggy's eyes. "Uh, yes, Ma'am."

"Thank you so much for what you did," Judith says. "Thanks to you, I am going home with my husband tonight."

"No problem," Henry says while looking at Don, "Go get out of here."

Judith and Don leave the bar as fast as they can.

Henry turns to Peggy. "Is it possible to walk you home?"

Peggy smiles and interlaces her arm with Henry's. "I wouldn't have it any other way."

Chapter 6 Football

"William," Margaret yells as she walks from the front door.

"Coming Maw."

Margaret turns to look out the door. Standing in front of the doorway are Will's friends. "Oh, Albert, I swear you are getting taller every time I see you."

Albert smiles big, showing the wad of tobacco in his mouth. The tobacco stretches his freckled cheeks as he carries a football. He tosses it up to about his chin level and catches it without looking. "Percy and I figured we could play some ball with Will. Is that okay?"

Margaret smiles. "It is Percy and I, Albert, not me and Percy."

"Ma'am, are you sure that just isn't a personal preference?"

"No, Albert, it is the proper English language. So don't come here making up your own language."

"Yes, Ma'am," Albert responds.

"Good," Margaret says.

"Hey Will, want to play some ball by the school?" Percy, a talkative individual, asks.

Will starts to answer but Percy doesn't stop talking.

Percy turns his head, avoids eye contact, then begins his chatty rant. "You know Mom told me to get out of the house and find something to do. So, I figured since your Paw died, I would run over to Albert's and get him so we could play. At first Albert was boring, but that is just Albert. You know he can be like that and all. I told him let's go over to Will's, and his Mom agreed. Albert's sister was annoying. I think she likes me, but I really don't like her. She is too quiet. I would rather have a conversation. So, we came here hoping you weren't hanging out with Helen." Percy turns back to look at Margaret as he catches his breath. "Oh, I hope it is all right, Mrs. Wood, if Will hangs out with Helen. Will would never do anything bad. On the other hand, Helen is a dame and all; you never know with her. She has a bit of a wild streak in her."

Albert coughs deliberately and elbows Percy.

A bit caught off guard, Margaret tries her best not to laugh.

"Thanks a lot, Percy," Will rolls his eyes and slaps at the ball in Albert's hands. Albert yanks it back. Will turns to Margaret. "Maw, I will be back later."

Margaret nods. "Take your time, William."

"Yeah, we all know you like my sister anyway, Percy," Albert blurts out.

The boys jump off the porch. Albert, a master of mimicking people, looks at Will and sarcastically puts on Margaret's voice. "Take your time, William."

Albert laughs. Will grabs Percy, who is thinner than Will. "Oh, a wise acre, I see. Telling Maw about Helen and all."

Percy starts to talk again, but Will pinches his index finger and thumb together in front of his mouth and acts like he is shutting his mouth. Percy grimaces as he understands the gesture. Will turns and reaches over to Albert for the ball. Albert tucks it away. "Nope, got to be faster than that."

All three walk side by side down a trail toward town. Albert and Will are the same height. Percy is about three inches shorter and skinny.

Albert looks at Will as they walk. "Hey Will, we just wanted to check and see if you are okay. We are sorry about your Paw."

Will nods his head. "Guys, I am okay. I miss him, but I haven't seen him for over two years, so there is not much difference. I know now that he isn't coming back, and I will never see him again if that makes sense."

Albert looks at Percy as he absorbs what Will just said. Then turns back to Will. Albert nods. "Okay, that makes sense."

"Hey Will, I think Gerald, Walter, Charles, and Ralph will be at the school when we play smear the man with the ball," Percy says. "Ralph is slow and clumsy. Gerald is the only nice one of the bunch. Maybe Walter sometimes, but Ralph and Charles need to be socked in the nose. Will have you seen Helen lately?" Percy stops talking abruptly.

Will looks at him for a moment.

Percy then turns to Albert and looks him square in the eyes, a rarity for Percy. "And I don't like your sister. Just because she likes me doesn't mean I like her. She kisses funny. Who puts their tongue in another person's mouth?"

Albert's chin drops in shock, leaving him speechless. Will starts laughing hysterically. He staggers around in dismay and uncontrollable laughter. "You kissed Ruth?" Albert is still speechless but looks for Percy's answer.

Percy looks down. "No, she kissed me twice. Then she told me not to tell you." Percy looks up at Albert. "My Mom said I shouldn't talk so much, so I figured I would stop right there."

"Well, Casanova, I think you have said enough," Will replies.

"When, when did this happen?" Albert asks.

"When I spent the night over your house. You were—

"Uh, I don't think we need details, Albert," Will says. "Besides, Ruth is a year older than us; what's the big deal?"

Albert tenses up and yells, "She's, my sister!"

Will giggles briefly while watching Albert's reaction, then nods. "Cool, although I am not a fan of Charles, either." Will puts his arm around Albert's shoulders to calm him down.

"Well, no one really is," Albert says as he exhales in frustration.

"As far as Helen." Will smiles, trying to move the topic far away from Ruth and Percy. "Yeah, I saw her yesterday and probably will see her later today."

Percy reaches into his pocket and pulls out an arrowhead. He looks at Will and says, "I wanted you to have this."

Will looks at Percy, "Why?"

Percy takes a deep breath. "You remember when we all went to the creek looking for gold when your Paw was here?"

Will nods.

"I was looking for tadpoles instead of gold. You know I like frogs and such. I think Albert was peeing on the side of the creek. You were looking for crawdads. Eventually, we were all wading in the creek, and your Paw walked up behind me. He almost scared the bejesus out of me. I thought my heart was going to pop out of my chest. I probably would have died right then. Anyway, he points to the creek water. He said, 'Today is your lucky day, Percy. Not everyone finds an arrowhead.' I reached down, and this was it. I looked up at him, and he gave me that wink he used to do. He always was a nice guy, Will. You know, I never heard him yell at anyone, but he didn't take crap from anyone, either. He just carried himself differently. For him, everything was fun, even when it wasn't. If that makes sense." Percy takes a deep breath, then continues. "So, I thought you should have it so you don't forget him."

Albert squints his eyes as he listens on.

Will takes the arrowhead from Percy, looks at it for a moment, takes a deep breath, and slides it into his pocket. "Thank you, Percy. It is something I will treasure."

Albert points up ahead as the trail comes out in a clearing. "Looks like we have some fellas there."

Will snatches the ball from Albert and takes off running towards the guys in the schoolyard.

Albert yells, "Will has the ball. Smear him." Then he takes off, running after Will, with Percy following.

Will tucks the ball in tight as he runs to the group of guys at full steam. His fingers squeeze the pigskin tightly, leaving indentions on the surface of the football. Frustration from the news of his Paw oozes into his steps. His stride gets longer and more deliberate as anger funnels through his body. He pants a little louder with each step, and his steps pound the ground loudly. Will is running like a madman.

One smaller boy lowers his body to get low on Will. With ease, Will extends his powerful, stiff arm that flings the boy to the ground. Dust flies as the kid hits the ground. He continues his ferocious run as another collides with Will at full force in the shoulders. Will spins from the collision as the would-be tackler falls to the ground. Will staggers around to maintain his balance. Two other fellas seize the moment, and one guy hits him low while another tackles him to the ground, stopping Will's run of frustration.

Everyone then piles on the tackle with Will at the bottom. A giant dust cloud hovers over the pile of bodies.

The boys untangle, dusts themselves off, and prepares for the ball getting ready for Will to stand up. He looks up, smiles, and in a calculating manner stands up. He is surrounded by six fellas his age.

Will looks at face to see who is the most nervous. He finds his victim and smiles as he suddenly tosses the ball. Ralph jumps high to get the ball, and instantly Will tackles him. Ralph shakes his head. "I didn't go nowhere, dang it. I think everyone was in cahoots against me."

Albert laughs. "It was only Will, Ralph. You are just slow."

Ralph shrivels his nose and agrees. He stands up and tosses the ball high into the air. As the ball comes down, bodies slap each other as they collide, trying to get to it. Gerald grabs the ball and tucks it in. Percy is close by and attempts to tackle Gerald. He sizes him up and lunges to him. Gerald jukes to the side. Ralph attempts to tackle him, but Gerald quickly sidesteps him. Suddenly, with great brutality, Will blindside tackles Gerald, almost running straight through him.

Will gets up and reaches down to Gerald. "You okay, Gerald? Or you a softie?"

Gerald smiles as he grabs Will's hand. "I'm good." A serious demeanor comes over Gerald's face. "You, okay?"

"I am," Will says.

Gerald is on his feet and smirks. "Good." Then puts the ball in Will's stomach. "Will has the ball."

Will gasps as everyone quickly tackles him. All the guys fall to the ground forming a dog pile with feet and butts in the air.

Slowly, each one gets off the pile and dusts themselves off. Will gets to his feet. "Not cool." Will takes a deep breath and tosses the ball up high.

The tiniest person, Percy, jumps up and grabs the ball. Percy is scrappy and shifty, scurries from out of the nest of guys, and finds an opening to getaway. He jukes past Ralph and starts to gather speed. Charles spears him in the chest, knocking the ball out of Percy's hands. As Percy falls to the ground, his right arm gets caught up behind him on the fall as he hits the ground. Percy screams in pain as he tries to support his right arm.

Like a lion over his prey, Charles stands over Percy with pride and prances around. He boastfully waves his hands in the air. Percy squirms on the ground in pain beneath him.

Will rushes over and pushes Charles back. "Not cool. You want me to bust your chops?"

Charles looks around for a moment, then steps back to Will. "Why are you in this? It is just a game. He shouldn't be here if he isn't tough enough to play."

Will leans into Charles. "Maybe we should respect his size and heart instead of preying on him." Will pushes Charles back and then closes the gap between them.

Percy screams in pain.

Albert rushes over to Percy. He looks down, and Percy is clutching his right arm. His forearm is broken.

Will realizes it and fully swings his right arm toward Charles's chin. Will's punch connects in the right spot under the chin, lifting Charles off his feet and buckling him to the ground. Charles is motionless and unconscious.

Ralph, Walter, and Gerald rush over. Ralph tries to stick up for Charles. Gerald quickly intervenes. "Hey guys, maybe we should call it a day." He looks down at Percy.

Will looks over, picks Percy up in his arms, and carries him as Albert leads the way.

Percy trembles as he cries.

"Albert, lead the way to Doctor Myers if you would."

Albert turns. "I will run up there and tell him you are on your way."

Will continues to carry Percy cautiously. Albert runs off.

Percy settles down and whimpers a little.

"Percy, this is the quietest you have ever been."

"That's not funny, Will. I guess I will live up to my promise to my Mom."

Will cuts him off. "Percy, just rest; we will be there in a minute."

They turn down a street, and Dr. Myers exits his office door. Will sets Percy down on the ground and Dr. Myers walks over and quickly scans over Percy. He turns as Albert is running up. "Albert, you don't mind going to get Percy's Mom, do you?"

"No, Sir, I will be back in a minute," Albert says as he runs off.

"Percy, how is the pain," Dr. Myers asks.

"It, it, hurts pretty bad."

"Yes, yes," Dr. Myers says, trying to soothe him.

He reaches down, picks up Percy, and carries him to his office. Will follows and quickly walks beside them. Dr. Myers looks over at Will as he walks to his office. "Will, I am sorry to hear about your Paw. Joseph was a good man."

Will nods his head.

The nurse holds the door open as they approach the doctor's office. Dr. Myers carries Percy inside and places him on the examination table. He looks Percy over and starts touching his arm. "Does this hurt?"

Percy grimaces.

Dr. Myers nods, then touches another part of his arm.

Percy screams.

"Yes, I understand that hurts." Dr. Myers moves his hand to relieve the pain. He is holding his arm by the wrist and right below the elbow. "Okay, it is definitely broken. In a little bit, I will need to set it. But we will wait for your Mom to arrive before we do that. How does that sound?"

Percy nods. "I can wait. That hurt bad. Almost as bad as when it happened."

Dr. Myers looks at Will and gives him a wink.

Percy continues, "I think this is the most pain I faced. But there was this time when I fell on—

Dr. Myers suddenly shifts Percy's arm, setting the bone back in place.

A haunting scream escapes from Percy's mouth.

The blood-curdling scream sends shivers down Will's spine.

Percy turns pale.

Will's eyes swell with shock.

Percy's Mom and Albert walk into the room. Percy's Mom frantically asks, "Is he going to be all right?"

Dr. Myers pulls out a cigarette and lights it. He puffs, then blows out some smoke and nods. "He will be fine, Ma'am. He has a broken arm. I just set it. We will put it in plaster, and he will have a cast for about eight weeks."

Percy shudders for a moment, and then the pain fades a little.

"I will prescribe him some pain medication for a few days. I got a shot that will make the boy feel good." Dr. Myers winks at Percy's Mom, then turns to Will. "You did good, Will. Thank you for bringing him to me."

Chapter 7 Potatoes

Margaret grabs her gardening fork. She gets down on all fours and moves the leaves back from the potato plant. She jumps back in fright and screams, "WILLIAM!" As a sizeable tan snake slithers from its hiding place, Margaret clutches her chest and exhales.

Will picks the snake up by the tail. "Just an ole rat snake, Maw."

The snake's head dangles around Will's knees as Will lifts his arm to shoulder level.

Margaret nods. "I don't mind those, but it caught me off guard.

Will smiles. "Snakes always do. This is a good one, just a rat snake. I'll put him out of the garden. He will find his way back later."

Margaret returns to the ground and removes dirt from the potato plant, exposing the tubers. She looks at Will and says, "I think these are ready."

Will pushes the wheelbarrow down the row close to the potato plant. Margaret carefully inspects another plant while Will retrieves a shovel.

"This one is ready as well, William."

"Yes Maw," Will says as he pushes the shovel into the ground. He carefully scoops the dirt and moves it to the side, exposing the fresh potatoes.

"Oh, William, be sure to use potato sacks. There is a shortage of tater sacks due to the war. Because of this, the store has increased the deposit for a sack from one cent to two cents. If we don't get tater sacks in return, we will start using boxes for now."

William scoops up a shovel of potatoes and dumps them in the wheelbarrow. He then reaches down with his hands and retrieves the rest of the potatoes from the ground. "Maw, this is a good plant. It looks like around twelve good-sized potatoes on this one."

"That's fantastic, William," Margaret says as she looks up. "I think all the ones in the first three rows we planted in late March are good. So, let's pull them up. That still gives us six rows from early April and six from late April. Let's leave those alone for now."

"Yes Ma'am. How much do you think that will bring us?"

"We will have about three full sacks and maybe some more. So over 330 pounds of potatoes to take in."

"Good, every potato counts. That will bring us over $16. Can't complain about that."

"No Ma'am, sure can't."

"Okay, I will do a wash load to hang them on the clothesline while you finish digging."

Margaret stands up, wipes her hands on her apron over her light green dress, and looks over at Will.

Will is on all fours on the ground, wearing his blue overalls. He is diligently digging up potatoes.

She looks on in admiration. *He is his father's spitting image and is hardworking, too.* A slight grin emerges as she walks to the back of the house.

Margaret grabs the washtub and the washboard and heads down to the creek. A bench lies along the bank parallel to the creek. She places the washboard on the ground next to the bench, then grabs the washtub, dipping it in the water to fill it. She struggles as it fills and pulls it back on the bank beside the bench. Margaret stands up straight, tidies herself, and then returns to the house.

There she grabs the dirty clothes, the red box of Duz laundry soap, and a scrub brush. Gracefully, she returns to the bench next to the creek. She places the dirty clothes on the ground. Margaret pours some of the Duz laundry soap powder into the washtub. She sets the soap on the ground, picks up the washboard, and uses it to stir the washtub, agitating the water. After a moment of stirring, Margaret admires her preparation and then grabs a set of overalls. She dips them in the water and then rubs them methodically against the washboard with a scrub brush, ensuring every inch of the fabric is washed. She wrings the overalls vigorously with both hands.

Margaret stands up, slings the overalls to loosen them, and rinses them in the creek. She then places them on the back of the bench to dry. Margaret follows the same procedure until all the clothes are clean.

Will pushes the heavy load of potatoes to the barn. He walks into the barn, grabs a potato sack, and slowly fills it with potatoes. As the bag reaches its full potential, he ties the end of the sack off to ensure they all stay inside. He grabs another sack and then fills it about halfway full. He leaves the sack next to the first one and returns to the garden.

Margaret clips the clean clothes onto the clothesline that runs along the side of the house. She places the pants, shirts, and dresses closer to the road. She places the undergarments on the clothesline closest to the house out of view. She rubs her hands on her apron in satisfaction and admires her work.

"Maw, we have almost four sacks full of potatoes," Will yells as he walks up.

"Wow, that is amazing."

"I have them stacked in the barn."

Margaret looks at Will and says, "It's good we can go grocery shopping today and have some extra money afterward."

"I will go load them up in the old Ford."

"William, that sounds great. Let me go freshen up before we go into town."

Margaret steps inside while Will pulls the black 36 Ford Deluxe to the barn. He grabs a sack of potatoes and places them in the backseat. Will cranks the car back up and drives it to the front of the house.

As he pulls up, Margaret stands on the porch, looking like a picture from a magazine and as if she hadn't done any chores this morning.

Margaret steps down the stairs like a movie star with everyone's eyes upon her. Will moves over to the passenger seat and Margaret sits in the driver's seat, looks over at Will, and then gives him a wink. "You ready?"

"Yes Maw."

As they travel down the road, Will rolls his window down. "Now, William, let me roll mine down, or it will mess my hair up." Margaret shifts into second gear and rolls her window down as they pass by a pasture of cows.

Will sticks his right arm out and rides his hand with the wave of the air flowing by him. He grins as he can feel the resistance from the air.

"Maw, do you like driving?"

Margaret glances over at Will. "I do, William. You know it was your father who taught me how to drive." As she reflects upon the memory, she smiles. "I remember Joseph looking at me saying, 'Maggie, now don't be bashful, but don't tear up my transmission either. Use the clutch before gear contact.' Then he would give me a wink and flash that smile." She grabs Will's arm affectionately, then downshifts as she approaches a T intersection.

She eases the car to a stop, looks both ways and then turns left on the larger dirt road. They pass by a couple of houses on each side of the road. Margaret then pulls onto the paved Main Street in front of Jimmy Hughes A & P grocery store. "Do you need help?"

Will gives her a look of surprise. "Naw Maw, I got this." He grabs a tater sack, then throws it over his shoulder.

Margaret walks inside the store and waves to a short, bald guy in his 50s. "Mr. Hughes, we got some taters for sale."

The bald man with a pencil between his left ear and skull, carrying a pad of paper, smiles and replies, "Oh, Margaret, perfect timing. We are running low. How much did you bring?"

"William, has almost four full sacks of them." She says with charm in her voice.

"Oh, wow, that is a considerable sum. That will be great." Mr. Hughes says as he walks up to Margaret. "You know we heard about Joseph and are truly sorry, Margaret."

Margaret thankfully grabs his arm. "Thank you, Mr. Hughes, but I can't fret about it forever. I miss my Joseph, and I love him dearly. But I got a boy to raise." She says that, as she turns, Will walks into the store with a sack of potatoes over his shoulder.

"Yes, you do," Jimmy Hughes replies. "If you need anything, don't hesitate."

"Oh, I won't," Margaret replies.

"Will," Jimmy yells, "place those on the scale in the back if you don't mind."

"Yes Sir, Mr. Hughes."

Jimmy looks at Margaret. "Fine, young man, right there."

"I would agree," Margaret replies. She pulls out her grocery list and hands it to Mr. Hughes.

"Wow, it looks like you're coming to the grocery store and leaving with more money in your pocket." He points at the list. "Now we are short on coffee. I hope you understand. The boys on the front line get it before us."

"As it should be, Mr. Hughes, as it should be," Margaret replies.

"The rest we will have right up for you," Mr. Hughes replies.

"Sounds good," Margaret replies as Will walks in with the last sack of potatoes. She follows him to the back of the store, where the scale is located at.

Mr. Hughes walks up. "Looks like you're leaving with almost $14 in your pocket today. We got your toothpaste, shampoo, Ivory soap, toilet paper, bleach, peanut butter, oranges, yellow onions, a dozen eggs, hot dogs, Crisco, and a loaf of bread. That comes to $3.04 minus $16.50 for almost four potato sacks, which leaves you with $13.46 to take home." Mr. Hughes pulls out his paper and begins to write. "Oh, you normally get a newspaper. Did you forget?"

"Uh, no, Mr. Hughes. Since Joseph has passed away, I no longer need to get a paper."

"Oh dear, I am sorry for being pushy."

"Oh, Mr. Hughes, I understand."

Will walks out of the store's front door and waits by the car.

"Mr. Hughes, I suspect we will have more potatoes in about three weeks or so."

"That will be perfect, Margaret." Mr. Hughes looks out the window, then points to Margaret.

She looks out the window. Will is leaning on the Ford and talking to Helen. He slowly slides his fingers through his hair as he speaks, and Helen twists her hair with her fingers.

"Reminds me of a younger Margaret and Joseph."

Margaret smiles. "I would agree." She turns to Mr. Hughes. "Were we really that young?"

Mr. Hughes smiles. "Yes, you were. Now, Margaret, forgive me for saying this, but you will have suitors knocking at your door in a few months."

"Mr. Hughes, that is a bit too much."

She gives Mr. Hughes the evil eye and smiles. "But if you hear of any suitors, you tell them to keep walking. I have no time for a suitor."

"Yes Ma'am." Mr. Hughes grabs the bag of groceries and two potato sacks and then carries them to the car. "Margaret, we only have two potato sacks. People have kept them instead of returning them."

"Thank you, Mr. Hughes," Margaret replies as she gets in the car.

Chapter 8 Church

Henry steps out of the Ford, closes the door, boldly flicks a cigarette onto the ground, and hurries to the passenger side. He sports a nice grey suit with a matching vest, which gives him a dapper appearance. He opens the door for Margaret to exit the car.

Margaret's green eyes and red hair radiate as she wears a dark black pencil dress, a black pillbox derby hat, and a black net veil. Black wrist-level gloves cover her hands as she grabs her black handbag. Like a Hollywood actress, Margaret always wears the latest fashion. The dress fits her perfectly, falling just below the knees, and stockings with a line in the back run down to her black stilettos.

Henry extends his arm and smiles. "Stunning as usual. Joseph would be talking about you in that dress for weeks."

Margaret smiles and grabs Henry's hand as she exits the vehicle.

Will, wearing black slacks and a dark grey button-up, collared shirt, pushes the seat forward and steps out of the car, following Margaret. He interlaces his arm with Margaret's and escorts her down the sidewalk to the church. Henry follows them.

"Maw, why do we have to dress nice on Sundays?"

Margaret smiles. "William, even though we are in Texas, where it is rugged, and fashion is sometimes forgotten about, when there is a choice, always choose to be fashionable, even in Texas."

The church, a rather prominent feature in Bennett Town, is made of tannish brick with an orangish-yellowish appearance. The three church towers are laced with white trim and the shingles are red.

As they approach the front white doors, a familiar face steps out. Henry groans for a moment. He whispers, "Margaret, I haven't had anything to drink today, as I promised."

Margaret's face grins with satisfaction.

Pastor Phillips appears cold and stoic in his black suit. He forces a smile as he notices Henry. "Margaret, it is good to have you and Will in the house of the Lord today."

Margaret smiles defiantly. "And Henry, Pastor Phillips."

"Oh, my apologies, Margaret," Pastor Phillips says, then looks at Henry with his hand extended.

Henry looks at the Pastor with disdain and begrudgingly shakes his hand.

Margaret looks at Will. "William, dear, I know you like to sit with your friends. Today, I would like to ask if you would accompany Henry and me for the service instead?"

Will nods. "Yes, Ma'am."

"Good, we shall sit as a family," Margaret declares.

Henry then looks at Pastor Phillips. "You wouldn't happen to have one of those fancy hand fans with Jesus on it, do you?"

Pastor Phillips grunts. "We do over there by the guest table. They are normally for the ladies."

Margaret walks over, grabs two, and then proceeds into the sanctuary. She hands one fan to Will and the other to Henry.

The church sanctuary has three sections of dark wooden pews, with twelve pews each. The front of the church has an altar with a green cushion on it and a wooden railing above it. Behind the altar is a podium and pews for the choir. All the wooden structures are matched in a dark wooden stain.

The windows are stained-glass. To the left of the sanctuary are three sets of stained-glass windows, with each top arched. The middle stained-glass windows are larger than the two on each side. The beautifully mosaic middle stained-glass depicts Jesus gazing upward to the heavens as he kneels. The other two handcrafted glasses have other religious figures, one in the fields and one in a building.

As Margaret walks down the church aisle, all heads in the congregation turn to her. She finds an open pew in the center section about halfway down. Gracefully, she walks down to the middle and sits down. Respectfully, Will and Henry sit to the right and left of her. Out of her purse, she pulls out a personal hand fan that matches her attire. She looks at Henry. "Wasn't going to let the Pastor get the better of you."

An elderly lady in a blue dress walks over and grabs Margaret's hands.

"Margaret dear, I am sorry to hear about Joseph."

Margaret nods her head. The woman releases her hands and turns around quietly.

The pipe organ begins to play as the service is about to start. Most of the town is in the congregation today. To the right section of the pews, Will notices Helen, Helen's mom, Joan, and Helen's dad, Earl. Helen smiles at Will. Sheriff Welch sits behind them. Will notices Percy, his mom, Frances, and his sister, Ruth. Gerald, Walter, Charles, and Ralph all sit in the back pews.

Henry looks around and then focuses on the Pastor at the front of the church.

The Pastor raises his arms gently and says, "Thank you all for coming to the Lord's house. It is good to see each of you here today. Our community has faced some tragedy, as we got word this week that Joseph Wood passed away in France while serving his country. We need to pray for the Wood family and extend our arms of love to help Margaret and Will. Let us pray."

Margaret fumes as she clings to Henry's hand. She whispers, "And Henry." She bows her head, and a flood of emotions comes over her. *I will never see Joseph again. It is over. We will never have what we had again. I have to carry on but without him. Oh, this is not going to be easy. I have to make the best of it for William's and Henry's sake. I never pictured life like this—*

"Amen!"

Margaret opens her eyes and lifts her head. She looks around, startled as the part of the congregation migrated around them. She gasps, then exhales. Two families are sitting next to Will. Three families have moved to sit next to Henry. They look down the pew at Margaret and nod in support.

The Pastor looks at the Wood family. "Our church is strong, Margaret, and we will be here for you."

Margaret smiles and then quietly says, "Thank you."

"Now let's turn to our hymnals to page 212 and sing ♪*In the Garden*♪."

The choir stands up, and the organ begin to play.

Henry looks over at Margaret as she reaches for a hymnal. She looks over at Will and points to the words.

Paw used to enjoy coming to church with Maw. Now, he will never sit next to her again. He slowly wipes his eyes as the song finishes.

"Please take your seats," The Pastor directs. "We will now have the ushers come by for the offering."

Margaret opens her purse and pulls out fifty cents. She hands it to Will for the offering plate. A older man with white hair and a white mustache that goes by Seth, smiles and nods as Will drops the change on the offering plate.

The church service ends.

"Maw, can I go over to Percy and Albert?"

Margaret nods.

"Margaret," a lady says as she approaches Margaret.

Margaret turns around. "Hello, Dolores."

"Itis good to see you, Margaret. If you need anything, please let me know."

They embrace briefly.

Another woman walks over. She is in her forties, and her brown hair falls over her shoulders and onto her green dress. She is a bit curvy and boisterous. She touches Margaret's arm. "I saw you at Jimmy Hughes's place yesterday, but I didn't say anything. You always light up any room you're in."

Margaret forces a smile.

"How is Will doing?"

Margaret swallows and says, "Alice, it's good to see you. Well, William misses his Paw, but he will be fine."

"Good," Alice replies. "If there is anything I can help with, just let me know."

"Thank you, Alice."

Will, Percy, and Albert walk behind the church, with Albert guiding them. As they get out of sight, Albert turns to them. "So, I just saw Helen's Paw, Earl talk to the Pastor and the Sheriff."

"You don't say," Will replies.

"The Pastor wants Earl to give money to the church so he can have a nice parsonage."

"Okay, the Pastor asks everyone for money. So, what's the deal?" Will asks.

"The Pastor also told Earl he can't stand your Uncle Henry."

"Are you pulling my leg?"

"Will, I wouldn't do that, and you know that. The Sheriff said your Uncle Henry is getting too big for his britches and Earl agreed with him. He then handed the Pastor an envelope full of money and patted him on the back."

"Holy mackerel, Will. What are you going to do?" Percy asks.

"What can I do?"

"I don't know," Albert says. "I don't think there is anything you can do except watch your uncle's back."

"Maybe I should attend church more often to get the scoop."

"Well, Helen is always here," Percy starts." So, there is a reason for you to come to church, Will. Albert and I are here too. However, you didn't sit with us today. You sat with your Maw. My Mom says your Mom always looks great even when she isn't feeling great. She says you must look out for her because of that. You could sit by Helen too if you like, I guess. But I wouldn't sit by Gerald and them guys. I'm not sure what the deal is with the Pastor. He seems more worried about himself than the people, but that is just me and how I see things."

Will looks at Percy. "Sometimes you are much smarter than you give yourself credit for."

Albert rolls his eyes and slaps Will in the stomach.

"You know I don't trust Helen's Paw, but she seems nice," Percy says.

Will grins, then nods.

Percy leans to Will and Albert. "You know the word on the street is your uncle embarrassed Earl and the Sheriff pretty bad the other night. That is just what I heard, but what do I know?" Percy throws his unbroken arm up in the air.

"Thanks, guys, but I probably should get back to Maw before the church ladies devour her."

"That is a pretty accurate statement," Albert says, chuckling.

Will walks back around the church and as he comes around the corner, Helen walks around. She grabs Will's arm and interlaces hers. "How are you doing, Will?"

"I am good," Will says. "How about you?"

"Me?" Helen places a hand on her chest, "Oh, I am fine as long as I have this dreamboat on my arm."

Will smiles, then turns and looks at her. "I heard Uncle Henry and your Paw got into a brawl the other night. Is this true?"

Helen pulls Will to the side of the church, and they huddle against the wall, their backs away from it. "Well, all I know is this. Paw came home, just a cussing the other night. 'That damn Henry has crossed the line. I will ruin his day if it is the last thing I do. I swear to God. That sorry Son of a Bitch, meddling in my affairs and all."

"Really?" Did he ever say why?"

"Nope, just went on for hours cussing, then he started yelling and cussing at Maw. I stayed in my room."

"I see," Will says and winks at her.

Helen lifts her head away from the wall and quickly looks around. She then leans over to Will and kisses him, leaving a lipstick stain on his cheek. She giggles. "I have to go, Will."

"Catch you later," Will says.

Helen runs off, and Will walks around the front of the church and spots Henry and Margaret. Henry looks over at Will and stares at him strangely. Will watches his uncle and then looks at his Maw.

Margaret turns to Will, and her chin drops. She looks around feverishly and then back to Will. She pulls out a white handkerchief. Then, she licks the handkerchief and frantically wipes his face.

"William, we are at church. This is not someplace to be smooching with the ladies."

Henry chuckles, pats Will on the back, and then gives an approving nod.

"Henry Wood, this isn't time to be the proud uncle," Margaret demands.

"Yes, Ma'am," Henry says, looking down.

"Maw, I was just standing there. She kissed me."

Henry winks at Will. "That's what I tell all the dames."

Margaret gives Henry a disappointing look. "You are not helping, Henry."

"No, Ma'am, I am not. You are right. Will stay away from girls at church. You never know they may drag you to the altar."

Margaret looks at Henry and then at Will, keeping a straight face. "That is true, William. Listen to your uncle."

"Yes Ma'am."

"Let's go home," Margaret directs.

Henry nods and walks to the car.

Margaret wraps her arm around Will. She leans on him as they walk. "Is this Helen that is kissing on you, William?"

"Yes Maw."

Margaret nods. "She seems like a nice young lady. A bit flirty, I might say, but still nice."

"She is nice, Maw."

"Good, I see her staring at you, with love in her eyes," Margaret says. "You have the same eyes on her, William. That is not a bad thing."

As they leave the town Margaret says, "Oh Henry, tomorrow, I have to stop by the bank and talk to Earl. Do you mind coming with Will and I?"

"I would relish being there."

"Good, I appreciate it, Henry."

"After you go to the bank, I think it is time for me to find a job. You don't mind if I go looking around, do you?"

"No, not at all, Henry."

"I figure the construction place is hiring," Henry replies. "Probably a good place for me to start."

Chapter 9 The Proposal

The next day, Will, Henry, and Margaret walk into the bank in Bennett Town. "Margaret, I just want to say, be careful with Earl. He is someone I don't trust."

Margaret, wearing a grey tea dress, clutches her purse. "I have high regard for your judge of character, Henry. I will take care of this if you don't mind waiting in the lobby with Will." She smiles. "If I need you, I will call you."

Henry nods. "Sounds good."

Henry opens the door to the two-story red brick building for Margaret. Margaret walks into the bank with her head held up high.

"May I help you?" Judith asks with a smile.

"Oh Judith, I like that baby blue dress you have on," Margaret says.

Judith smiles. "Don likes it, too."

"I bet he does," Margaret says.

Judith notices Henry, rushes over to him and hugs him quickly. "Thank you, Henry."

Margaret and Will look on with curiosity.

"Hmm, something you need to tell us, Henry?"

"Oh, no, Ma'am, just doing what Joseph would have done is all."

"What can we help you with?"

"I need to see Earl regarding our home," Margaret says.

"Just a moment, his brother, Butch, is in there with him. They are discussing a land purchase," Judith explains.

"I understand," Margaret replies.

Henry walks around the bank, pacing back and forth.

Earl's office door opens, Butch steps out like a man on a mission and walks directly to the front door of the bank.

Earl walks out of his office and looks over at Judith.

"Mr. Bennett, we have Margaret Wood here to discuss her house."

Margaret stands up as Earl approaches. He looks at Margaret and says, "Please come to my office."

Earl shuts the door behind her and sits down behind his desk.

Henry asks Judith, "Has Earl left you alone?"

Judith nods her head. "He has so far."

"Good. Let me know if something changes."

"I will."

A cigarette burns in the ashtray on top of Earl's desk. Earl leans forward with his fingers interlaced together. "First thing, Margaret, I am sorry about your loss. It is just sad."

"Well, Mr. Bennett, I appreciate that," Margaret says. "Life has to go on for all of us."

Earl picks up his cigarette, takes a puff, puts the cigarette back into the ashtray, and exhales. "So, Margaret, how much is your house payment?"

"It is $30 a month, and we still owe 18 years on it."

"You have been in it for about 12 years now, yes?"

"Yes, that is right."

Earl looks at his cigarette. "Has the army paid you anything yet?" Earl eagerly turns, anticipating the answer.

"No, not yet," Margaret responds. "I am supposed to receive a gratuity check this week. Then I need to file a claim for his life insurance policy."

With an evil grin, Earl leans forward. He looks Margaret over from head to toe, filling with lust. "Now, Margaret, I would hate for you to lose your house because you are waiting for the government to pay you."

Margaret gasps, "What do you mean? I have always paid the payments on time."

"I know this, Margaret, but if you miss a payment, I may be forced to foreclose your place. It is what it is. Then we would sell it to the highest bidder that covers the loan."

"Are you kidding me? I lost my husband, and now I am about to lose my house?" Margaret asks as she trembles.

"Oh, Margaret, there are ways around things like these troubled times," Earl says while watching her.

"What do you mean?"

"Can I be frank here, Margaret?"

Margaret nods. Earl picks up his chair, moves it to Margaret, and sits down beside her. He places his hand on her knee as he looks at her in the eyes.

Margaret shudders.

"So, Margaret, we all know you weren't exactly the best girl out there. I mean, you had Will out of wedlock."

Margaret slaps Earl and pushes his hand off her leg.

Earl smiles smugly. Then, he licks his lips. "Margaret, we all know you weren't married when you had Will. Whatever your reasons, but we also know you didn't marry Joseph until after he was drafted—"

Margaret interrupts with anger. "Mr. Bennett, first, William is Joseph's boy. Joseph was my husband, and I have been with him since we met."

"That may be so, but you are not an innocent woman. If so, you would have married him before you got pregnant. The whole town knows this and talks about it whenever you're not around. You know they even suggest that Henry and you are lovers."

Margaret gasps.

Earl places his hand on her leg again and smiles. "So, this is easy. You're a woman who hasn't had a man in some time. I am a man who can help you keep your house, just depending on how badly you want it." Earl slowly pushes her dress up.

Margaret trembles, then stands up and quickly steps away from Earl. "Mr. Bennett, you can address me as Mrs. Wood from now on," Margaret demands as she straightens her dress. "I will not cater to some bribery tricks. Either the bank takes my money, or so be it. How would it be if I told people what just happened in this office?"

Earl grins and moves closer to Margaret. "No one will believe the town trollop but they will believe the man the town is named after. Think about it," Earl says with a condescending grin. "Mrs. Wood."

"Mr. Bennett, I don't care what the town says about me. I loved and still do love Joseph. I have never been a tramp, nor do I have any plans to start now." Margaret points her finger at Earl. "What would Mrs. Bennett think about all this? Would she believe a woman, or would she believe her man?"

"Oh, Mrs. Bennett likes where the money comes from."

"I think our conversation is done here," Margaret says as she walks to the door. Earl places his hand on the door to keep it shut.

Margaret smiles, tilts her head to the side, and lifts her eyebrows. "Do I need to call my brother-in-law? From the whispers at church, you are not so bold with him in the equation?"

Earl looks at Margaret stewing. Margaret pushes him out of the way and walks out the door. As she leaves the office, "Henry and Will," she snaps.

Henry and Will jump up from their chair, look at each other briefly, then run to her. "Is everything all right, Margaret?" Henry asks.

"We will discuss it later," Margaret says as she storms out of the bank.

Chapter 10 Jobs

"Henry, take William home. I need to go to Drum's and see Mr. Drum," Margaret directs.

"Is everything all right, Margaret?"

Margaret shudders for a moment as she exhales, squinting her face as she collects her thoughts. Then she briefly looks at Will and then back to Henry. She grabs Henry's arm, forces a smile, lifting her chin up proudly, and swallows hard. "Henry, you are a good man. Everything is fine. We will discuss it later."

Henry, processing Margaret's energy, says, "Okay, Margaret. You want a ride to Drums?"

"No Sir, I can walk. It is good for me."

Henry opens his driver's door. "Do you want me to pick you up?"

"No, I will get a ride home. You go find a job. As a matter of fact, William, you can also look for a job. It will be good for you, son."

"Yes Maw," Will replies.

Margaret lifts her chin and smiles. "Good, then it is settled. I will be home before you know it."

Will looks at Henry. "Something got into Maw. I don't know what it is, but something was said or happened."

Henry shrivels his lips briefly. "Do I need to go confront Earl?"

"I don't think so, not yet," Will says.

"Hmm, okay, what about looking for a job? I plan on going to Trevor's construction company. You got any other ideas?"

"I know they used to hire people my age at the old Ice Plant," Will says.

"That sounds good. I will drop you off there, and then I will run to Trevor's. Afterward, I will swing by and pick you up."

Margaret walks down the street to Drum's Department Store. She gets angrier with each step she takes. Even though angry, Margaret still walks with unmatched grace, her head high, focusing on the horizon instead of what is in front of her. It's almost like walking into the royal court, with everyone watching the queen making her entrance.

She stops in front of Drum's Department store as she passes other stores on the street. Margaret grabs the door handle, pauses, takes a deep breath, and opens the door.

Cling!

Lucy looks up at the door chime and smiles as she recognizes Margaret. She stops everything and walks over to Margaret. "Margaret, dear, how are you doing?"

Barely able to contain herself, Margaret nods. "Is Mr. Drum in?"

Lucy points to the back. "He sure is. He is back in his office."

"I will be back here in a few. I need to see him."

"Okay," Lucy says as she walks back to the counter.

Margaret makes her way past the mannequins in dresses and to the back of the store. She steps in front of Mr. Drum's office, and sees him sifting through paperwork behind his desk.

"Hmm, Mr. Drum."

Mr. Drum looks up and cheerfully exclaims. "Oh Margaret, do come in. What brings you in so early?"

Margaret sits down, clutching her purse. She takes a deep breath, and tears start flowing down her cheeks.

Mr. Drum, in disbelief, looks around, grabs some tissue, and hands it to her.

Margaret gladly takes the tissue. "Mr. Drum, I am so sorry for crying in your office. Please forgive me."

"Margaret, there is nothing to forgive. Hell, you lost your husband."

Margaret shakes her head. "It is more than that."

Mr. Drum listens attentively.

"I just left the bank talking to Earl Bennett."

"What did that sorry bastard do now?"

"He told me they would foreclose the house if I missed a payment. Then he told me he could make special arrangements with me since I am the town trollop. Basically, if I slept with him."

"He said that?"

Margaret nods while sobbing.

"Lucy," Mr. Drum yells.

"Yes, Robert?"

Mr. Drum stands up and opens the closet behind his desk. He pulls out a pistol. "Lucy, I need you to stay here with Margaret while I head down to the bank."

Margaret's eyes grow in fright as she stands up as well. "Please, Mr. Drum. No. I need you to listen to me."

Mr. Drum looks at Lucy and slowly sits back down, placing the pistol on the desk. "So apparently, Earl is telling Margaret she can lose the house if she misses a payment and then propositioned her to accommodate her situation. Is that right, Margaret?"

Margaret nods.

"Okay, Margaret. Joseph had insurance, right?"

"Yes Sir, but from what I understand, it could take up to six months to receive the check."

"Will the insurance cover enough?"

"Yes, it is a $10,000 policy. I could pay the house off immediately and live comfortably."

Mr. Drum pulls out a handkerchief and coughs into it. He looks into the handkerchief and notices blood. He wipes his mouth quickly and conceals the handkerchief. He looks at Lucy, and she nods.

"You pay your house payment, Margaret, and if you are short, let me or Lucy know. You can pay us back once you receive your insurance payment. That will put Earl out of the equation. You know I never liked his sorry butt, anyhow. When we bought this place, we were also going to buy the place next door as well. Earl found out about it and beat us to the punch. He did it just to be a damn pest."

"I will also still get six months pay from the army for Joseph."

"He was in the 4th Infantry Division, wasn't he?"

Margaret nods.

"Yep, I was in the 4th in the Great War. The old Ivy Division." Mr. Drum smiles. "Joseph may be gone, but I must look after a fellow 4th Division Member and their family. So don't you fret on Earl. He and Butch are just a bad bunch."

Henry stops at the Ice Plant and looks over at Will. Will combs his hair. "Do I look all right to ask for a job?"

Henry chuckles. "You should mess your hair up and grab some dirt to rub on your shirt and cheeks. That way, they'll know you're not afraid to get dirty."

Will looks at Henry, not sure if he is joking or not.

"Will, my nephew. I am not goofing you on this. You don't want to go in there all decked out. That is a working man's job, not a dandy's job."

Will steps out of the car, looks down, and smiles back at Henry. As Henry suggested, he leans down and rubs dirt on his shirt and face. Then he stands up and says, "Don't worry about me, Uncle Henry. I will see you when I get home."

"That is the way to go. Now go in there like an ace and take that job."

Will walks to the front of the Ice Plant, and Henry drives away. He opens the door, and a sudden chill comes over Will. The factory is cold from processing ice, and the ice saw machine is loud inside.

"Frankie, we want the block cut to 25-pound slabs."

A wiry man replies, "Got it, boss."

The boss turns and looks at Will. "Are you here for an order?"

"No, no, Sir. I am here to work."

The boss, a stocky man in his early forties, looks at Will, his brown eyes peering out from his thick eyebrows. "Looking for work, you say?"

"Yes Sir."

"You look like a strong boy. Do you think you can handle slabs of ice up to 100 pounds and such?"

"Yes Sir," Will replies confidently.

All we have are blocks that weigh 300 pounds, but we have pulleys and such. This is hard work, son, but we could use you. How old are you?"

"Sir, I am fifteen. I will be sixteen in October."

"You're not a man yet. I will hire you, but not at a man's wage. It will be a boy's wage."

"Yes Sir."

"I will pay you .65 cents an hour. Fair enough. I pay men 1.10 to 1.20 an hour."

Will looks at the boss, "Yes Sir."

"You can call me Gus. I am Gus Foster. What is your name, son?"

"I am Will Wood."

Gus's face and demeanor change as he recognizes the last name.

"You Joseph and Margaret's boy?"

"Yes Sir."

"I knew Joseph. He was a good man. I will pay you .70 cents an hour starting out. I will bump you to a man's wage when you turn sixteen. Is that a deal?"

Will nods.

Gus extends his hand, and Will grabs it firmly. He looks into his eyes as he shakes it. "When can I start, Mr. Foster?"

"You call me Gus. Let's get you started now. How is that?"

"Thank you, Gus."

"Okay, so in the summer months, you will mainly help cut and load slabs of ice on the truck for delivery. Most think we don't work much in the winter, but we live in Texas, where the winters are still hot at times." Gus looks at Will. "You know what they say about Texas, don't you?"

"No Sir."

"They say the devil himself used to live here in Texas, but he fled to hell to cool off."

Will laughs.

"Now they also say that God had the devil leave Texas because this is God's country." Gus takes a deep breath, then wipes his brow. "You know, I think both of them have a bit of truth to them."

Henry stops the car in front of Trevor's Construction. He pulls his liquor bottle out of his pocket, takes a swig, and wipes his lips with his forearm. He leaves the bottle in the car and walks to the back of the construction company.

Out back is a lumber yard and Henry walks to where a couple of guys are loading lumber. "Hey fellows, you know where I can find Trevor Morgan?"

They both point to the door. One man answers, "He is in the office inside."

"Thanks, fellas." Henry walks inside to the office and knocks. "Trevor."

Trevor looks up and smiles, "Oh my, Henry Wood. How the heck are you?"

Trevor quickly walks around the desk, patting Henry on the back.

"What brings you down this way, Henry?" Trevor points to a seat for Henry to take.

Henry sits down and says, "Well, I am looking for a job, my friend. I need to work."

Trevor sits back down, pulls out a cigarette, and offers one to Henry. Henry takes one. Trevor strikes a match and lights his cigarette, then leans over to help Henry light his. Trevor takes a puff and exhales. "Well, Henry. I could use you and know you would be a hard worker. I've known you my entire life. We do have one pesky issue, though."

Henry takes a puff and then exhales. "What is that?"

"Well, it is this little issue of embarrassing the man the town is named after, ole Earl Bennett." Trevor smirks. "Now, I liked it. Someone finally put him in his place, but listen to me, Henry. Earl wields a lot of power in this town and is never one to be made fun of. He will always get up on someone when it is over. He brings us a lot of business. That's the problem. Probably half my business is dealing with Earl or his clients."

Henry nods. "Trevor, I don't want to put you in a bad way. I understand. I can go out to the steel mill and probably get a job.

Trevor leans forward, grabs Henry's hand, and winks. "Just hold on, old friend. You and Joseph, we all used to run around together. Joseph got the best girl in town. You and I were left chasing the others. I am glad you are back, Henry. I am sorry to hear about Joseph. He was a really good guy. I can hire you if you can lay low on Earl for a bit. Because of the war, I need another adult here. Most of my workers are teenagers. They like to play grab ass too much."

Henry leans back and waves his hand. "Trevor, I don't want to put you in a bad way with business."

Trevor laughs. "That's why I want you. You are looking out for me right now as we speak. Earl doesn't have any other place to go for construction materials. He can huff and puff all he wants. I can start you out tomorrow. How is that?"

"Deal," Henry says proudly as he stands up and stubs out his cigarette in the ashtray.

"Good, how is Margaret doing?"

"She is hanging in there. You know she is solid as a rock, keeping her head up."

"What about you? Found yourself a dame?"

Henry smiles. "Well, there is Peggy Ward."

Trevor is a little caught off guard. "Peggy is one of the few women in this town that I haven't heard anything bad about. It sounds like you may have yourself a keeper there, Henry. Who knows?"

"Time will tell."

"Let's walk the yard." Trevor points out the doorway.

"I just want some adult conversation. I am around these teenagers all day trying to be men. Most of them are all doll dizzy and can't get them to think straight."

"Haven't we all been there, Trevor?"

Trevor chuckles. "Yes, we have." He turns to Henry. "I remember you used to like to get into confrontations. So how did it feel with Earl?"

Henry smirks. "Well, you know, everyone is different. But in the army, I found that I thrived in confrontation. This sounds strange, but all my senses come to life and are at their peak. During a fight, I can smell things like never before. I can sense every moment as if it is slowing down just for me. I am in total control. I am at my peak. I'm not sure what all you heard about Earl, but I was in complete control, and everything was at my pace. If that makes sense."

"It does. Oh, the whole town knows about it. I heard it from several people. I even heard that Earl went home so pissed that he smacked Joan around. Now, she ain't ever done anyone wrong, but she is Earl's punching bag."

Henry breathes heavily. "There is no reason for him to hit a woman."

"I agree, but the Sheriff ain't doing nothing for this. Earl owns him."

As a customer pulls up in the back of the yard. Trevor and Henry shake hands. "Henry, I will see you tomorrow at six. Is that good?"

"Sure is."

"Mr. Drum and Lucy, I need to get back to work tomorrow. Is that okay?"

Lucy looks at her husband and back at Margaret.

"Hmm," Mr. Drum coughs, "It is perfectly fine, Margaret."

"I would also like to pick up sewing dresses and such in the evenings here on the sewing machine if that is okay."

"It has never been a problem. Besides, those dresses you make help bring the latest fashion to our small town," Lucy replies.

"I will start tomorrow. Thank you both for listening and understanding."

Chapter 11 The News

Margaret pulls the casserole dish from the oven and places it on the table. The steam and aroma of the chicken pot pie fill the air. Will sits down next to Henry at the kitchen table, while Margaret gracefully sits down next to them.

Henry leans over the chicken pot pie and inhales the aroma. "Smells great, Margaret."

"I wanted a nice meal tonight. It has been six months to the date since Joseph passed away. So much has happened since then. Although Joseph is gone, we still have a lot for which we are thankful."

Will looks on attentively.

Henry grabs a plate as Margaret scoops the pot pie onto his plate.

Margaret smiles, then scoops up some for Will.

"Maw, school is about to be out for Christmas. Gus told me I could get some extra hours in if I wanted to. If it is all right, I will take him upon that."

"William, I think that is a good idea, but don't let your chores fall behind."

"I won't, Maw."

"Margaret, I would like to bring Peggy over for Christmas."

Margaret smiles. "Wow, Henry, I have never seen you bring a lady over."

"Well, maybe it is time to start."

"I would say so."

Henry takes a bite of the pot pie and closes his eyes as he savors the taste in his mouth. His grins and chews the food while nodding in a euphoric fashion. "This is mighty tasty, Margaret."

"Thank you, Henry." Margaret looks over at Will and says, "So, I have a couple of things that we need to discuss."

Henry and Will immediately pay attention to her talking.

"I will stay longer at Drums for the next few weeks. I have several ladies who want some dresses made." Margaret smiles. "They want to look like someone between Bette Davis and Ingrid Bergman, with the dresses to boot, so I get the privilege of dressing them up."

Henry chuckles. "You mean to doll them up."

Margaret grins. "I guess that is one way of putting it." Then she looks over at Will. "That means you two hard-working fellas may have to fend for yourselves. Is that okay?"

"Sure thing, Maw, I will probably go over Helen's and sweet talk her into cooking for me. Or maybe I will get her mom to cook for me."

"As for me, Margaret, you know I can fend for myself, but I think Peggy will take care of me."

Margaret takes a deep breath. "My men are growing up." She briefly glances off at the kitchen counter.

Will and Henry look at each other in confusion.

"So, I got a letter from Western Union today."

Henry and Will turn to Margaret.

"It is from the insurance company. It is a check for $10,000. Tomorrow I will go to the bank and cash it. I plan to pay off, roughly $2100 on the house, and deposit the rest in savings. I will put $50 each into your savings account."

"Margaret, you don't have to do that. That is your money."

"I know Henry, but you have been a good brother and uncle. This is not up for an argument."

Henry doesn't know what to say.

"I would like each of you to meet me at the bank around 3:30 before it closes at 4:30. I plan on paying it off immediately."

"Margaret, you never told us what Earl told you that day."

"Nope, I didn't, but this should put an end to Earl in our lives." Margaret looks at Will. "William, yours is a bit different. Don't let him interfere with you and Helen."

"Oh, I won't, Maw."

"Good, I raised you right. A man always protects his lady."

Henry looks around for a moment. "You know Margaret, once the word gets out that you have received that check, people will come out of the woodwork wanting money."

Margaret nods. "That's why I am doing everything tomorrow. What is left over, which will be a considerable sum, will be used for unforeseen catastrophes or helping William or you, Henry, if you purchase a house, and so on. I am not sharing it with anyone else, nor will I spend it foolishly. I will remain frugal and live within my means. My job will provide a comfortable living without a house payment."

Henry takes a bite from his plate, chews slowly, and wipes his mouth with a napkin. "Margaret, you owe no one anything. It's just you and young Will here."

"That is why it is going into savings. So, it is settled. Tomorrow will be a good day."

Chapter 12 Bank Dilemma

Margaret walks to the back of Drum's Department Store wearing a yellow suit-style peplum dress with matching yellow suede pumps. The yellow ribbon in her hair makes the red hair more prominent and noticeable. She knocks on the door and pushes the door open slightly. Margaret gasps as Mr. Drum lies on the floor, curled up in a ball, shaking.

Margaret calls out his name as she shakes him.

Mr. Drum grabs his chest and coughs. Blood oozes from the corner of his mouth. His eyes make contact with Margaret's. He trembles in fright.

"I will be right back. I am getting Dr. Myers."

Margaret runs out of the store and heads to Dr. Myers's office down the street. She sprints down the sidewalk at a pace that any Olympic sprinter would respect. She quickly slides, breaking the heel of her yellow suede pumps. Margaret flings open the door to the doctor's office and yells at Nurse Beverly. "I need Dr. Myers immediately. Mr. Drum is lying on the floor of his office, shaking in pain. He can't speak."

As soon as Dr. Myers hears the news, he darts out of his office and down the street with Margaret following. She quickly removes her pumps and runs after him. They enter the department store and hear Mr. Drum coughing.

"In the back, Dr. Myers," Margaret commands as she guides him to the back office.

Mr. Drum is still on the floor, and blood is oozing from his mouth down his chin. Dr. Myers nods, then looks at Margaret. "Get Nurse Beverly down here and tell her to bring my bag."

Margaret moves over to the phone on the wall in Mr. Drum's office. She picks up the receiver and takes a deep breath while waiting for the operator to answer.

Dr. Myers grabs Mr. Drum's wrist and checks the pulse. "Steady old friend. Just try to relax."

"Operator, can I help you?"

"Yes, this is Margaret at Drum's Department Store. I need to be connected to Dr. Myers's office."

"Sure thing, I will patch you through." The operator waits on the line."

"Well, you have color in your face. That is a good thing." Dr. Myers smiles as he places his hand on Mr. Drum's chest. "And your heart isn't racing."

Nurse Beverly picks up the phone. "Dr. Myers's office."

"You have a call from Margaret at Drum's," the operator says before leaving the call.

"Nurse Beverly, Dr. Myers needs his bag down here at Drum's."

"On my way, Margaret."

Margaret hangs up the phone.

"Those are good signs. Why don't you go fetch Mrs. Drum if that is okay?"

"Yes Sir, I am on my way."

"You don't have to run, Margaret. Take your time. It lets me catch up with my ole friend while Nurse Beverly and I look him over. We will get him down to my office after checking everything out."

Margaret hurries out of the department store and heads to the Drum house. She briskly walks barefoot down the street. Walking, she ponders *Why Dr. Myers didn't seem to worry too much about this. Either he already knew what was happening, or it wasn't serious. Hmm, I hope Mr. Drum will be okay.*

Margaret arrives at the Drum house, and knocks on the door. Lucy opens the door wearing a red robe. "Yes, Margaret?"

"Mrs. Drum, Dr. Myers is at the store with your husband. I found him on the floor coughing up blood. Dr. Myers is there but he doesn't seem as concerned as I am."

Lucy's jaw drops for a moment. "Please come on in, Margaret."

"Let me get a dress on. Follow me, dear."

Lucy heads to their bedroom, and Margaret follows. Lucy gets a grey peasant dress out of the closet. She drops her robe, exposing her naked body. Margaret politely turns away. "Oh Margaret, don't be shy. It is just us girls."

"Now, Robert has been sick for some time. We have not told anyone this, so I don't want the town talking about it later. But Dr. Myers says he has lung cancer and thinks he may only have a couple of years left to live."

"Oh my goodness, Mrs. Drum. I didn't know. I am sorry to hear this."

"How does this dress look?"

Margaret, a bit confused says, "Hmm, it looks fine."

Lucy grabs Margaret's arm. "Listen to me, Margaret, we said we wouldn't let it control our lives and are not starting now. You know all too well about grief and death. I am not grieving my husband before he is gone. I hope that makes sense."

Margaret nods.

Lucy hugs her. "Good, and you can call my husband Mr. Drum, but you call me Lucy. Understand?"

Margaret smiles.

"Now, let's go down and make sure Robert is okay." Lucy slips on her matching shoes. "Wait, where are your shoes?"

Margaret chuckles. "Oh, I broke the heel off my pumps running to Dr. Myers's office."

Lucy takes a moment to think. "Well, make sure you pick a nice pair of shoes from the store today. If we have to order them, that is fine, too. We will put that on Robert's tab."

Lucy interlaces her arm with Margaret's, and they head out the door.

"So, Margaret, what is new at the Wood house?"

Margaret looks around to make sure no one is around. "Well, I got the insurance check yesterday. At 3:30 today, I will pay my house off and put the rest in the bank."

"Hot diggity dog. That is great news." Lucy looks around. "Don't let anyone else hear me say that crude hot diggity dog saying, but it is needed. You know you will have to be on your p's and q's now. Every suitor in a 50-mile radius will be knocking at your door looking for a potential rich wife."

"I know. Henry warned me."

Margaret opens the door to Drum's Department Store, and Lucy walks in with Margaret.

"Robert, dear," Lucy yells.

Margaret walks to the back. On Mr. Drum's desk is a note, which reads.

Lucy and Margaret, I got Robert at my office. Dr. Myers.

Margaret hands Lucy the note.

"Okay, Margaret. Looks like I am heading to the doctor's office. You have the fort. We will be back in time for you to go to the bank. Thank you for looking out after my Robert."

Lucy quickly hugs Margaret and leaves the building.

As Lucy leaves the department store, Margaret takes a deep breath and cleans Mr. Drum's office.

Time is passing slowly. Margaret tries on a set of pumps, walks around in them momentarily, and then looks into a mirror to see if they complement her attire. She gives them an approving nod.

Mr. Drum approaches Margaret and says, "I think you have something to do now, don't you?"

Margaret's chin drops. "Mr. Drum, are you okay?"

He smiles. "Oh, I will be fine. So, this is our little secret. Only Lucy, you, and the doctor know. No one else needs to know."

"Oh yes, Sir. Certainly."

"Now, from my understanding, I think you are due at the bank."

Margaret smiles. "Yes, Sir." She hugs Mr. Drum, separates from him, and joyfully hops around. Suddenly, she stops. "Mr. Drum, are you going to be okay?"

"Oh, I will be fine," Mr. Drum reassures her. "I might not have a lengthy stay left on this earth like planned, but I will be just fine. I think that phrase of making the most of each day will suit me fine." Mr. Drum smiles at her. "Now you go get out of here."

A somber and respectful tone sets in with Margaret. "Yes, Sir."

Margaret walks down the street in her new shoes. They are not the yellow suede pumps she had before. Instead, they are black suede with a rosette on them. Walking down the street, she proudly clings to her yellow purse. Pedestrians pass by, smiling and waving at her. As she approaches the bank, she notices Henry and Will standing by the car, both wearing dirty overalls.

Henry flicks a cigarette butt to the ground, then both men walks towards Margaret.

Margaret winks at them and then pats her purse. "I have both your savings account books in here."

Henry chuckles. "Thank goodness, I would have forgotten it."

"I know." Margaret smirks.

Henry walks to the bank door and opens it as Margaret walks through, with Will following. She then walks to the desk where Judith is sitting at.

Judith is wearing a green dress, wearing bright red lipstick, and smacking on some gum. "Hey Margaret, how are you today? Can I help you?"

Margaret smiles and says, "Yes, I would like to find out the remaining balance on my house today." Margaret removes the check from her purse. "I would like to pay it off with this. The remaining will go into my savings account." She pulls out her savings account blue booklet. "Except for $100. I want the $100 split evenly to William and Henry's savings account." She hands the check and the savings account booklets to Judith.

Judith gasps. "Wow, that should not be too hard. I need a few minutes, if you can excuse me," she says as she stands up.

"No problem."

Judith steps away and walks over to the teller counter. She discusses it with Floyd Cooper, who takes the check and steps away into a closed office. Judith returns smiling. "He will be just a few moments. Mr. Cooper has to get the exact numbers for your loan so you can close it out."

Henry smiles. "So, how is Don?"

Judith grimaces. "I, I don't know. We, uh, separated about a month ago, Henry."

"I am sorry to hear that."

Will and Margaret casually pace around the bank.

"Didn't have anything to do with Earl, did it?"

Judith looks down for a moment, then back up to Henry. "Well, it does. I have seen Earl now a few times."

Henry takes a deep breath and shakes his head. He looks directly into Judith's eyes and says, "You know, Judith. Don is a good man. There is nothing good with Earl."

"I agree with that. But look at Earl; the whole town revolves around him. Don just works on cars."

Henry looks down. "So I guess that makes you nothing more than a little gold digger."

Judith gasps as Henry walks away.

Floyd walks over to Judith's desk with some paperwork. "Margaret, I have everything you need here," Floyd says politely. "I need you to sign the back of the check." He hands Margaret a pen. She turns it over and signs it, then hands it back to him.

"The remaining balance on your home is $2074.85. Placing $50 into William's savings account and $50 into Henry's account leaves a balance of $7825.15 deposited into your account."

He opens each savings account booklet to show where it is written the deposit. Then, he hands her a receipt for the house payment and a separate receipt for each savings account deposit.

Margaret grins. "Good." She hands all the paperwork over to Henry except the house loan receipt. "Hold onto these for the moment."

Floyd looks at Margaret. "If you wait a few minutes, I will have the closed-out loan paperwork for you, or we can mail it."

Margaret smiles. "I think we will wait. Oh, Mr. Cooper, I would like a second copy of this receipt for the house. I know you have several carbon copies in your ole receipt book."

"Yes, Ma'am, give me a few minutes," Floyd says as he steps away.

"Henry and William, just find a place to sit down for a few." Margaret turns to Judith. "Is Mr. Bennett in?"

"Yes, he is Margaret." Judith stands up. "I can let him know you want to see him."

Margaret motions with her hand. "No need, I got this."

Margaret walks over to Earl's office and opens it without knocking. She steps inside and gracefully shuts the door.

The chunky man from behind the desk doesn't even look up. "Yes, Judith, what is it?"

She stands across the desk from Earl. "Oh, Mr. Bennett, I am not Judith," Margaret says as she notices red lipstick on his collar.

Earl lifts his head and grins. "So you need to come see me to make an arrangement to keep that house of yours, I see."

"No, Mr. Bennett, you have it all wrong." Margaret lifts her chin as she slides the receipt across his desk.

Earl looks down at the paper and pauses. He looks back up at Margaret. "Well, congratulations, Margaret. It looks like you own a house." Earl grabs the receipt and stands up. He walks around the desk and hands it to Margaret. She quickly places it in her purse. Earl steps closer to her, intruding on her personal space.

Margaret takes a deep breath. Earl suddenly grabs her around the waist. She resists by leaning back, but Earl still has a firm hold on her. "Now Margaret, this doesn't fix the matter of a lonely woman who has been around."

Earl looks her over with lustful eyes. With his free hand, he grabs her breast.

"No, no, Earl."

Earl licks his lips.

"HENRY!" Margaret yells.

Earl suddenly releases her and is caught off guard.

The door opens, and Henry barges in. He looks at Margaret as she tries to gather her composure. She points to Earl and doesn't say a word. Earl begins to backpedal as Henry walks aggressively to him. Henry grabs Earl by the shirt with his left hand. Earl falls back to the desk and Henry reaches behind his head as far as he can with his right hand and brings it down with a thunderous smack to Earl's right eye.

Will comes rushing in. "Maw, Henry, they are calling the Sheriff."

Henry turns and says, "Be sure to tell the Sheriff my full name." He turns back to Earl.

"WHERE IS HE JUDITH?"

"I WANT EARL BENNETT NOW!"

Everyone turns to see who is yelling. Will looks out of the office, and Margaret follows. Don Ross walks past Judith's desk with a pistol drawn.

"William, get out of here now," Margaret yells. Will runs into the bank's lobby.

Margaret turns to Henry and commands, "Henry, let him go. We need to leave now."

Henry looks at Margaret as she steps out of the office, then he turns to Earl, and yells in his face, "This isn't over by a long shot."

Earl is trembling.

Henry releases him, walks out of Earl's office, and accidentally bumps into Don. Don looks at Henry with sweat beading on his face. Henry is caught off guard by seeing Don.

Don fires a shot into Earl's office.

Everyone in the bank squats down in panic.

"You are never going to touch my wife again, you, you, you, damn marriage wrecker." Don squeezes off another round.

The Sheriff comes running in, and Judith points to Earl's office. Sheriff Welch tackles Don, dislodging the pistol from his hand. He then has Don face down on the ground and quickly handcuffs him. He slowly pulls Don up to his feet.

Earl boldly walks over to Don and looks him in the eye. "While you are at home, Don, I am snuggled up with your wife, and you can't do anything about it." Earl chuckles as his words set Don off into a frenzy.

Don fights vigorously while the Sheriff holds him in place. Don spits on Earl. "I swear before it is over with, I will kill you, Earl. I will watch you die."

"That's enough," Sheriff yells, as he tries to control Don.

Earl laughs. "I am not worried about you. Hell, Don, you walked in here, shot twice, and missed twice."

Henry looks at Judith and says, "You see this right here. You and Earl caused this." He shakes his head and walks away.

Floyd steps out from behind a counter. "Margaret, here is your second copy."

"Thank you, Mr. Cooper." Margaret lifts her head. "Henry and William, we are done with our business here today. It seems like the bank has more pressing matters to deal with."

Henry walks to the door, opens it, and guides Margaret with his arm. "After you, Margaret."

Chapter 13 Duncan House

Henry puts the car in gear and drives away from the bank. Margaret looks over at Henry. "Is it possible for you to swing by the liquor store and pick up some brandy? I prefer you get it for me, Henry."

"I would be honored to," Henry says with a smile. He turns the car down the back alleyway.

Margaret turns in her seat and looks at Will. "You don't mind if we take a little detour, do you?"

"No, Maw."

"Good."

Henry pulls the car in front of the liquor store. "Just give me a minute," Henry says, jumping out of the car and darting into the store.

Henry walks down the aisle, picks up a bottle of whiskey, and a bottle of brandy.

The cashier is an older man in his fifties. He looks at Henry. "Henry Wood, right?"

"Yes, Sir."

"I hear your family has just received some new wealth."

"You did, hey?"

"Sure did."

"Wow, news travels fast."

"This is Bennett Town, Henry. There are no real secrets here."

"I will take note of that," Henry says as he places money on the counter. "Keep the change." Henry nods at the attendant, grabs the bottles, and walks out of the store.

Back in the car, he hands the bottles to Will, and gives Margaret a wink as he puts the car in gear and heads down the road.

"Okay, Margaret, what happened back at the bank?"

"I showed Earl that the house is paid off, and he made a pass at me."

Will's face turns red as his anger brews. Henry looks at Margaret. "Margaret, I can end this but must leave afterward."

"No, no need for that. It seems Earl has burnt a few bridges."

"Yep, apparently, Judith and Don are separated. Judith is playing the role of Earl's mistress."

Margaret frowns. "It seems Earl likes to have several mistresses."

"It would seem so."

"I don't get it. Are women drawn to money and power because Earl is no catch regarding his appearance?" Margaret shakes her head.

Henry looks around and remains quiet.

Margaret smirks. "I did like that punch, though, Henry. It was very impressive."

Henry chuckles. "Yeah, I landed a good one on him. You know Joseph would have been proud of that one."

"Yes, he would have," Margaret says, then turns to Will. "William, it was a good punch."

"He should have bashed his brains in," Will replies.

Henry pulls up to the house, runs out of the car, and opens the door for Margaret. Margaret steps out and walks to the house. Henry waits patiently for Will.

He places his arm over Will's shoulder. "You know Will. It is only a matter of time before Earl gets his. Don't fret over it. His time will come soon."

Will takes a deep breath and looks at Henry. "I would like to be there when it happens."

Henry smiles. "Oh, wouldn't we all? Now you, my nephew, have to be careful with him. You are seeing his daughter. She may look at him differently than you do. If you like Helen, you must see her viewpoint too."

"She hates him."

"Really?"

"Yep, he beats her mom, and I am sure he hits her too."

"I never understood a man who hits a woman. Is it a control thing? I don't know, but something is wrong," Henry points to his head, "in that head of his. You should be careful around him and Helen and always get me if he thinks he is tough. I will take care of him."

"Yes, Sir."

"So, when are you seeing Helen again?"

Will smiles. "Uh, tonight."

"Good, you go do young people things then. Let me get those two bottles from the car."

Will walks into the house as Henry grabs the bottles.

"Maw, is it okay if I go see Helen tonight?"

Margaret smiles. "William, my working man. Of course." She walks up and rubs her hand through his bangs. "You know your Paw wrote me and told me that the front of the hair in England is called fringe, not bangs. That sounds a bit whacky, don't you think?"

"I do, Maw." Will takes a deep breath. "You know, Maw, for some reason, I miss Paw today."

"Me too, William."

"That deal at the bank makes me wish he was still here."

"Oh, I agree. You know your Paw would have killed Earl."

"I think Uncle Henry was about to kill him."

Margaret chuckles. "Yep, I agree. I must keep him from doing that. We need him around here too much for that. Now you get changed and have fun. I will work on that ole quilt I was preparing for your Paw. I figure you may want it one day."

Henry walks in. "Where do you want me to put your bottle, Margaret?"

"Oh, just set it on the table." Margaret rolls her eyes. "I think I may have some tonight. You going to see Peggy?"

"Yes Ma'am."

"Good."

Will, wearing denim jeans and a light blue long-sleeve button-up shirt, walks around the side of Helen's house and looks up at her bedroom window. He grabs a couple of small rocks and tosses them until one hits the windowsill. The window opens, and Helen looks out. She quickly motions for him to be quiet by placing her forefinger over her lips.

Helen surveys the area, discreetly slides out the window, and shimmies down the water drain onto a support post. Her pink dress flaps in the breeze. As she makes her way down, Will grabs her and helps her to the ground. Helen gives him a peck on the cheek. Then quietly says, "Let's go."

Will grabs her hand and then runs down the street like two burglars trying to avoid detection. As they pass two houses, Helen starts giggling.

"What is so funny?"

"Us, sneaking off into the night," Helen says flirtatiously. As they walk along the street, Helen skips and hops every few steps. "So, what do you want to do tonight?"

"Hmm, I dunno, maybe walk the tracks."

Helen shrivels her face.

Will looks around as they walk. "Too cold for skinny dipping."

Helen squeezes his arm. "Yes, it is."

"How about we go to the old, abandoned Duncan house and snoop around?"

"I like that idea," Helen says excitedly as she hops up and down. "A discovery adventure awaits us."

Will lifts his chin and extends his arm out. Helen interlaces it, and they slowly walk out of the town in unison.

"You know Helen, I don't have a flashlight."

She smiles. "I think we will be okay."

"We can take the tracks to get there. They run close to the old house."

"Sounds good."

"You're not offering me a cigarette?"

"Nope, I figure I can do without them."

"I see. Did you hear about the commotion at the bank today?" Helen asks.

"Hear about it, I was there."

"Tell me about it."

Will stops walking as they approach the railroad tracks. "Are you sure you want to hear this?"

The moonlight beams down as Helen nods her head. They begin walking along the tracks.

"Okay, but don't shoot the messenger," Will says reluctantly. "My Maw got the check for my Paw's passing away. We went to the bank, my Maw, Uncle Henry, and me, to deposit it and to pay off the house."

"She paid her house off?"

"Yes, she did."

"That is wonderful."

"So, after she received her receipt, she went into your Paw's office to show him, and I guess he made a pass at her."

Helen stops in her tracks and gasps. "Will you're not cracking wise, are you?"

Will looks at her in all seriousness. "No Ma'am. I wouldn't do that when it comes to something like this."

Helen watches him as he talks.

"I guess your Paw grabbed my Maw, and she screamed for Henry. He came running in and punched your Paw."

"That is where the black eye came from," Helen replies.

"Then suddenly, Don Ross walks in with a pistol, looking for your Paw. He was screaming his name. He went into his office. Uncle Henry left your Paw's office when they heard the Sheriff had been called. Don fired a shot and, I guess, missed. Then he fired another one, and the Sheriff tackled him."

"Do you know what it was about?"

Will looks down momentarily and replies, "Supposedly, Judith is your Paw's mistress."

Helen gasps and clutches her hands to her mouth. "I knew it. I knew it. Paw has been leaving the house at night, and when he comes home, he fights even more with Maw. She has accused him of having an affair." Helen looks at Will. "She found lipstick on his collars and women's perfume on his clothes. Oh, how I hate him, Will. I could kill him."

"You don't mean that, do you?"

"I do. He beats Maw. He has knocked me around before. He blames her for anything, and I guess he is cheating on her too."

"I am sorry to tell you this, Helen."

"Let's go to the old Duncan house. I don't care about him. I care about my Maw."

"Okay." Will is trying to think of a way to change the subject. "You know, I hear the old house is haunted or something. Young couples go in but never come out."

Helen elbows Will in the ribs.

"Ouch! I am only repeating what I heard."

"Ha, ha, ha. I am not scared," Helen says as she clings to Will.

Will points out, "There it is. An old three-story house." He takes a deep breath. "It probably has a couple of dead bodies in there."

"Will, I am coming here with you without a flashlight. Don't be giving me the heebie-jeebies."

They chuckle as they step away from the railroad tracks and cross the backyard. The front tower and chimney are visible from the back. The wind blows slightly, causing the window to shudder and creak.

Helen clings tighter to Will's arm.

"Are you scared, Helen?"

Helen shakes her head but doesn't say a word. She points to the back door.

"Are you sure you want to go in? We don't have a flashlight. All we have is the moonlight that will beam through the windows."

"I'm sure," Helen whispers as her heart races.

Will steps on the back steps with Helen right next to him. He looks around and then reaches for the door. The back door has an old brass doorknob. Will grabs it and turns it slowly, and the door opens. He looks at Helen and takes a deep breath.

"I will go first, then you can come in."

"Nope, you will go in with me holding onto you. We go together."

Will nods, then starts to walk forward. Helen grabs Will's belt that is above his buttocks. She hangs on tightly. Will walks in and realizes they are in the kitchen. He exhales as Helen looks over at the sink.

"It is dark, but it looks very dusty in here."

"You want to stay here, Helen, or go check out the rest of the house?"

"Let's go see what else is in here."

She grabs his belt again as Will walks through a doorway without a door leading out of the kitchen. It opens to the dining room to the right and another room to the left. Directly in front of them is an open door that looks like a tiny closet under the stairs. Will points to the dining room. "The moonlight is better on this side of the house."

Will walks into the dining room and jumps back. Helen screams as Will steps on her. Will quickly wipes cobwebs from his face. "Oh, I don't mind spiders and such, just not cobwebs and spiders on my face."

Helen laughs. "Well, if anyone else is here, they know we are here." She gets serious and says, "That might not be a good thing, Will." Suddenly, she giggles.

"Oh, you are having fun with this," Will says.

"I am."

They slowly walk into the dining room as Helen is still holding onto his belt. Will turns to the center of the house. "The staircase is there." He walks towards it but notices a room at the front of the house within the tower. He pulls Helen with him as he heads to the room. He slowly opens the door, and his mouth drops slightly.

"Look, Helen, an old library. This is incredible."

Helen separates from Will and stands next to him. She walks over and pulls a book from the bookshelf. "Too bad, I have no idea what the book is. Next time, a flashlight is a must for this adventure. Maybe earlier tonight. I should have shimmied my butt back up to the window escape and got a flashlight."

"I agree." Will chuckles. "I like looking at your butt when you do your window escapes."

"Ha, I bet you do," Helen says, smiling at him.

Will pulls a few books out, slowly flips through them, and then puts them back where he found them. He looks over at Helen standing by the bookshelf. The moonlight shines on her, high-lighting her pink dress, short blonde hair, and pretty smile as she looks through a book.

"Hmm, you want to go upstairs?"

Helen closes the book, puts it back where she found it and turns to Will. "Sure." She grabs Will's hand. "Lead the way, Will."

Will's heart starts to beat a bit faster with excitement. He walks to the staircase with Helen holding his hand. He steps on the stairs, and it creaks. With each step they take, the stairs creak more and more. Helen takes a deep breath with each step. They reach the top of the stairs. A hallway that leads to a bedroom on the dim side of the house. The hall goes around the staircase, leading to a small nursery above the library and a smaller bedroom above the dining room.

The bedroom above the dining room has a full-size bed with a chest at the foot of the bed and a dresser along the wall.

Will walks in, holding Helen's hand. He turns to her, pauses for a slight moment, and then kisses her. Time slows down as they are lost in the kiss. Slowly, they break from the kiss. Will bends down and picks up Helen. He carries her and lays her down on the bed. Will crawls on top of Helen. They start kissing and petting.

A light flashes through the window. Will jumps up off Helen. Helen sits up. "What is it?"

"I, I don't know. It looks like someone is driving up to the house."

"This is not good," Helen says.

"We just have to remain quiet. Hopefully, they will leave."

Will and Helen creep over to the window and squat down so they can see.

The car turns off, and the driver's door opens. A chunky man smoking a cigarette steps out of the vehicle. He walks over and opens the passenger door, and a busty woman steps out of the car.

Helen looks at Will and whispers, "Is that my Paw?"

Will whispers, "I think so, and he is with Judith."

Helen shakes her head. "My Paw is ruining my family, and now he is ruining my night."

"Helen, we have to figure out how to get out of here. They didn't come here for the library."

"Will, I may be blonde, but I am not dumb. I realize that. Let's sneak into that nursery. They ain't doing anything in there."

"Tiptoe, try not to creak."

"I know, I know."

Judith giggles as she and Earl approach the front door.

"People don't know that this house was almost completely paid for, but the Duncan family didn't pay their taxes so that I could get the house out from underneath them. They only had three or four more payments. I pay the taxes on it yearly, that's all," Earl explains to Judith.

"That is smart, Earl."

Helen rolls her eyes as she hides behind the door with Will.

The front door opens, and Earl and Judith stroll up the stairs. The stairs creak with each step.

Will looks at Helen, then leans to her ear. "I am not sure if we will be able to leave until they do."

Helen whispers in Will's ear, "If I have to stay here and listen to them, hmm, you know, I will throw up."

The hair on Will's neck stands up from Helen's breath. He whispers, "We may be able to sneak out the window and shimmy down."

Helen whispers next to Will's ear, "No, Will, getting a window open will be louder than walking down the staircase. I'll take my chances, either running down the staircase or waiting. Anyway, I am here with you. That is the saving grace." She kisses his neck behind his ear, then whispers, "You just want to look at my butt, is all."

Will suppresses the urge to laugh.

"Earl, are you sure no one ever comes here?"

"Oh, everyone thinks it is haunted. So, no one comes here. This is better than your place. I think your husband has people watching in on your house."

Helen fumes as she listens.

Will can hear Judith smacking her gum.

"Enough talking, Judith; it has been a day."

Will and Helen can hear Earl and Judith kissing and moaning.

Will whispers in Helen's ear, "They are in the master bedroom. If we tiptoe, as long as we reach the staircase, we can either dart off or quietly try to get down the stairs."

Helen moves her head and looks at Will. "Okay, Will"

Will kisses her quickly and grabs her hand. They start to move.

"Oh, Earl," Judith moans.

Helen takes a deep breath as her anger brews. She is fuming and ready to explode. They tiptoe out of the nursery. Helen thinks *just tune them out, Helen. Just get out of here.*

Will takes the softest steps possible, with Helen following. They approach the primary bedroom door and stop. Will turns to Helen.

Judith moans.

Helen fights the urge to scream. She nods, and they walk past the bedroom and slowly reach the top of the stairs. Will leans to Helen's ear and whispers, "If it starts to creak badly, we run."

Helen nods.

Will takes the first step successfully. Helen follows. They take another step and can still hear Judith and Earl in the background. Each step brings them closer to their goal, but each step seems like an eternity. They finally reach the bottom step and walk to the front door. Will slowly opens it, and they walk out the front door. They start walking away from the house and Helen suddenly stops.

Will turns. "What?"

"Will just wait a second, but be ready to run. We are running back to the tracks."

Will looks confused. Helen reaches down to the ground and picks up a rock the size of two fists. She walks over to her Paw's car and throws it. It crashes through the windshield. Will gasps.

Helen starts running. "Let's go." They run to the backyard.

"What was that, Earl? I thought you said no one comes out here."

"I don't know, but let me find out."

Will and Helen make it to the railroad tracks, a good distance away. They start laughing. "Oh my goodness, Helen, that was whacky."

Helen lifts her chin proudly. "Yep, I did that."

Will and Helen walk at a fast pace down the tracks.

Helen turns to Will. "Will when I get home. I am waking my Maw up and telling her everything."

"Do you want me there?"

"No, I got this, but I will stop by the Ice Plant and see you tomorrow."

"Okay, but I'm walking you back to your house."

"Uh, your darn right you are."

Chapter 14 Moonlight

Peggy adjusts her apron as she looks around the diner. It is almost empty. She walks over to one table and wipes it clean.

The door opens, and the chimes ring. Henry walks in wearing a nice pair of grey slacks, a white long-sleeve button-up shirt, and his brown jacket slung over his shoulder.

Peggy turns and smiles. "Thought I would see you here around closing time."

"There is no other place I could think of right now. How much longer do you have?" Henry sits down at the bar.

"Oh, about fifteen minutes. You want some coffee?"

Henry looks around. "Don't mind if I do."

"Give me a sec." Peggy finishes wiping the table and walks behind the counter. She grabs the pot and pours it into the coffee mug. She turns. "Black, right?"

"Oh, you know me all too well now."

Wearing a grey peasant dress with two front pockets and a sewing bag, Margaret opens the front door to Drum's Department Store. She turns the lights on and walks to the back of the store. Across the hall of Mr. Drum's office is a small room with a sewing machine and a seamstress mannequin. A cheval mirror stands behind the mannequin to help the seamstress.

She glances down at her watch and notices it is 9:30 in the evening. Margaret puts her sewing bag on the top of the sewing machine. She looks around, pulls out her bottle of brandy, takes a sip, sits down behind the sewing machine, and adjusts her position as she moves the wheel slightly. She threads the needle on the machine and pulls her fabric under the machine needle.

"Henry, it is time to go," Peggy says as she takes her apron off. She hangs it on a hook in the kitchen, turns out the lights, and walks to the front door with Henry. She locks the door as they leave.

Henry hands Peggy his jacket, and she puts it on. Henry pulls out a cigarette, strikes a match against his heel, then lights the cigarette. He takes a puff and then hands the cigarette to Peggy. She smiles and takes a puff, then hands it back.

"The stars are out tonight, Peggy," Henry says. "I figure we could walk down to the lake tonight. Just relax and enjoy the evening."

Peggy interlaces her arm with his and says, "It has been a long evening. That sounds good. Do you mind playing something soothing on that harmonica you have in your pocket?"

He gasps. "How do you know I have a harmonica in my pocket."

Peggy turns to him, stops Henry from walking, and places her hand on his chest. "Isn't a lady supposed to know everything about her man?"

Henry smiles and leans down to Peggy, giving her a peck on the lips. They turn and walk down the street and head out of town.

Margaret pushes the white fabric through the sewing machine and cuts the thread. She stands up and then adjusts the dress on the mannequin. Walking slowly with three pins sticking out of her mouth, she surveys her work. She pulls the bottom of the dress down a bit and then pulls out a pin from her mouth. Margaret tucks the bottom of the dress up a little and sets the pin to hold it in place. She does the same on the other side of the dress.

Margaret tilts her head to the side. "That is better. If Mrs. Simpson wants a Hollywood dress, a Hollywood dress is what she will get."

The moonlight is bright, and it reflects off the lake. Henry pulls his whiskey bottle from his back pocket and hands it to Peggy. She smiles and takes a sip. Henry leans back on the ground and lies down. Peggy screws the lid on the bottle, places it next to her side, and snuggles up on Henry's chest.

"Oh, this is peaceful, Henry."

"That it is. You know December nights in Texas aren't too bad, and normally, you get a clear night to have a good view of the stars."

"You like looking at the stars?"

"I do. I spent many nights around the world looking up at those stars, wondering if I would see the sunrise."

"That had to be scary."

"In some ways, scary. In other ways, it is peaceful. Peering up at the stars, you realize there isn't much purer than looking at the sky at night. It is you and nature. Nothing else. No radio, no yacking, no cars, just you and the sky. For once, you take a moment to observe it and truly realize the element you are in. Other times, you're too consumed with non-natural things. That is how I see it."

Peggy smiles. "I like that, but do forgive me, Henry, as I ask you to ruin this evening of peace and maybe play me something nice on that harmonica, ruining this quiet moment."

Henry smiles. "Well, Peggy, I will have to get up for this."

"Oh, I was so comfortable," Peggy says as she sits up.

Henry sits up and pulls out his Mississippi saxophone. He leans over, grabs the bottle, takes a drink, looks at Peggy, and says, "I had to wet my lips."

Peggy chuckles, shaking her head.

Henry puts his lips over the edge of the harmonica and blows out, then starts in with the ole Irish tune, ♪*Molly Malone*♪.

Peggy sits back and watches in awe as Henry plays effortlessly. The Irish dance tune tantalizes the evening stars. The moon's reflection dances to the small ripples in the water. Almost in unison with the melody emitting from the harmonica. Peggy grabs Henry's arm.

"That one is too fast, Henry. You know what I want to hear."

Henry takes a breath. "I know, it is what everyone loves. It is one of my favorites as well. I guess for a romantic evening, I can't go wrong with ♪*Danny Boy*♪.

Peggy smiles, then sips the whiskey. "No, you can't go wrong with that beautiful song." She places a hand on Henry's arm and nods.

Henry moves his lips over the harmonica and plays the old tune as if he came from Ireland and grew up playing it every day. The captivating melody arouses Peggy's emotions, and she wipes a tear from her eye as Henry plays. He belts out the final notes.

Peggy claps enthusiastically.

"You ready to go home?"

"No, I don't think so, Henry. Maybe we can just lay here tonight and see that sunrise you fretted over when overseas," Peggy suggests.

Henry smiles. "I like that." He lies back on the ground, and Peggy snuggles back onto his chest.

Margaret gazes at her watch and notices it is 1:25 in the morning. She looks her dress over one more time and nods in satisfaction.

"Mrs. Simpson will pass for a Hollywood star in this dress."

She grabs her sewing bag, turns out the light, and walks to the front door. Margaret yawns and quickly walks home.

Chapter 15 Aunt Beatrice

Will pulls a block of ice from the vat using a chain hoist and guides it to the cutting table.

Gus approaches Will. "Will, there is a Joan Bennett here to see you."

Will is not sure what to make of it. He ensures the ice block is secure on the table and follows Gus.

They walk to Gus' office, where Joan is casually looking around. Her dress complements her short blonde hair.

Joan turns as Gus and Will walk in. "Awe, Will, my daughter's beau." Joan walks over and tries to hug Will, but he steps back and looks down at his overalls.

"Mrs. Bennett, I am filthy."

Joan hugs him regardless. "It is all right. A woman must respect a man who works hard. A little laundry later is all."

She turns to Gus. "Mr. Foster, I do apologize for being so presumptuous, but would it be okay with you if Will and I had a rather short conversation in your office? I will certainly return him to his duties most urgently."

"Oh, Mrs. Bennett, no problem. Take your time." Gus steps out of the office and closes the door.

Joan grabs Gus' chair and pulls it around the front of the desk next to the other chair. "Please, Will, have a seat."

"Yes Ma'am," Will replies as he sits down.

"Will, I know much more about my daughter than she gives me credit for. I know she smokes, and I know she is very fond of you." Joan looks directly at Will. "I know when she sneaks out her window."

Will is getting uncomfortable as Joan's eyes are peering down at him.

Joan puts her hand on Will's arm. "Will, you are both young, and she adores you, so these things don't surprise me."

She takes a deep breath and pulls a cigarette from her purse. Joan strikes a match and carefully lights the cigarette. She takes a puff and then hands it to Will. As she exhales, Will takes a puff. He exhales and hands it back to Joan.

"What is surprising is that I underestimated my husband. Helen came to me last night when she got home. She explained everything, I believe." Joan pauses as she looks into the distance, then turns to Will. "And I believe her."

Will breathes out with relief. "Mrs. Bennett, I am not trying to start anything. I am also not lying. I wanted to beat him myself when my Maw called out."

"I understand. I have given him far too much liberty. More than any wife should. Is it true he made a pass at Margaret?"

"Yes Ma'am."

A tear runs down Joan's cheek. "Is it true that Don Ross tried to shoot Earl because of Judith?"

"Yes Ma'am."

"Is it true that you saw him with Judith at the Duncan house, and you could hear them acting like they were the ones married to each other?"

"Yes Ma'am."

Joan takes another big puff of the cigarette and then snubs it in the ashtray on the desk. She wipes her eyes and sniffles momentarily, trying her best to keep her dignity. She surveys the office and then looks at Will, forcing a slight grin. "Did Helen throw a rock through the car windshield, or did you?"

"Ma'am, Helen did."

"She told me she did, but I thought she may be trying to cover for you."

"No Ma'am, if I would have done anything, I would have beat him."

"Sounds like it is something that Earl needs. I cannot stand that arrogant asshole. Oh, how I wish he were dead. He is good at dishing those out to women but gets intimidated by strong-willed men. Hmm."

Joan looks around for a bit, then suddenly stands up. "Mr. William Wood, thank you for your time."

Will quickly stands up. "Yes Ma'am."

"Promise me this, Will."

"Ma'am?"

"You will always treat my daughter like the respectful Will, never like Earl would."

"Oh, that is a promise you can take to the bank."

"I am proud of you, Will. You have been through a lot and are still a teenager but far more a man than some men I know." Joan hugs him. As she walks out the door, she yells for Gus. "Mr. Foster!"

Gus runs back to the office.

"Thank you for allowing me to use your office. You have a fine young man working here."

"Yes Ma'am."

"Good day, Mr. Foster." Joan walks out the door.

Gus steps back into the office and looks at Will. "Is everything okay?"

"Yes Sir. All is good."

"Good, we have some ice waiting on you."

"I'll get right on it, Gus."

Margaret is out on the porch with her sewing bag, yarn, and part of a quilt. She sits in a rocking chair and starts stitching the quilt, little by little.

Henry walks up the steps. "Good day, Mrs. Wood."

Margaret smiles. "Good day, Mr. Wood. Did you have a good time last night?"

"Sure did, a rarity for me. It was uneventful. It was just Peggy and I relaxing by the lake."

Margaret looks up at Henry. "You sure it was," she pauses, "uneventful?"

"Now Margaret, I am never a man who brags about things. I am also one not to lie much, so yes, it was uneventful." Henry laughs. "I was just playing the harmonica and watching the stars."

Henry walks over and sits on the porch swing while Margaret continues stitching.

An older lady walks up to the house. She is short in stature, has grey hair, and wears a brown dress with a matching coat and purse.

Henry looks at her for a moment, then back to Margaret. "Aunt Beatrice?"

"Is that her?" Margaret asks.

The woman slowly steps on the porch steps and lifts her head. "I am looking for Margaret Wood."

Margaret looks at Henry, puzzled.

Henry asks, "Who is looking for Margaret Wood?"

"Beatrice, Beatrice Wood, I am her aunt."

Margaret stands up and helps her on the porch. "I am Margaret."

Beatrice smiles. "Oh dear, I didn't recognize you. It has been a long time."

"Yes, it has been since I was pregnant. I remember it well. You told me that I was not a Christian lady for being pregnant out of wedlock."

"Oh, let bygones be bygones," Beatrice says, waving the criticism off with her handlike swatting a fly.

Henry looks down and shakes his head in disappointment.

"You know, dear, I heard about Joseph and have wanted to come by. I just never found the time."

"Yes Ma'am, he passed away well over six months ago," Margaret coldly replies. "It has been hard on William, Henry, and me."

"Is that Henry?"

"Yes Ma'am, he came back early. He was wounded in the war."

"Oh dear, bless his heart. We have all had our hardships. You know misfortunes have struck us at our place. I could sure use a little help with some money and all."

Henry stands up. "So you didn't come comfort, Margaret or Will, once, couldn't even send a note since his tragic passing. I know you knew about it, but still, you did nothing. But you dare to come over here because you heard the insurance company paid her. I see right through you, Beatrice. My eyes are wide open. The clarity of what I see is beyond comprehension. Some may call it enlightenment. I call it cyphering from the bullshit you're selling, Beatrice, and seeing one for the scoundrel you are. I'll be damned if I call you Aunt Beatrice."

Beatrice's face turns beet red.

Henry looks at Margaret. "I got this. You go sit down."

Margaret walks back over to the rocking chair and picks up the stitching.

"You go back home the way you came, and don't let the door hit you in the ass as you go. You tell anyone that wants to come mooch off Margaret. That they will get no such thing here; they didn't lose their husband or father to the war."

"Or brother, Henry or their brother," Margaret injects. "You have grieved as well."

Henry turns to Margaret for a moment and then back to Beatrice. "Margaret is right. You should have been here the first week, looking out for young Will and Margaret." Henry points to the steps. "Now go."

She slowly walks down the steps. As she gets to the bottom step, she no longer walks feebly but with a normal stride.

Henry sits back down on the swing and looks at Margaret. "First the family, then it will be the local men in town. You better brace yourself, Margaret."

"Thank you, Henry."

Earl arrives home early from work while Joan sits on the front porch swing, smoking a cigarette and holding a shotgun. Her face angrily stews as Earl walks along the sidewalk to the house. He steps towards the edge of the porch.

Boom!

Joan fires a shot from the double-barrel shotgun, forcing the swing to sway. She stands up, tosses her cigarette on the porch, and steps on it to extinguish it. "Not another step closer, asshole. You are a two-timer and have embarrassed me and your daughter for the last time."

Earl quickly raises his hands in the air. "Helen, please, it has been a rough night." Earl edges closer to the steps.

"STOP!" Joan yells as she points the shotgun at Earl.

He stops in his tracks and begins to shake.

"You know I have another shot in this, and I will not miss. Go back to your car and stand by the door."

"What?"

"You heard me, you little two-timer. Step back, NOW!"

"I'm going. I'm going," Earl says as he hurries back to the car.

Joan smiles and pops the shotgun open. She replaces the fired and unfired shells and closes them back up. "Listen to me, Earl, two-timing, Bennett. The days of you coming over here are long gone. You are no longer welcome at this residence. You will not come by to see me or your daughter."

"But, Joan, she is mine too."

"Not anymore. She is not after she saw you in the sheets with another woman. No daughter should ever have to see that. We are done. You will pay all the bills and live elsewhere. I will live just as comfortably as before. Don't you slide on your responsibilities. If you cross me, I will tell the town about you, Earl. Are you listening?"

Earl nods, with his hands in the air.

Joan points the shotgun to his passenger headlight and pulls the trigger.

Boom!

Glass flies everywhere.

"Do I have your attention?"

"Yes, yes!"

"If you cross me or approach me, I will kill you, Earl. No one tarnishes my name or pride. Now go." She waves the shotgun for him to move.

Earl rushes into his car and drives away.

Joan lifts her chin with satisfaction as she watches him flee the house and driveway.

Chapter 16 Suitors

Will tosses his apron on the table at the Ice Plant. "You got anything else, Gus?"

"Nope, sure don't. Have a good night, and don't get in trouble. See you Monday."

"Yes Sir," Will replies, walking out the door. As he steps out on the street, he notices Percy and runs over to him.

"Whatcha doing tonight, Percy?"

"Uh, probably nothing. There ain't much to do this time of year. You like working at the Ice Plant?"

"It pays," Will says with a smile.

"I have been staying out of trouble, is all. I am making my Maw happy. She still says I get in trouble or talk too much. I don't talk too much, do I, Will?"

Will chuckles. "You don't want me to answer that, do you?"

Percy briefly looks down at the ground, then kicks a rock. "I guess I just have a lot to talk about."

Will nods. "Have you seen Albert?"

"No, but I can find him. Do you have any plans with Helen for tonight? I heard her Paw moved out. I also heard her Paw is no good. My Maw talks about it. Does it get cold in the Ice Plant when you work there?"

Will smirks. "Yeah, it is a bit cold, but in the summer, it is perfect." Will pats his pockets, looking for a cigarette. Then he looks back at Percy. "Hey Percy, let's meet tonight around 9:00. You, me, and Albert if you can find him. Maybe we can get into a little trouble to pass the time. What do you think?"

Percy's eyes light up. "Yes, it has been so boring around here. I feel like time has stopped with nothing to do. Let's have some good ole Will and Albert fun. Maybe I will invite Gerald too?"

"Only Gerald, not his other pals. They are not to be trusted."

"Sounds good."

Will steps away, then turns. "Oh Percy, we need flashlights tonight."

"We have some at the house. I will bring them."

148

"Mr. Drum, you have yourself a good day," Margaret says. "I may be back tonight. I am working on a new dress for Sara Hopkins." Margaret smiles. "She wants to have that Starlight look from Hollywood. I think I can help her out."

"Margaret, you have a nice day as well," Mr. Drum replies as Margaret walks out.

Margaret strolls down the street, clinging to her purse. She looks ahead towards the bank as she gracefully glides down the street.

"Hey there, lady," a familiar voice yells.

She turns to see Henry running across the street.

"You need an escort home," Henry asks as he extends his arm.

Margaret interlaces her arm with Henry's. "That would be nice, Mr. Wood."

"Have you seen Will today?"

Margaret turns and looks at the Ice Plant. "No, I think he will probably be at home by the time we get there. They close earlier on Saturdays than we do."

They proceed down an alley that leads out of town.

"Busy day today?"

"Not so much. But I will be back at the store later tonight. Working on a dress for Sara Hopkins."

Henry tugs her arm. "Do I need to pick up some more brandy?"

Margaret smirks. "Now, now, Henry. I can survive without a drink each night." She rolls her eyes, "But it does soothe the soul."

Henry chuckles. "I find that it is very soothing."

They walk down the road with the house in sight. Henry leans over to get a better view.

"Hmm, Margaret, someone is waiting for you on the porch."

"Who is that?" Margaret replies.

"I don't know. I don't recognize him. But he is in a suit and has flowers. He seems like a wishful suitor to me. Do you want me to handle it?"

"No, I got this," Margaret says with a smirk. She looks over at Henry inquisitively and toys with him. "He seems quite confident as he sits in the swing."

Henry shakes his head. "That he does."

"Henry, let me go ahead, and you can follow along. Let me address this, and you can come up as we talk."

"Yes Ma'am," Henry replies as he pulls out a cigarette and lights it.

Margaret walks up to the house. As she approaches the porch, the gentleman stands up with confidence. He peers down from the porch wearing a dark grey suit and matching vest, with a white pinstripe shirt under his vest. His shoes are shiny and match his suit. His black hair is slicked back.

"Margaret Wood," he says as he walks toward the steps.

Margaret stops in her tracks. "Yes, I am Mrs. Wood. Why are you on my porch?"

"Oh, Mrs. Wood, I was waiting for you to return home."

She lifts an eyebrow. "And your name is?"

"I am sorry, Mrs. Wood. I am Gary Brooks. I live in Steel City."

Margaret looks around and then back to Gary. "Mr. Brooks, I would like to know why a handsome man like yourself would come from Steel City to Bennett Town to sit on my porch and see little ole me. What do I have to offer that would lure you this far?"

"Well, Mrs. Wood, your beauty is known throughout the area."

"So, you came purely because of my beauty? That seems like such an adolescent thing to do. Well, Mr. Brooks, I am sorry you traveled this far. I am a married woman. Maybe it is time for you to leave my porch."

"Hmm, Mrs. W—

"Excuse me, Gary," Henry interrupts. "I think this nice lady asked you to leave. Is there a problem with that?" Henry tosses his cigarette butt to the ground as he walks to Margaret.

Gary's frustration shows in his face as he steps off the porch. He looks at Margaret and Henry as he walks by, then drops his head as he walks away.

Henry watches Gary's every move. Margaret casually walks up the steps and sits on the porch swing.

"Margaret," Henry says as he turns towards her. "He won't be the last, you know."

"I know, but I got this."

"What happens when one of these so-called suitors shows up to Drum's at ten at night when you're sewing?"

Margaret stops swinging, "You know, Henry, I haven't given it much thought. Do you think that will happen?"

"I do, Margaret. You are now considered a woman of wealth, and everyone knows it. They are just waiting for the ideal time to approach you."

She bites her lip. "Henry, I am still going to live my life and not put it on hold from these predators."

"Will and I can take turns checking in on you when you are sewing at night. How does that sound?"

Margaret smiles. "That sounds fine."

Albert and Gerald walk up to Will. Will looks around. "Where is Percy?"

"Oh, he ran back to get one more flashlight. He has a tater sack with three of them in it, but you know Percy," Albert replies.

"Percy is fun," Will says as he looks at his watch.

"What do you have for us, Will?" Gerald asks as he pulls out a comb and combs his hair.

"Oh, just wait, my friend. I think it will be fun tonight. Then again, it could be boring," Will replies.

"Hey guys." Percy waves as he walks past a streetlight. He runs to Albert. "I got us all a flashlight for tonight. I am excited. What cool thing are we doing tonight, Will? Are we going to the cemetery? Going to do some sneaky army stuff? Peep in on the dames?"

"Yeah, you would like that," Gerald says. "Peeping in on Ruth, I bet."

"I don't need to peep in on Ruth. Ruth—

Will slaps Percy quickly in the stomach.

Albert's eyes grow in anger.

"Guys, it may be nothing, but then it may be something. Tonight, we will sneak in the back door of the Duncan house."

Gerald holds the flashlight under his chin and turns it on. "Boo, spooky spooky!" Then laughs in a haunting manner.

Will grabs a flashlight and says, "Follow me, fellas." He starts walking down a trail to the railroad tracks.

Gerald slaps Will in the chest. "So Percy, you are being quiet back there." Gerald winks at Will. "Tell us what you meant about Ruth back there."

Albert walks next to Percy and gives him the evil eye, Percy utterly oblivious to it. "Well, Ruth and I, you know, I have grown to like her kissing me. She is good at keeping secrets. My Maw told me I should always respect someone who can keep a secret. You know Maw has always guided me, right. I can't say that about others, but it seems to me all she wants is to protect me."

"Percy!" Gerald yells. "We want to know about Ruth. Don't we, Albert?"

"I don't know if I do, but Percy, stay on the topic."

"Well, she told me if I showed her mine, she would show me hers."

Will and Gerald stop in their tracks and turn to Percy and Albert. They all look at Percy with anticipation of his response.

Gerald smirks. "Well?"

Percy nods in a non-guilty manner. "Oh, yeah, I got to see her unmentionables."

Albert gasps and struggles to get the words out. "And you showed her yours?"

Percy nods his head. "Yes. I thought that was a good swap. Ruth said we could do that again anytime I wanted. I have thought about taking her up on that several times, but something always comes up. I was going to tonight, but Will mentioned this."

Gerald busts out laughing hysterically. "You came with us instead of seeing some dame's privates?"

"Oh, I didn't see her privates. I saw her undergarments. Anyway, tonight sounded like too much fun with you guys to pass up. What did I do wrong?"

"Nothing," Gerald says as he rolls his eyes. Then he walks over to Albert and slaps him in the chest. "Don't worry; it seems your sister is safe with Percy."

"It seems I have to keep my eye on Percy," Albert replies.

They approach the railroad tracks.

"Okay, fellas, we got to keep quiet from here on out. I am pretty sure Percy will divulge every detail," Will says. "Lights out along the tracks."

The moon peers down on them from the evening sky, lighting their path.

Will stops and turns. "Okay, we will all scoot quietly to the back door. Once in, we can use our flashlights. We can check things out for a few minutes, but after about twenty minutes inside, I want us all to make our way to the second floor of the nursery."

"Why the nursery, Will?" Percy asks.

"Because there we can see when someone pulls up. We may have a visitor tonight," Will smiles.

They rush to the back door. Will turns the brass knob and opens the door. He shines the flashlight around. *Wow, it looks slightly different, with some light shining on things.* Albert steps in and moves through the kitchen. Percy and Gerald make their way in. Percy is a bit nervous. Gerald touches him on the shoulder, and Percy jumps.

Will walks through the dining room and then heads to the library. He walks up, pulls down a book, and breezes through it.

Then he pulls down another old book, *The Picture of Dorian Gray*, and flips through the pages. About halfway through the book, he stops flipping the pages and sits in a chair. He slowly starts reading as everyone moves around throughout the house.

Will shines his light on the page. It begins to dim a little. *Dang it.* He closes the book, turns off the flashlight briefly, and then places the book back on the shelf.

Gerald and Percy start walking up the stairs, creaking with each step. Albert walks into the library and shines the light on Will.

"Are you okay from what Percy said?"

"Will I'm fine."

"Good, let's get upstairs." Will leads Albert upstairs.

As they top the stairs, Gerald greets them. "Will, this bedroom right here. Someone has been using it for some adventures, it seems. The rest of the house is coated with dust, but this bed has newer linen, which is not made like the rest of the stuff in the house. It is out of place."

Will smiles. "Yep, I know. Let's all go to the nursery and hang out. Once in there, let's turn out the flashlights."

They approach the nursery, "Will, did anyone die in this house or get murdered here?" Gerald asks.

"Uh, not that I know of," Will replies.

"Well, I feel better now," Percy replies as he sits in a wooden chair in the nursery.

Will walks to the window and waves for everyone to gather around.

"Okay, let's just sit down and lean up enough to peer out the window."

"What are we looking for?" Albert asks.

"The other night, Helen and I were up here."

"Ha, that's why the bed is messed up," Gerald replies.

"No!" Will says scornfully. "We were up here kissing, but in the other room. Then we heard a car pull up. It was her Paw and Judith from the bank. They went into that bedroom and did what you suggested."

"Wait!" Gerald replies. "You mean Judith Ross?"

"Yeah," Will replies.

"She is an aunt or something. She is married to my Maw's brother, Don Ross, the mechanic."

"I am sorry, Gerald. I didn't know," Will says sympathetically.

Headlights shine on the road approaching the house.

"Okay, everyone, we must be quiet—even you, Percy! Someone is coming down the driveway."

They all huddle at the windowsill with their eyes peering over the edge. The car stops in front of the house, and Earl steps out of the driver's seat. He looks around momentarily and then leans on the car's hood.

Will looks at Gerald and whispers, "He is by himself. Last time Judith was with him."

Headlights emerge on the road approaching the house. As it gets closer, they recognize the car.

"That's the Sheriff's car," Percy says, trying to whisper as he talks. "We are going to jail."

"Percy, just wait," Albert whispers reassuringly.

Sheriff Welch steps out of the car and adjusts his belt. He walks over to Earl, briefly looks up at the Duncan house, and looks back at Earl.

"So, Mr. Bennett, you wanted to meet out here?"

Earl pulls out a hand-rolled Maduro Perfecto Cigar. He cuts the tip, letting it fall to the side, and then pulls out a box of matches. He strikes the match and lights the cigar methodically. Then, he takes a big puff, looks at the Sheriff, and blows out some smoke.

Will looks at Percy and holds a finger to his mouth to be silent. They all listen attentively.

"I got something for you," Earl says as he pulls out an envelope full of cash and he hands it to the Sheriff.

Sheriff Welch takes the envelope, looks through the paper money, and quickly places it in his pocket.

Earl motions with his cigar in his hand. "Now, Sheriff, I need Don Ross to stay in jail for another couple of weeks to finish what I want to do."

The Sheriff nods. "You still having secret rendezvous with Judith?"

Earl smiles as he brings the cigar to his face. "Yep, almost every night, and she has no idea."

Gerald looks at Will and whispers, "No idea? What is that?"

Will shakes his head. "I don't know."

"I figure I can enjoy Judith for a couple more weeks, then fore-close on her house. Another property falls into my hands, and she has no clue. Her husband rots in jail and misses his house payments. Not once did it occur to her. She is too fixated on having a fling and her marriage being done."

"Mr. Bennett, you are one dastardly man, if I might say so myself," the Sheriff replies.

"Well, Sheriff, you don't get the town named after you unless you are doing some shady things. I am a master at it. Oh, I will find another victim after her. You keep him in jail until the deed is done." Earl smiles. "Sheriff, I have secured about fifteen properties this way. Now, Judith is the only one as my secretary, and as for the rest, I have fun with their wives. It distracts the husband, so no one watches the payment missing, and then I foreclose on them—just an easy real estate transaction for me and nice money in my pocket. The late-night rendezvous is just the icing on the cake, is all. Oh, how I like my icing."

"Yes, you do, Mr. Bennett, yes you do. When do you see Judith again?"

"Oh, I go pick her up in about an hour. I will bring her back here and continue our little fling. She is a fiery one in the sack, if you know what I mean," Earl boasts as he puffs on his cigar.

"Mr. Bennett, if that is all tonight. I figure I would head on home."

"Sounds good, Sheriff; go have fun tonight."

Gerald lowers himself below the windowsill and takes a deep breath. He looks at Will and whispers, "Did you hear that?"

"I did, Gerald. That isn't why I brought you out here. I had no idea about this."

A car pulls away from the front of the house.

"I know Will. You know there are four of us. We can take Earl out right now if we want."

Will looks around for a moment. "God, I would love to. He is out of control."

The second car pulls away from the front of the house.

Will stands up and looks at Percy, Albert, and Gerald. "I have a plan."

Chapter 17 A Well-Executed Plan

Percy hides in the bushes outside the house while Albert remains in the nursery. Percy flickers his flashlight to the window in the nursery, and Albert does the same to Percy.

Will and Gerald are hiding in the library. "You ready, Gerald?"

"I am, Will. I think this will work out for all of us."

They turn and look out the window. In the distance, a set of car lights is heading their way.

"It is showtime." Will and Gerald hide behind the door of the library.

Albert squats down and looks over the windowsill as the car pulls up in front of the house.

The car stops, and Earl gets out. He hurries over to the passenger side and opens the door. Judith steps out of the car, smiling. She steps away as Earl closes the door, then interlaces her arm with Earl as they walk to the house.

Earl opens the door and guides her through the front door. Judith giggles as they walk into the house.

Gerald is trying his best to maintain his composure.

"Come on, Earl, it's cold. I need you to warm me up."

Earl and Judith swiftly move up the stairs.

Will whispers to Gerald, "Let's give them a few minutes."

Time moves slowly as they wait. Passionate sounds resonate throughout the house from the upstairs bedroom.

Gerald breathes heavily and looks at Will. Will steps from behind the door, and Gerald follows. Will stands before the library window and flickers his light to Percy. Percy flickers back. Will and Gerald quietly leave the library and walk out the front door. Both stand on the front porch with their back against the wall and the door between them.

Percy walks over to the car, opens the driver's side door, and sits in it. He smiles briefly, then turns the headlights on and honks the horn repeatedly—the horn blares.

"Earl, what is that?"

"I don't know, but I will go find out. You stay here." Earl grabs his clothes and walks out of his room. He then proceeds to stumble in the clothes. Albert listens attentively from the nursery.

Earl walks to the edge of the stairs and starts walking down.

Albert discreetly moves from the nursery to the bedroom. He shines a flashlight on Judith's exposed body. She quickly pulls the covers over her.

Albert shines a light on his face and holds a finger to his mouth to make her quiet. "Now, I have to talk to you, and I only have a few moments."

Earl steps off the bottom stairs and opens the front door. Percy turns the car lights off.

"Who the hell are you?" Earl yells.

Percy turns the lights back on, and Earl blocks the lights to his eyes as he steps on the porch.

"NOW!" Will yells.

Gerald kicks Earl's feet out from underneath him. Earl's body crashes to the porch, and Will kicks him in the kidneys.

"That is for my Maw, you bastard," Will yells as he kicks Earl in the stomach. "Next time, I will kill you."

Gerald stands up and kicks Earl in his tenders. Earl screams in pain.

"You are lucky I don't kill you, you sumabitch," Gerald yells as he proudly walks around Earl who is curled up in the fetal position.

Judith frantically clings to the blanket as she pulls it up to her chin.

Albert shines the light on his face as he cautiously extends his arms nonconfrontationally and approaches the bed. "Mrs. Judith, it is me, Albert. We all heard Earl and the Sheriff talking. They are setting you up."

Judith's demeanor changes slightly.

"Earl is keeping you distracted while your husband is in jail. No one is paying the house payment. He is swindling the house out from under you."

Judith gasps and angrily stands up. The blanket falls to the floor.

Albert's eyes swell up to the size of silver dollars as he gets an eye full.

"Albert! Turn around while I get dressed. You can fill me in while you look away."

"Yes Ma'am."

Earl looks up at Gerald, and Gerald kicks him square in the nose, and Earl loses consciousness. Gerald quickly fumbles through Earl's pockets. He pulls out his keys and raises them high. "I got them."

Will kicks Earl again in the chest, but Earl doesn't move.

Gerald and Will look at each other. "I think we sent a message," Gerald says.

"I believe so," Will replies.

Percy runs up. "Is he still alive?"

"Oh yeah, he is breathing. He is just out of it, is all," Gerald says.

"Awe Shucks!" Percy exclaims.

"Percy! I didn't see that from you," Will says.

Percy looks around. "Well, after he tried to have his way with your Maw, he has ruined Gerald's family. He deserves it."

"I agree," Gerald says.

Albert and Judith slowly walk out the front door. Everyone looks at Judith. She looks back. "I know now. I am such a fool."

Gerald looks at Judith, holding the keys in the air. "Do you want to drive us home, or do you want me to drive?"

Judith smiles, "I will drive."

Albert looks at Will and Gerald. "What about him?"

"Leave him, he can walk home," Will replies.

Percy moves over to Earl, removes his shoes, and throws them into the bushes. He looks at Will and says, "It is a long walk home for him and serves him right on this cold night."

Albert chuckles as he walks to the car. Gerald gets in the front passenger seat while the other three pile into the back seat. Judith gets in the driver's seat and cranks the car. Her perfume saturates the air in the confined space of the vehicle. She puts the car in gear and lets out of the clutch, spitting dirt as she turns the car down the dirt road.

"What are you going to do, Aunt Judith?"

She looks over at Gerald. "First thing I am going to do is take all of you home. Then, I am going to confront the Sheriff on what I know and get my husband out of jail. Once we get home," Judith takes a deep breath, "Well, that is none of your business, but I assure you he will never doubt his Judith again. I am going to the bank on Monday to make the last two payments. I have the money. Earl had been giving me money. Well, I will use his money."

Gerald smiles.

"I just hope your Uncle Don will have me back. I have done him wrong. No man should be treated the way I treated him." Tears flow down Judith's cheeks.

Margaret grabs the balance wheel on the sewing machine and rotates it slightly, then takes her scissors and cuts the thread.

Cling!

The front door chimes at Drum's rings.

"Henry, is that you?"

"Uh, no, Ma'am. My name is Fred Hester."

Fred walks to the back of the department store. He is wearing black slacks and a tucked-in grey long-sleeve dress shirt. He has blond curly hair and appears to be in his late 30s.

Margaret quickly stands up behind the sewing machine and removes her sewing apron. "Can I help you?" she asks as she steps out of the sewing room.

Fred almost runs into Margaret as she steps out.

She clutches her chest. "Oh my goodness, you about scared me. Can I help you?"

"Oh, I just came to enjoy the pleasure of your company."

"Ugh, look here, Mr. Hester, is it?"

"Yes, Ma'am, it is."

"I don't know what you have heard, but I am married. I plan on remaining a married woman. Nothing has changed in that matter."

Fred tilts his head. "Margaret!"

Cling!

The door chimes ring.

Margaret steps to Fred, points to his face, and angrily says, "Do NOT call me Margaret. I am Mrs. Wood to you."

Fred quickly grabs Margaret by the wrist.

"I think Mrs. Wood has expressed her displeasure in your company," a familiar voice says.

Fred turns. "Who the hell are you?"

Henry smiles. "A man who loves confrontation." Henry steps in between Margaret and Fred.

"Margaret, are you okay?"

She nods. Henry turns back to Fred. "Now, you can leave and never come back, or we can settle this in a less gentlemanly fashion if you choose."

Fred looks around, steps back, and hurries out of the store.

Margaret exhales. "Thank God you were here, Henry." She hugs him, and he holds her as she shakes.

"Margaret, do you want to walk home?" Henry asks with a slight grin.

"You know, Henry, that would be a good idea." She looks around. "Do you think he will come back?"

"I don't know, but maybe I'll stop by more often."

"I agree."

Henry sticks out his arm, and Margaret quickly interlaces it. "Let's go home."

Chapter 18 A Disappointed Seth

Henry opens the church door for Will and Margaret walk, and all three walk through the doors to the sanctuary.

Pastor Phillips cuts off a conversation in mid-sentence and rushes over to Margaret. He shakes her hand and says, "It is so good to have you, William, and Henry here today."

Margaret looks at the Pastor suspiciously. Then, she makes her way to her usual seat in the church.

Henry sits down and leans to her. "What was that about?"

Margaret whispers to Henry, "I have no idea."

Will looks around and notices Helen and her Maw sitting up front. He then looks behind him and notices Percy and Albert sitting together. Albert grins from ear to ear.

As he turns, he notices Earl Bennett, with a bruised face, talking to the Pastor and the Sheriff. Earl watches Will as he talks to the Sheriff.

A cold chill runs over Will as he worries that Earl is telling the Sheriff about the previous night. The Sheriff turns to Will and nods his head.

The Pastor starts the service as Earl and the Sheriff sit beside each other.

Will's mind races. *Oh my, what if the Sheriff arrests me? That will be too much for Maw. Would he do that here? Would he wait? Maw would be so disappointed in me.* He internally chuckles. *Now, Uncle Henry would be proud of me. Even Helen would be proud of me. She would even be mad that she wasn't there to participate. I can't wait to tell her.*

"I ask the ushers to come up as we pray for the offering." The ushers start to walk up to the front of the church. "Dear Lord, thank you for our wonderful patrons in this church. Sharing their wonderful 10% to ensure your message is delivered properly. In Jesus name, Amen!"

The ushers make their way down the aisles, and Seth, the tall, lanky usher, stops at the pew with Henry, Margaret, and Will. He smiles and nods at Margaret as he passes the offering plate her way. She places a dollar bill in the offering plate.

Seth grunts aloud in disappointment as he sees what she has placed on the plate. Henry starts to stand up, but Margaret grabs his arm and stops him. He takes a deep breath as Seth walks by.

Margaret pats his arm to calm him. He looks at Margaret, then leans to her. "That is disrespect in the House of the Lord, Margaret."

"It's okay," Margaret says.

Seth and the ushers return the offering plates to the Pastor. Pastor Phillips surveys the contents of the offering plates. He turns and looks at the congregation in disappointment. He takes a deep breath and looks at Margaret. "It seems we are short of our 10%. Would you like to resolve this?" He keeps his eyes on Margaret.

Henry stands up and opens his mouth.

"Henry! Please sit down. I will handle this," Margaret replies.

Henry takes a deep breath, adjusts his belt, and sits back down.

Margaret stands up gracefully. "If you are referring to me, Pastor. I do believe my account with the Lord is even. He got something far more worth a measly 10% from me. You go ahead now and preach." Margaret sits back down with confidence.

A hush swallows the sanctuary for what seems like an eternity. Margaret is not deterred one bit.

Pastor Phillips fumbles through the pages of the Bible. Then he begins his sermon.

Henry grins from ear to ear. *That slimy fake preacher just got put in his place. He probably doesn't even talk to the Lord like he pretends to. I am so proud of my brother's wife. She is far stronger than people realize.*

Will grabs Margaret's hand and beams with pride. He leans to her ear and says, "Way to go, Maw. Paw would be so proud."

She smiles. "I am quite sure he is smiling down from heaven at this very moment."

Henry cranks the car and puts it in gear. He lets out the clutch as they drive away from the church.

Will sits in the back and runs his fingers through his hair. He takes a deep breath. "Maw, Uncle Henry. I need to talk to both of you."

Margaret turns to look at Will. "William, what is it?"

Henry looks at Will in the rearview mirror. "Will, do I need to pull over?"

"No, I need both of you to listen to what has happened the last few days at the Duncan house."

Margaret takes a deep breath. "Wow, William. I'm not sure I like you and Helen going to an old house and making out."

"Maw, this isn't about that."

"I know, William. This is pretty big."

"Did Earl get a look at you?" Henry asks.

Will nods. "He did. He got a look at me and Gerald."

"Hmm, well, if the Sheriff hasn't stopped by yet, I take that as he either wasn't told or Earl didn't want him to pursue it based on what you and Gerald may know."

"I don't think he knows that we know about trying to steal the house from the Ross'," Will says. "Now, come Monday, he will know. Mrs. Ross says she is paying the house note up to date."

"Well, William, you need to be careful. Stay away from such mischief."

"Margaret, I agree, but he just saved a couple from losing their house and maybe their marriage."

Margaret nods. "It seems there are some ugly things in this town."

"That may be an understatement," Henry says as he pulls the car in front of the house. "Hey Margaret, I am going to run to Peggy's. Is that okay with you guys?"

"Sure, no problem."

Henry steps out of the car and shuts the door. He turns to an old white house with steps in front of it. An old bicycle is leaning against the wall. The bike has a basket on the front and a metal-framed steel seat behind the main seat.

He smiles for a moment, then whistles loudly.

Peggy walks out the front door wearing a green shirt-waist dress. Her brown hair falls over her shoulders. Bashfully, she says, "You looking for me?"

Henry smiles. "You know it."

She runs to him and hugs him. "You get all that religion you needed this morning?"

"Oh, probably would have to stay many days for that."

Henry slowly puts his hand on her hip, steps back, and shakes his head. "You do look beautiful, Peggy. So much so that it is blinding my eyes."

She thinks momentarily. "I don't know how to take that. Is that a good thing or a bad thing?"

Henry smirks. "It's a good thing, trust me." He looks over at the bicycle and then back to her. "Do you want to go for a ride on the bicycle?"

Peggy shrivels her face. "I don't know about that."

Henry walks over and moves the bicycle around. He nods his head and pats the handlebars for her to sit on. "We can make this happen."

"Are you sure?"

"Trust me, Peg."

"Okay, how do we do this?"

Henry sits on the seat and waves for Peggy to come over. Peggy walks over and sits on the handlebars with her feet up. She giggles. "Henry, don't get us killed."

"I'll give it my best." He pushes the peddle down, and the bicycle starts moving.

"Henry! Henry!"

He peddles faster.

Peggy takes a deep breath as he balances them down the road. A grin stretches across her face as her brown hair flows in the wind.

"You having fun yet?"

"YES!" Peggy screams.

He leans his head to the right so he can see past Peggy.

"Go faster, Henry."

Henry thrusts his legs down to push the peddles faster and faster. They approach an intersection and notice a car approaching.

"Henry, a car is turning," Peggy says nervously.

Henry sways a bit and guides the bicycle into the ditch. Peggy flies into the air as the bike flies over them. Henry falls to the side of the impact. Quickly, he gets up and rushes to Peggy, her dress over her face.

"PEG! PEG! Oh Peg."

She lies motionless on the ground.

He reaches down and touches her stomach. "PEG!"

She flings her dress down away from her face and laughs hysterically.

Henry looks to the sky and gasps. Then looks back down to her. "Oh, you scared me."

She grabs his suspenders and pulls him to her. "Come here, my stuntman." She kisses him passionately. They are lost in the moment, intertwined in each other's embrace. Slowly, Henry breaks from the kiss. He looks into her caramel-brown eyes.

Peggy grins. "Let's do it again?"

Confusion comes over Henry. "The kiss? Or the bicycle?"

"Both." Peggy pulls him to her as she kisses him again. She wraps her hands over his head and rolls him over. Peggy breaks from the kiss and sits on top of Henry.

"You know I love you, Peggy," Henry says.

Peggy gasps, hands are over her mouth. She quickly stands up, and Henry gets to his feet. He looks around and puts his arm around Peggy. "Peg, you know I don't always do things traditionally." He turns to her, holding her hand, "But I want to make you my wife."

She freezes in place. "Are you?"

"Yes, I am."

Her emotions come over her as she jumps up and down. "Yes, Henry. Yes." She wraps her arms around Henry's neck and squeezes him tightly.

Peggy breaks from the embrace. "I have been waiting for my ole soldier to ask me. I love you, Henry."

They walk side by side as their arms are around each other's waist.

"You pick the date," Henry says. "But I will not get married in that church under Pastor Phillips."

Peggy smiles and rolls her eyes. "Oh, you might need that Pastor to bless you after the honeymoon."

Henry chuckles.

"So, another bicycle ride?"

"Yes, let's go."

Chapter 19 Earl's Revenge

"How was your lunch, Mr. Drum?" Margaret asks.

"Oh, it was good. Lucy left early and is running down to the bank," Mr. Drum explains, looking a little dizzy.

"Mr. Drum, you look pale," Margaret replies. "Are you okay? Do you want to sit down? Here, let me help you." Margaret walks over and helps guide him as they return to his office.

He sits down behind his desk. "Thank you, Margaret. I am just weak, is all."

"You let me know if there is anything you need. Are you good?"

"I am Margaret. You go on now."

"Yes, Sir." Margaret walks back to the front of the store.

She walks up to a mannequin and adjusts the dress on the mannequin.

Cling!

The door chime rings.

Margaret looks up, and Lucy walks in with a smile. Lucy turns and locks the door. She then motions for Margaret to follow her.

Lucy walks swiftly, and Margaret tries to catch up.

"Robert, you will not believe what I just witnessed."

Lucy steps into Mr. Drum's office. Margaret follows her in.

Mr. Drum looks up from his desk. "Lucy, dear, what is it?"

"I was at the bank, and Earl Bennett was throwing the trash can out of his office. Judith was there with receipts, proudly displaying them before him. He was trying to steal her house from her and Don, as he had been sleeping with her. I guess she got wind of it and let him have it after paying off the late balance."

Mr. Drum shakes his head. "That is something that Earl would do. He is evil."

"Oh, he was slinging stuff off his desk and tossed his trash can in the hall. He was irate. Earl kept yelling, 'Someone is going to pay for this.' I'm not sure what that means. Not only that, but they moved Judith's desk to be by the manager instead of by Earl."

"I wonder who he is going to make pay?" Margaret asks.

"I don't know," Lucy replies.

"Hmm, let me tell you what I know," Margaret says.

Mr. Drum and Lucy look at Margaret.

"Wow! That is deep," Lucy says.

"I know, and it seems that everyone is tied to this guy some-how—even my William," Margaret says.

Mr. Drum collects his thoughts, then looks back at Margaret. "This guy is out of control. You need to be careful, Margaret."

"I know, Mr. Drum."

Lucy takes a deep breath. "Robert, you need to go home and rest a bit. You still look a little weak."

Mr. Drum shakes his head.

"Mr. Drum, please do. I will lock up here. I think I will be back later tonight. I am finishing the dress for Sara Hopkins, and I think Betty Sue wants a dress. She is stopping by."

"You have been making the ladies in Bennett Town look elegant, Margaret," Lucy says as she touches Margaret's arm. "We are leaving for the night."

"Sara, stand still for just a second," Margaret says as she walks around Sara. She pulls out a pin from her green pinafore dress pocket. "I think this light pink pencil dress fits you fine. You will be a regular Bette Davis right here in Bennett Town. I need to hem about an inch off this, and it will be perfect."

Sara smiles, and the light pink dress compliments her tan skin complexion and brown hair.

"Go ahead and get out of the dress. I will finish up, and you can take it home."

"Really? I can have it tonight?" Sara asks with enthusiasm.

"Of course," Margaret says as she threads her sewing machine. "Oh, let me help you with the zipper."

Margaret walks behind Sara and unzips the dress. Sara shimmies from the dress, and Margaret takes it to the sewing machine.

"Any big plans, Sara?"

"Oh, I want to wear this when Danny comes home," Sara explains. She pauses and looks at Margaret, and her demeanor changes. "Oh, I am sorry, Margaret. I shouldn't have said that with Joseph and all."

"Oh, it is fine, Sara," Margaret says reassuringly. "You deserve to be excited."

A little uncomfortable and hesitant, Sara asks, "Have you ever thought of someone after Joseph or moving on."

Margaret pushes the dress through the sewing machine. "Oh heavens no. Joseph is still my love. I don't know if that will change one day, but the answer is definitely no right now."

Margaret turns the spinning wheel slightly and then cuts the thread on the dress. She looks back at Sara. "I think we have a dress. I am pretty sure one that Danny can't keep his eyes off of."

"Thank you, Margaret," Sara replies as she gently grabs the dress. "I am looking forward to that day. I may need a few more dresses if you don't mind."

"No, not at all."

"You have a good evening. Are you leaving?"

"No, I am expecting another lady shortly. I figure I will work on one of my own as well while I wait."

Sara nods, walks out of the sewing room, and heads to the front door.

Margaret changes the spool that is attached to the sewing machine.

Cling!

The door chime rings at the front door.

Margaret smiles as she pulls out a roll of ruby-red material. She unrolls some of it, places it over the mannequin, and then smiles. "I think this will do just fine."

She thinks to herself, *I will look lovely in this dress and a matching derby hat. I can pull it off. Yep, let me work on this.*

Margaret lays the material on the ground and gets her sewing chalk out. She gets down on all fours and starts marking the material.

Cling!

The door chime rings.

"Betty Sue, I am in the back," Margaret yells. "Just come on back here."

Margaret pulls her scissors out of her pocket and cuts the material.

"Well, if this isn't just interesting," a familiar male voice says.

Margaret jumps to her feet, adjusts her dress, and turns around. Earl is standing in front of her with a liquor bottle in one hand and a cigar in the other. He wears grey slacks and a stained white collared shirt with black suspenders.

"You know, Mrs. Wood," Earl says snarly. "I told you, I know you. Oh, I know you, so, well. You are not all that saintly as people like to think."

Earl takes a swig of his liquor and then puffs his cigar. He leans his head slightly and looks Margaret over from head to toe. He is relishing what he sees. He blows smoke out and then licks his lips.

Margaret nervously says, "Mr. Bennett, you have no business here, and it is time for me to go home. You, you need to leave."

Earl grins and steps closer to Margaret. She steps back and into the sewing machine table. Earl pushes up against her and crudely snubs his cigar out on the table. Then, he brings his face close to hers. She clinches the scissors in her right hand tightly.

"Hmm, a war widow, or is it," Earl pushes his hand on her thigh, slightly pushing up her dress, "the town trollop?"

Margaret thrusts the scissors forward, but Earl blocks them and drops the liquor bottle. He leans forward and forces a kiss on her lips. She squinches her lips shut and swings her arms into his torso. He pulls her tight with one arm and pushes his hand to her unmentionables. Margaret thrusts her knee forward, hitting Earl in the right spot. He releases his grip, and she breaks from his hold. With all her energy, she starts to dart out of the room, but Earl reaches back and catches the bottom of her dress, pulling her back.

It starts to rip, and Earl chuckles. "You won't be needing that anyway."

He quickly wrestles her to the ground. Then, with the weight of his body on her, he grabs her arms and pulls them over her head.

"NO! NO! Earl Bennett, NO!"

Earl smiles as he pushes her hands together over her head and secures them with one hand. "I like it when you call me Earl."

With his free hand, he pushes her dress up over her waist and unfastens his suspenders. "Margaret, you are a beauty. You can't tell me you don't like this?"

Margaret spits in his face.

Earl moves back and slaps her across the face. Then he releases her arms. His eyes are in a rage.

Cling!

"I have been waiting to show you what a man can do for some time now. Tonight, you will know what a real man is."

Earl unfastens his pants. Margaret closes her eyes and squirms relentlessly.

Suddenly, Earl is off her body. She opens her eyes in amazement. Henry is on top of Earl. He reaches back to the heavens and brings his mighty fist down on Earl's nose.

Margaret hurries back to the corner of the room and shakes in fright.

"You lousy bastard. I knew the day would come when I end you. Tonight is the night." Henry pummels Earl's face relentlessly. Each punch seems more powerful than the previous, drawing more blood.

Cling!

"Maw, you here?"

Margaret's eyes bulge. "Uh, Uh, William."

Will walks into the room and takes one look at Margaret. He sees her dress torn and blood on her face. Rage fills every pore in Will's body. He clinches his fist as the hair on his back stands up.

She turns to Henry, who is still beating Earl. He quickly pulls Henry off Earl. Earl is woozy. Will lunges to Earl's throat with his hands. They grip like a vice around Earl's throat. Earl's eyes bulge as he is gasping for air.

Margaret jumps to her feet and grabs Will by his shoulders. She pulls him off. Earl's lungs are trying to fill with air. Henry pulls Margaret away.

"No more, Henry. I don't need you or William to land in jail."

Henry looks at Margaret and points to Earl. "This man hit you, Margaret. He tried to rape you. He deserves to die."

Margaret's lips quiver. "That he does, Henry. Just not by your hands or Williams. I don't care after that, but I lost Joseph, and I can't lose one of you two."

Cling!

Margaret looks at Henry. "That will be Betty Sue. William, stop her and tell her to go get the Sheriff now!"

"Yes Ma'am," Will says as he runs out of the sewing room. A lady in a yellow dress who is barely five feet tall walks in.

"Mrs. Betty Sue, there has been an emergency. Can you go get the Sheriff?"

"Is everything okay, William?"

"The Sheriff, please!"

"I'm gone. I'll get him here as soon as I can."

Cling!

Henry leans down to Earl. "You know, Earl. I don't understand you. You have power in this town, but you like to prey on women folk. Why is that?"

Earl sits up from his pool of blood. As blood pours over his eyes and from his nose, he lifts his head. "Sometimes the king likes to play with the peasants."

"Henry, just leave him be. He isn't worth our time," Margaret says.

Will returns. "She is gone to fetch him, Maw."

Earl smiles. "The Sheriff will do what is right."

Henry and Margaret both look at Earl in shock.

Cling!

"Margaret, you have to tell him what happened," Henry says.

"Oh, I will."

Earl stands up, and the Sheriff walks into the room. He looks at everyone, and Margaret starts to speak. The Sheriff raises his finger. "Just a moment, Mrs. Wood." He looks at her torn dress and her bloody face.

He takes a deep breath, then looks over at Henry, then Earl.

"Okay, I need a statement from Mrs. Wood, Mr. Bennett, and Henry."

"Hmm, Sheriff, if there is a Mr. Bennett here, then there is a Mr. Wood here as well," Margaret states.

"Yes, Ma'am," Sheriff replies.

Earl adjusts his throat. "Sheriff, that Will also assaulted me. I was assaulted by Henry and Will. They tried to take my life. Margaret arranged for me to be here tonight. She told me she was lonely and didn't want her family to know about us having a little rendezvous."

Margaret stands tall. "Mr. Bennett, that is a lie. You came here to rape me. If I wanted to entertain you sexually, then why is my dress torn to shreds and my face bloody?"

Earl grins and takes a step forward. "Because you told me that you wanted a real man, that your Joseph didn't know how to handle a woman."

Margaret and William lunge toward Earl. Henry stops Margaret, and the Sheriff stops William.

"You see, Sheriff, the boy and Margaret are trying to assault me right now in front of you."

Henry looks at Earl with disdain, then looks at the Sheriff. "Sheriff Welch, anyone with an honest bone in their body can see that Earl was trying to rape Margaret. When I came in, he had her on the ground ripping her clothing."

"That is because she told me to be rough. I thought it was whacky, but I went along with it," Earl says proudly. "Sheriff, who are you going to believe? A man that is a reputable businessman, and the town is named after, or the town trollop who has been lusting for a man for some time?"

"Okay, okay, everyone stop. Mrs. Wood, did anyone else see this encounter with you and Mr. Bennett?"

Margaret cringes her lips. "No, Sheriff. Henry came in when Mr. Bennett was ripping my knickers against my will and trying to get in them." She closes her eyes and shudders.

"Now, Sheriff, we all know Margaret here had Will out of wedlock. Hell, we don't even know who the father is."

Henry shoves Earl against the wall. "Mark my words. I will watch you breathe your last breath before this is over with."

"You see, Sheriff, he is threatening me right now."

Henry moves back.

"Okay, this is what is going to happen. Henry, Will, and Mrs. Wood, you have a no-contact order to be around Earl. You can do your daily business, but other than that, no closer than 100 feet. Is that understood?"

Henry nods as he seethes in anger.

The Sheriff turns to face Earl. "Mr. Bennett, you have the same no-contact order. You cannot be within 100 feet of Mrs. Wood, William, or Henry."

"Wait, the boy is dating my daughter," Earl says.

"He can date your daughter. He can't be around you."

"Hold on," Henry says. "Sheriff, he tried to rape Margaret, and you are going to brush this aside?"

"I don't have any evidence of that," The Sheriff replies. "Mr. Bennett, you are free to go."

Earl smiles and pats the Sheriff on the back as he walks out. The Sheriff follows.

"Maw, are you okay?"

Margaret shakes her head. "Just my pride is hurt." She looks at Will, "William, I want you to know this. Your father has been the only man for me. I have never desired another. So please don't listen to that gibberish from that bad man."

Henry moves around, cleaning the place up. "Margaret, let's get you home."

Chapter 20 A New Kid in Town

"That no good, dirty scoundrel," Mr. Drum shouts as he looks at Margaret.

Margaret nods her head. "I am sorry all this happened back here in the sewing room, Mr. Drum."

"Margaret, don't you worry about that. I will talk to the Sheriff today about his perverted benefactor that he has supporting him."

Margaret puts her head in her hands. "I don't think it will do any good."

"Maybe not, but it puts him on notice. I have half a mind to go down to that bank and rid this town of that trash once and for all."

Meanwhile, a tall, slender man in a blue business suit with a dark red kerchief sticking out of his left pocket, a black Fedora, and brown leather shoes opens the bank's door. He has wavy blond hair, a flawless tan complexion, and captivating amber-brown eyes.

Confidently, he walks into the bank, holding his hat.

Judith looks up and smiles. "Yes, Sir, can I help you?"

"I am looking for the owner of the bank."

"Oh, that would be Mr. Bennett." Judith's grin changes to a serious demeanor. "Right this way." Judith walks across the foyer and stops by Mr. Bennett's office. She points. "He works here, Sir. Your name?"

"Oh, my apologies; my name is Thomas Stevenson, and yours?"

Judith smiles. "I am Judith Ross."

She looks into Mr. Bennett's office and says sternly, "Mr. Bennett, there is a Mr. Stevenson here to see you."

Mr. Bennett waves him in. Mr. Stevenson looks around and walks right in. He points to Mr. Bennett. "Bennett, right?"

"That is a fact." Mr. Bennett says as he stands up and extends his hand.

Mr. Stevenson shakes his hand. "Well, I am Thomas Stevenson."

They break from the handshake.

"Nice to meet you, Thomas." Earl points to the seat opposite him across the desk. Please have a seat. You can call me Earl. You are not related to Governor Stevenson, are you?"

Thomas laughs. "Oh, yeah, that is my uncle."

Earl chuckles. "Yeah, right. So, what brings you to Bennett Town?"

"Oh, I don't know. I just heard so much about it and figured I had to visit this place." Thomas leans forward, "You don't happen to know a lady named Margaret Wood."

Earl's demeanor changes as he reaches for a cigarette. "You mean the Town Trollop?" He strikes a match and lights his cigarette.

"Excuse me, Earl. I must have missed what you said."

"Oh, the Town Trollop, the local whore, or whatever term you want to use."

Thomas stands up, places his hat on Earl's desk, then turns his back to him. He walks to the door, shuts it, then locks it. He turns back around and steps to Earl's desk. "Mr. Bennett, I am not sure how things are in this town, but from my understanding, they are much more cordial than how you portray them. You see, I am from Texas. For some reason, in my part of Texas, we were taught to never talk down about women."

Earl stands up. "Listen here, Mister. I own this town, and I can do as I please."

Thomas looks at him calmly and then retrieves his hat. "That may be so, but I am here to tell you this. If I ever hear of you speaking a derogatory word regarding Mrs. Margaret Wood, I will personally kill you. I will not mince words, so I need you to understand that." Thomas looks at Earl with a stern and forceful look.

Earl suddenly jumps, shaking his right hand as the cigarette burns his hand. "Damn it!"

"Mr. Bennett, you seem peculiar, but I believe we are done here."

Thomas turns, unlocks the door, and walks out. As he walks towards the front door, Judith smiles at him. Thomas puts his hat on and walks down the main drag of town.

"Margaret, why don't you go home and call it a day?" Mr. Drum asks.

"You know, I think I will. William is back in school, and I can straighten things up around the house. I may be back tonight. I need to find out whether Betty Sue is stopping by."

"I can tell her not to come tonight if that is okay?"

"No, it keeps me busy."

"Okay, well, I will see you tomorrow. Oh, please have William or Henry up here when you come by tonight. If need be, I can come up here too."

"Oh, I think Henry will be just perfect for the job. I guess I will see you tomorrow." Margaret walks out the front door.

She heads down the sidewalk, thinking about last night. *I genuinely wish Joseph was still around. This would never have happened.* Walking down the street, she notices people staring at her like never before. Their eyes peer at her in such a judgmental way. A few huddle together, whisper, and point at her. *Am I having a panic attack, or am I hallucinating? People have always been so friendly, but now everyone looks critical and scary.* She turns and looks back at the store while she walks and suddenly bumps into someone. She clutches her chest in fright. "I am so sorry, clumsy me."

The gentleman smiles. "Mar, Margaret Wood, I would recognize you anywhere."

A bit dumbfounded, Margaret looks the stranger over for a moment and then says. "Do I know you, Sir?"

He tilts his head, tips his hat, and grins. "Oh, no, Ma'am, you don't, but I do know you."

"How is that?" Margaret asks cautiously.

"You see, I served with Joseph in France. My name is Thomas Steven—

"Tom Stevenson," Margaret says with a smile.

He nods his head. "Yes Ma'am. Joseph talked about you all the time."

"What are you doing in Bennett Town?"

"Would it be too forward if I could walk you where you're going?"

Margaret's stature straightens, and she looks at Tom. "Well, I would say no, but I am heading home."

"Would it be okay to meet you somewhere else? Maybe tomorrow?"

With a suspicious eye. "How do I know you are who you say you are and not snooping around just to get money?"

Tom briefly pushes his hat back, looking at Margaret. "Hmm. Well, Mrs. Wood, I don't know anything about your money. I can only presume that it is from Joseph dying next to me. But I have my own money. My last name is Stevenson. My uncle is the Governor." He smirks.

Margaret carefully looks at Tom and slowly says, "Sure he is."

"Okay." Tom reaches into his jacket pocket, pulls out a photo, and hands it to Margaret. "This is Joseph and me in England at a pub. He requested ♪*DannyBoy*♪ because Henry plays it well on the harmonica, and you sing it so well."

Margaret looks at the photo and recognizes Tom in the photo. She sniffles for a moment. "That doesn't prove anything. You could have found this somewhere."

"I agree, but I am next to him in the photo. I also know you are Joseph's only love, and he is yours. I know you call your son William, where as Joseph called him Will. Joseph called you Maggie, and he loved dancing with you to the song ♪*Cheek to Cheek*♪."

Margaret gasps loudly as a tear runs down her cheek. She quickly hugs Tom and sobs as she embraces him. Abruptly, she breaks from the embrace. "Then what do you want?"

Tom takes a deep breath. "I want to fulfill a promise to my best friend. We both promised each other if one of us were to die, that the other would visit the family."

"Are you married?"

"No Ma'am. I am just here because I promised to visit you and Will to ensure both of you are okay. After a few days, I will probably return to Austin."

"What's in Austin?"

"Nothing, just some family, is all."

Margaret nods, then lifts her chin. "Maybe you could walk me home. William should be there soon from school and his job."

"I would be honored, Mrs. Wood."

"It's Margaret. Now, don't get any ideas. My husband is Joseph."

Tom smiles. "Oh, I would never be so audacious when it comes to putting you or Joseph in a bad way."

"Good."

The school bell rings to end school for the day. Will looks across the room and smiles. He grabs his books and walks over to Helen. He grabs her books, and they walk out of the classroom. As they walk down the hall, Walter, Charles, and Ralph stand next to their lockers, laughing and pointing in Will and Helen's direction.

Will notices and hands his books to Helen momentarily. "Give me one second, Helen."

He asks Walter, "What are you cracking wise about?"

"Ha." Walter looks at Charles and Ralph. They all step to Will. Walter points his finger into Will's chest, "You are a son of a whore. Your Mom is out there trying to wreck Helen's family, whoring herself around, just like she did when she got pregnant with you."

Will takes a deep breath and swings his right fist towards Walter. Charles catches Will's arm in full swing and then hits Will in the stomach. Will doubles over, and Walter punches Will in the head. Will falls to the floor, and Ralph kicks him several times in the gut.

"NO!" Helen screams as she tosses her books to the ground and runs over to the scuffle. She jumps on Walter's back, wrapping her arms around his head.

Ralph laughs. "You got your dame fighting for you. Figures, the son of the town slut couldn't do anything. Why are you with this guy, Helen?"

Will's anger surges, and he lunges up, grabbing Ralph by the throat and slamming him against the locker.

"Oh shit," Walter says as he slings Helen off.

She falls to the floor and yells, "Help."

Walter grabs Will from behind around his neck. Will lifts Ralph off the ground. His feet dangling as he gasps for air. Charles quickly tackles Will to the ground.

A male teacher moves in and starts slinging people to the side.

"We got to go, Ralph," Walter yells.

Charles, Ralph, and Walter run from the scene, like bandits fleeing a robbery, as Will lies on the ground with blood dripping from his nose.

Helen rushes over to Will and cradles his head.

"Di, did you hear what they said, Helen? About my Maw being a whore and a homewrecker?"

"I heard it all, Will. Your Maw is the nicest person I know. Trust me, I know who my Paw is," Helen says as she helps him up. "Are you okay?"

"Just my pride is all that is hurt."

"Let's get you home, Will. I will walk you."

"I got to go to work."

"Nope, I will let them know once I get you home," Helen replies as they leave the school.

Will wraps his arm around Helen as they walk away.

Helen leans to Will and kisses his cheek.

A smile comes across Will's face.

Chapter 21 Swing Time

Henry looks at the house and notices Margaret sitting in the swing and a gentleman on the steps. Margaret is smiling.

Something is wrong with this picture. Who is this money thief now? Henry thinks to himself. As he walks up the steps, the man stands up and looks at Henry.

"Henry, this is Joseph's battle buddy from the war. His name is Tom Stevenson," Margaret says.

Henry stops. "Tom Stevenson, I heard that name before." He looks at Margaret and then cautiously back to Tom.

"So, how do you know Joseph again?"

"Well, I figure I would wait until Will gets home until I got into all the particulars, but I was there on the beach with him when he died."

Henry's face turns white.

"Look, Henry, I am not here to bring any trouble. I am here because Joseph and I made a promise that if one of us were to die, the other would check in on their family."

Henry nods his head as he collects his thoughts.

Tom extends his hand to Henry. Henry looks down and shakes his hand. Then walks up the stairs and sits next to Margaret. Tom sits back down.

Henry leans to Margaret. "It seems Will got himself into a little fight at school today. That is why I came home early. Something tells me the hospitality in this town has turned."

Margaret nods in disappointment. She slaps Henry's leg. "As long as we stick together, we will be fine. I do have a dress to complete for Betty Sue tomorrow evening. If you or Will could chaperone me, that would be great."

Henry nods. "Not a problem," then looks at Tom, "So where are you from, Tom?"

"Oh, I grew up around Austin."

"I see. This is a good way from Austin."

"That it is. Over 300 miles."

"Tom, I am sorry. Would you like some tea?" Margaret asks as she stands up.

"Oh, I would love some tea."

Margaret turns to Henry. "And you, Henry?"

"Yes Ma'am."

Margaret walks into the house.

Tom looks over at Henry. "Just to ensure you know I am who I say I am, Joseph told me a rather humorous story that I chuckled over for some time."

Henry squints his eyes.

"Now, of course, I could never tell it like Joseph. He was a master of telling stories. But he told us how he convinced you to go up and kiss this girl named Betty and that she didn't like you. His words were something like, 'She attacked him like a mama bobcat protecting her little ones.' I believe that was his words."

Henry shakes his head while chuckling. "That would be something he would say. Come on up here and sit in the chair, Tom."

Margaret comes back out with a tray and three glasses of sweet tea. She hands one to Tom. He stands up, says, "Thank you," and then sits down.

She walks over to Henry and hands him a glass. Margaret grabs the last glass, places the tray under the swing, and sits back down.

Henry takes a sip and then looks down the path to the house. "What in tarnation is that?"

He quickly stands up and places his glass on the porch by the swing. Swiftly, he moves down the stairs and runs up to Will and Helen. He checks out Will's bloody nose and bruised eye. "Are you okay, Will?"

Margaret's eyes grow in fear. She runs down the porch and checks on Will.

"Uncle Henry, Maw, I am okay. It was just three of them."

"Three of them," Margaret exclaims.

"Yes, Ma'am," Helen interjects. "They were calling you all sorts of names and such."

"Fighting over foolish names, William?" Margaret asks.

"Maw, no one in this town is going to call you a whore," Will exclaims.

Margaret gasps.

"Mrs. Wood, they said that you were a homewrecker to my family. I know better, but Will was not having it," Helen explains.

"Margaret, Will did the right thing," Henry looks at Will and says, "I want names later, Will."

Helen interjects, "He was fighting Walter, Charles, and Ralph."

Henry looks around. "Should have known."

"Mrs. Wood, I am running back into town and letting the Ice Plant know Will is home."

"Okay, thank you, Helen," Margaret says.

Helen leans over, stands on her tiptoes, and kisses Will on the cheek before heading back down the trail.

"William, go sit on the swing. We got some company tonight," Margaret explains.

Tom stands up as Will walks by. He looks at Henry and Margaret and says, "Oh, my, he is the spitting image of Joseph."

Margaret sits down next to Will in the swing. Henry stays on the porch steps and pulls out his harmonica. He wipes it slowly as Tom sits down in the chair. He looks over at Will.

"Will, I served with your father. We were battle buddies, and we made a promise to each other to check in on each other's family if one of us was to die."

Will looks at Margaret in disbelief.

Margaret places her hand on Will's hand for reassurance. "It's Tom Stevenson. Your Paw wrote about him often."

"I would like to start by saying that Joseph had an incredible nature about him. He didn't let anything get him down. He also had a good moral compass about him. Some of the married fellas would forget that when going to a pub in England."

Tom looks at Margaret. "Joseph never forgot that."

Margaret nods her head and fights the tears back.

"Will, he thought the world of you. Every day, he was bragging about you. He was very concerned with seeing you grow into a man."

Tears flow down Will's cheeks.

Tom looks over at Henry. "And Henry, he thought you had wonderful talents. Joseph would tell me that, then say he was great at defending people, consuming alcohol, and playing the harmonica."

Henry looks down, smiling. "Oh, he knew me all too well."

Tom takes a deep breath. "Look, I will explain how he died if you want me to. I will be around for a few days, then hurry out of here and not be in your hair. I greatly respected Joseph, and he was my best friend."

Margaret looks around for a moment, then back at Tom. She lifts her chin reluctantly. "No, I think we would like to know what happened."

Tom looks down, thinks for a second, nods his head, then looks up with his lips squinched tightly. He takes a deep breath, "Joseph and I had landed on the beach with our squad. The crazy thing is we survived the beach where many didn't. We were attached to the hip so that it would seem. The engineers broke through the wire, and we ran up on one of the pillboxes. We rested against it, still standing, and a German tossed a grenade out. Joseph pushed me away, and it exploded. He died immediately. Whereas I was wounded in the leg." Tears flow from Tom's eyes, and he tries to talk, but no words come out. His chin quivers. "He saved my life."

Will's head is in Margaret's chest, sobbing. Margaret's eyes fill with tears. Henry stands up and walks away, rubbing his eyes.

"It should have been me, not Joseph," Tom says as he wipes his face. "I don't know why he died and not me."

Henry turns and walks over to Tom. He grabs his hand and pulls Tom to his feet. "I understand how you feel." Henry hugs Tom tightly.

Margaret pushes Will off her lap. "Are you okay, William?"

He nods. "I am, Maw."

"Good, we needed to hear how Joseph died. It would have killed me not knowing."

Margaret walks over, leans in on the group hug, and kisses Tom on the cheek. "I am glad Joseph was with someone he cared about." Margaret takes a deep breath and steps away.

Tom and Henry break from the embrace.

"Oh, I have something for Will." Tom reaches into his pants pocket and pulls out a watch. He looks at Will.

"Joseph, wanted you to have this."

Will rushes over and places it on his arm.

Margaret smiles. "You know your Paw wouldn't wear jewelry, but he was proud of that watch."

Will lifts his head.

Margaret looks at Tom. "Tom, where are you staying?"

"Oh, there is a little hotel outside of town."

"How long are you in town for?" Henry asks.

"Oh, I don't know. I figure about a week or so." Tom tilts his head. "You know, play it by ear."

Henry nods, looks at Tom, and pulls out his liquor bottle. He takes a small swig and then offers it to Tom.

Tom winks at him. "Don't mind if I do." He takes a swig and hands it back to Henry. Henry twists the top on it and says, "You keep it, Tom. I have another."

"Well, Tom, why don't you let us figure out what happened with William? Can we see you tomorrow?"

Tom grabs his hat and tilts it to Margaret. "Of course. I would be glad to." He turns and steps off the steps, then walks away.

Margaret looks at Henry. "What do you think?"

"I think he is sincere," Henry says. "Joseph made an impression on him, and he respects him enough to come here. That says a lot. He isn't one of those money grabbers."

Margaret thinks momentarily. "William, what do you think?"

"I agree with Uncle Henry, Maw."

"I do, too. Henry has always called someone exactly for what they are within minutes. Henry, you have never been wrong when judging someone's character."

Chapter 22 Helping Hand

"Maw, I got to run. I am walking Helen to school." Will grabs his books and jets out of the house.

"You be careful, William."

"Yes Ma'am."

Will runs under the willow tree and makes his way down the street. As he walks, he looks down at his watch. The brown leather band fits snuggly against his wrist. The white face of the watch allows the minute and hour hand to be seen easily. *I wonder when Paw last looked down at this watch face. What were his thoughts as he gazed upon it? Was he on the beach with Tom? Or was he on a landing craft or in England?* He looks up, and there is Helen's house.

Will runs up the path to the porch, hops over the steps, and walks to the door.

Knock! Knock!

"Just a moment." He hears Joan yelling.

Will smiles.

When the door opens, Joan opens the door in a green button-down dress with a big smile. "Good morning, Mr. Wood." She turns to look back into the house and yells, "Helen!"

"Yes, Maw, coming." Helen runs down the stairs in a blue and white polka dot shirtwaist dress. She quickly slides on her black and white Oxford shoes and hugs her mom. "See you later, Maw." She grabs Will's hand as she walks down the porch.

Will looks over his shoulder and yells, "Bye, Mrs. Bennett."

Joan winks at him. "You have a great day."

"You trying to score brownie points with my Maw?"

"No, just being nice. Anyway, what's the hurry, Helen?"

"Oh, nothing, just figure we could get going, is all. You okay from yesterday?"

Will smiles. "Oh, I am fine."

They turn down the street. Helen is full of energy and unable to contain her excitement as they walk.

"So, who was that man on the porch when we came up yesterday?"

"That was Thomas Stevenson. He was with my Paw when he died."

Helen stops, and her demeanor changes. "Oh, Will, I am sorry."

"No, no, it was good. He told us how Paw died and even gave me Paw's watch." Will turns his wrist, and it turns Helen's hand as he shows her the watch.

She looks at Will. "I know that is something you will cherish." She gives him a peck on the cheek and hugs him.

They separate and continue to walk down the street. As they approach the T intersection, they cut across someone's yard. They move fast until they meet the next street and continue walking.

"What time is it, Will?"

Will looks down at his watch. "It is 6:45."

Helen smiles. "So every time someone asks you what time it is, know that your Paw is checking on you."

Tom leaves the hotel as he puts his Fedora on his head. *Let me see this town with people around,* he thinks. He starts walking down the street that connects to the school. Slowly, businesses open their doors and prepare for their day.

He lights a cigarette as he walks down the street.

"So, anything new with your Maw or Earl?"

"Nope, you know she kicked him out." Helen laughs. "She shot at him with the shotgun a couple of times. I think Maw can be the craziest of us all."

Helen twirls her hair and says, "Will, what time is it?"

Will looks down at his watch, then smiles as he looks back at Helen.

"Ha, you see. He is looking down on you."

Honk! Honk!

A car pulls by them and Will and Helen look over and see Earl as the driver. He leans out the window with a bottle in his hand.

"You two think you're so cute walking down the street. Helen, get in my car now."

Her face grimaces and turns red. "I will not. You are dead to me. You're not even my Paw anymore. You are simply a guy named Earl."

Earl stops the car and gets out. Swiftly, he moves towards Helen. Will steps in his way. "Sir, you need to leave NOW!" Will says, pointing away from them.

"Boy, who do you think you are?" Earl says as he pushes Will to the ground and grabs Helen by the arm.

Tom hears a scream and looks down the street. *Is that Will and the girl from yesterday?* Tom flings his cigarette to the side.

Will manages to get on his feet and tackles Earl. They tumble to the ground, and Helen falls back. Earl rolls over on Will, reaches back to deliver a punch to his face, and starts to punch Will, but his arm stops. Tom has a grip on the arm and he quickly pulls Earl off Will.

"Mr. Bennett, I see. It seems you like to hit youngins. Is that a popular thing around here, or is it just what you like to do?"

He pushes Earl to the ground and extends his hand to Will. "Sir, I believe a fine young man like yourself should be on your feet. That little lady would prefer a man standing."

Will, in shock, grabs Tom's hand. Tom winks at him as he pulls him up. Then, Tom places his arm over Will's shoulder. "You go tend to her. I got this."

He runs over to Helen and hugs her.

Tom turns to Earl, who is getting to his feet. "I do believe Mr. Bennett that I told you, "if you ever said a derogatory word regarding Mrs. Margaret Wood again, that I would kill you."

Helen and Will both turn to listen to Tom's words.

"Let me adjust that if you ever put any of Mr. Joseph Wood's relatives in a bad light or hurt them. I swear to the good Lord above that I will take your life from you personally."

Earl snarls his face. "What is that family to you?"

Tom steps toward Earl. "That family to me, in some ways, is family. I served with Joseph Wood. He was my battle buddy and he gave his life for me to live. He taught me how to be a good man, but rest assured, there is a man inside of me you don't want to meet."

Helen wraps her arm around Will's waist.

"Do I make myself clear?"

Earl grunts as he gets back into his car, cranks it up, and spins the tires as he leaves.

Tom turns back to Will and Helen. Will has his arm around her waist, and she has a hand on Will's heart. Tom tips his hat. "My dear lady, I apologize for not introducing myself earlier. I was a bit detained. But I am pretty sure you are an incredible young woman if Will has taken a liken to you."

Helen smiles, and Will is speechless.

Tom winks at Will. "Hmm, Mr. Wood, I believe you and the lady were on a blissful walk together."

"Uh, yes, we were," Will says, smiling.

Tom tips his hat again. "Good day," then walks away.

Helen and Will walk down the street. "Wow, he was great," Helen exclaims.

Will nods. "Paw can pick 'em."

"Let's go by your Maw's work and see if she is there yet."

Will looks at his watch. "Okay, we have time."

Helen grabs Will's wrist, which has the watch on it. She looks at Will. "Your Paw was looking down on you. That is why Tom came."

Will gasps and nods.

They turn down the street and notice Margaret walking to Drum's. She is wearing a light blue peplum dress with a matching light blue ribbon in her red hair.

Helen squeezes Will's hand. "Your Maw is always so graceful and elegant looking."

"Paw used to brag about that all the time. He said, 'She made doing dishes look like something out of Hollywood.' Then he would give me a big wink."

Helen waves to Margaret, she breaks from Will's grip and runs to Margaret. Margaret smiles as Helen runs her way.

"Mrs. Wood, you won't believe what just happened," Helen says as she stops in front of Margaret.

Margaret turns her head slightly to listen.

"Will was walking me to school. Earl, my so-called Paw, stopped in his car, and Will defended me. Well, Earl and Will were on the ground, and Tom, who was on your porch, ripped Earl off of Will. He told Will to take care of me, and then he told Earl if he ever said or did anything to your family again, he would kill him."

"Oh my," Margaret says. She walks over to Will as he walks up. "Are you okay?"

"I am fine, Maw. Tom wasn't playing around with Earl. He just happened to be walking by."

Margaret smiles. "Well, I am glad everything worked out. You two got to get to school and all."

"Yes Ma'am," Helen says.

Will looks at Margaret, and she nods.

Margaret looks down the street to Drum's Department Store and notices Tom standing by. Walking down the street, she notices people pointing at her and whispering again. *Wow, just a few days ago, they offered me a greeting for the day. Now, I am a leper. At least my family loves me.* She approaches Tom.

"Good morning, Mrs. Wood," Tom says as he tips his hat. "I hope this isn't too forward."

Margaret smiles. "Good day, Mr. Stevenson. No, not at all. From what I understand, you already had a busy morning."

Tom smiles. "I guess you could say that. So, this is the famous Drum's Department Store."

Margaret smiles as she unlocks the door. "I don't know about famous." She asks Tom, "Do you plan on working with me today?"

"Actually, I have no plans."

"The way Joseph explained it, everyone comes in from miles around to see what you're wearing for the latest fashion and for you to make them a dress."

Cling!

The door chime rings as Margaret opens the door.

"Well, I can't have you work with me. The store officially doesn't open for another two hours. I normally come in early so I can catch up on some sewing. I do that and normally return late in the evening after I have supper with Henry and William to finish up on some dresses."

"I see. Do you mind if I accompany you while you sew? Or is that being too forward or anything?"

"No, I don't mind at all. Just don't expect it to be fun or anything special."

"Oh, no. Just sitting and talking is fun enough for me. I spent a lot of time just talking with men." Tom frowns. "That did get old."

"So, you came here to pick up on your ole battle buddy's wife?"

"Uh, no, not at all. That is not my intent. Joseph was my friend. I would not dishonor him that way."

Margaret smiles on the inside as she enjoys Tom's nervous banter. She walks to the back of the store, and Tom follows her.

"Something tells me you are having fun at my rambling."

Margaret stops before the sewing room door and looks over her shoulder at Tom, raising her index finger. "That much is true." She turns on the lights and looks around briefly.

"Just give me a moment," Margaret says.

She walks into Mr. Drum's office and pulls the chair from across his desk to these wing room. She pats it and says, "Here you go, Tom."

"Oh, I could have got that."

"I know, but I don't need a man doing everything for me."

Tom smiles and sits down in the chair. Margaret walks over to the dress mannequin and looks everything over. She fidgets around the mannequin. Tom watches her every move. She knows his eyes are on her. He can see her reflection in the mirror by the mannequin.

"So, Tom, what do you want to talk about?"

Tom grins. "That is putting a fellow on the spot now, isn't it." He looks around the room, "So, what is this thing with Earl?"

"Oh, you went from us having a good conversation straight to the unwanted conversation, Mr. Stevenson." Margaret walks around the sewing machine and sits down. "I will make a deal. I will tell you about him, but you must go after that. I must get some work in."

"Fair enough," Tom replies.

Margaret looks down for a second and then back to Tom. She thinks for a moment. *Should I even bother? He has been friendly and helped out this morning, but should I even bother?*

A grin comes over her face. "If I tell you about Earl, you can come tonight around 9:00 for the rest and for you to tell me about you. How is that?"

Margaret, what are you doing? You are definitely going out on a limb now. Are you flirting with this guy?

"Okay, the short version. I went to the bank to ensure everything was in order when Joseph died. Earl Bennett informed me that if I didn't make the house payment, the bank would foreclose on the house, but he would give me an alternative. That was to sleep with him in exchange for payment forgiveness."

"Are you serious?" Tom asks angrily.

"Oh, I am, and it gets even better. William and Helen, Helen is his daughter, caught him shacking up with his secretary. William caught him giving the Sheriff a payout. Apparently, the payout was for the Sheriff to keep his secretary's husband in jail while he slept with her and conned her house out from under them. When that got exposed, he then came down here and tried to rape me."

Tom gasps.

Margaret shudders. "Right here in this room. Henry beat his face in. William saw me with my dress ripped and all. In a way, no son should ever see their mother. Then, when the Sheriff came, Earl told the Sheriff that I was the town trollop, a lonely war widow, and a homewrecker. Basically, I was a whore and wanted him. His word is gold with the Sheriff."

Tom stands up. "I am so sorry, Margaret. This should never have happened. Where I come from, we respect women. I was far too easy on him. I will fix this, Margaret."

Margaret stands up quickly and grabs Tom. "No, it should all be over with now."

Tom looks at Margaret. "What can I do to help you and your family with this?"

She is taken aback and thinks. "I don't know if there is anything you can do except just listen. I have Henry and William, but I can't talk all those things with them if that makes sense."

Tom nods. "It does."

Margaret looks at Tom. "I want you to know it is comforting to have you here. I do have to work."

"I see that is my cue to leave," Tom says.

"Exactly." Margaret smiles. "Tonight at 9:00?"

"Yes Ma'am."

Margaret opens the door to Drum's. She looks down at her watch and realizes it is already 8:50 pm. She looks around and then pushes the door open.

Cling!

She walks to the sewing room and stares at the dress on the mannequin. "This will be perfect for Betty Sue."

She looks at her watch again, at 8:55. *Oh Margaret, what are you doing? I'm all nervous about whether a man is coming by. He has better things to do anyway.*

Margaret sits down behind the sewing machine table and fidgets with the spool.

Cling!

The door chime rings. Margaret stands up enthusiastically. *Settle down, Margaret, and don't throw yourself out there.* She adjusts her dress.

Tom walks into the sewing room with a smile on his face. "Good evening, Mrs. Wood."

Margaret smiles. "Good evening," She points to the chair.

Tom nods and sits down. "So how is Henry and Will?"

"Oh good, Henry is going to see Peggy tonight. They have been a thing since his return. William will run over to Helen's."

"Helen seems like a nice young lady."

"I would agree." She moves the wheel on the sewing machine slowly, now and then, looking over at Tom from the corner of her eyes. "So, Tom, tell me more about Joseph."

"I think I said once that I never saw Joseph get down. He was always chipper. Even when we were going to battle, he was just chipper in nature."

Cling!

Margaret raises a finger. "That's the door chime. It should be Betty Sue."

Margaret listens to the footsteps. A short lady walks into the sewing room. She looks over at Tom and then at Margaret.

"Oh, I didn't know you were entertaining guests," Betty Sue says with a snarky tone of voice.

Tom looks at her oddly.

Margaret stands up and says, "Oh, this is Joseph's ole war buddy." She looks at Betty Sue suspiciously for a moment. "I have your dress done; would you like to try it on."

Betty Sue lifts her chin and clears her throat. "Uh, no, I would not. I came to tell you that I will not be doing business with a homewrecker."

Margaret gasps. "Excuse me."

"You heard me. It is all over town that you are trying to be a homewrecker to the Bennetts."

"Oh, dear Lord. This town can spread a lie better than the best of 'em."

"I must go now," Betty Sue says as she turns and walks away.

Margaret, at a loss for words, sits down.

Cling!

The door chime rings as Betty Sue walks out the door.

She shakes her head. "This is why William was in a fight at school. This is so dumb." Her hands tremble. "All of this because Joseph died. All of this because of that crude, ugly man, Earl."

Tom starts to get up. "Margaret, is there anything I can do?"

Margaret shakes her head. "No, once someone tarnishes your reputation, I guess it is pretty much done." A tear slides down her cheek. She takes a deep breath and looks up at Tom. Forcing a smile, she says, "You know there are times I just want to pack up and leave, but I would not do that because of William and Henry." She stops and looks around for a moment.

Tom sits quietly, watching Margaret.

"You know Tom, I am so glad you came here. It gave us some closure, but you don't need to be drawn into all this mess. You have your own life to live."

Tom stands up and looks at Margaret. He walks around the sewing machine and extends his hand. "My best friend was Joseph Wood, and his wife is a bit distraught right now. Do you think I will abandon her and her family at this time of need? I don't think so, Mrs. Wood. You don't know Thomas Stevenson, but that is not who I am."

Margaret chuckles and takes his hand. She stands up.

"Now, we can sit here and chat or go somewhere else and chat."

She smiles. "You know, I would like a drink."

"So, to the bar?"

"No, no, Sir. This town would go into a frenzy over that."

Tom reaches down into his coat pocket and pulls out the bottle Henry gave him. He looks at Margaret bashfully, "Will this do?"

She grabs the bottle and says, "It most certainly will. That looks to be a Henry special." She unscrews the lid and takes a sip. As the liquor runs down her throat, she closes her eyes, feeling the warmth fill her lungs. Slowly, she opens them and grins, handing the bottle back to Tom. She holds a finger up. "Stay here."

Margaret walks to the front of the store and locks the front door. She pauses for a moment. *Is this the right thing? I mean, all we are doing is talking about Joseph. So, this can't be bad.* She smiles and walks back to the sewing room.

Tom looks at her. "Margaret, I don't want you to get the wrong idea. I am only here to look after you. Not to pray upon you at a vulnerable time."

Margaret looks into Tom's eyes. "I know. And I for you. Let's sit back against the wall and chat. Something tells me we will both get a good cry out of this, that is much needed."

Tom smiles. "I think that might be much needed."

Margaret sits down with her back against the wall and pats the ground next to her so that Tom can sit down. He sits down beside her and takes a swig from the bottle.

"So, you and Joseph went to the pubs, and you say he didn't frolic with the ladies."

She takes the bottle from him and sips. Then she looks at Tom. "What about you? You said you weren't married. Did you frolic with the British ladies?"

Tom gasps jokingly. "Now we are getting deep here, Margaret." He takes the bottle from her hands and takes a sip.

Margaret yanks the bottle from his hands and nudges him with her elbow. "Now, Tom, I told you all the ugly details about Earl, and trust me. A lady is not happy to share ugly things like that." She looks into his eyes, smiling. "Back to the question, Mister."

"A few flirted with me but I didn't find them to my liking."

Margaret stops and looks at Tom. "You mean you don't like women?"

"No, that is not it. I do adore women. They were just a bit less than elegant if I should say."

Margaret's speech starts to slur. "I see, Joseph's battle buddy has standards." She takes another sip.

Tom takes the bottle. "That is exactly it." He takes an other drink.

Margaret looks around as the room starts to spin a little. "So, what kind of woman meets Tom's standards?" She finishes the bottle.

"Well, someone who carries themselves with grace and confidence," Tom says as he feels something on his shoulder. He closes his eyes as he feels a bit tipsy. Slowly, he opens them and looks at Margaret, who is passed out on his shoulder. He grins from ear to ear and thinks, *This poor woman has been through hell.* His eyes slowly drift shut.

Chapter 23 The Morning After

Tom opens his eyes. He looks around at an unfamiliar setting and notices the sewing machine. Margaret's head is on his lap. He looks down at the empty bottle in her hand. *Oh my, I wonder how late we stayed up talking. Man, she has had a rough go at it. Joseph would have killed Earl over this. Maybe I should do them all a favor and do it for them.* He slowly moves from under Margaret's head.

Margaret stirs briefly. Tom moves her carefully, and she is entirely lying on the ground. He looks her over. *Now I know why Joseph fell for her. She is beautiful, graceful, and a very strong woman.* Her dress is up over her knees. *Oh, that will not do.* He pulls it down to cover her knees.

Tom glances at his watch. It is 4:50 a.m. He picks up the liquor bottle and puts it in his coat pocket. Then he grabs the chair and carries it to the front door of the department store. He unlocks the door and opens it.

Cling!

The door chime rings. Tom looks up at the chime, "Quiet now."

He carries the chair out the front door and sits by the front door overlooking the street. *Margaret, Will, and Henry have a predicament here. Joseph would have remedied this if it were my family. I have to do the same. That is what brothers in battle do.*

Tom pulls out a cigarette and lights it. As he takes a puff from the cigarette, he is trying his best to stay awake. The streets are empty. There is no movement in town.

Cling!

The door chime rings.

Margaret steps outside. She looks at Tom, and he quickly stands up.

"Here, Margaret, have a seat."

"Oh, thank you. I don't need to sit down. I do need to get home and get ready for today. I've got to get William and Henry taken care of."

"Of course," Tom replies. "Let me put the chair back."

Tom picks up the chair and leans into the door.

Cling!

Margaret looks around at the street quietly. Suddenly, she thinks. *He stayed protecting me. Joseph knows how to pick 'em, that is for sure.* She yawns as the morning cool air wakes her up.

Cling!

Tom walks out the door. Margaret locks the door and looks at Tom. "Why didn't you go home?"

"I figure you needed looking after."

Margaret admires his comment, tries not to smile, and nods. "You know most men would have tried to take advantage of me."

Tom swallows hard. "While you are easy on the eyes, Margaret, I would never do anything to you."

She places her hand on the side of his face and smiles. "Walk me home?"

"Of course."

They start walking away from the store.

"You know Margaret, you got a lot going on around here with Earl and all. You don't mind if I stay around longer to ensure Earl doesn't try anything else. I mean, you have endured more than most."

Margaret flirtatiously glances at Tom and says, "You think I can't take care of myself, Thomas Stevenson?"

"No Ma'am. Something tells me you can handle your own—you shouldn't have to." *Is she flirting with me?*

"Hmm, now I spilled my guts on what has happened around here since Joseph has been gone. Maybe you can tell me a bit more about you."

"Okay, I have two brothers. Both are in the military, one in the Pacific and the other in Europe. My Dad was a hardworking businessman. He worked in the oil fields and later became an oil investor. Is that what you want to know?"

Margaret pushes his shoulder, "I want to know what you want to tell me."

"Oh, that is not specific."

Margaret bites her lower lip and says, "Are you a man that a woman must be specific with?"

"No, not at all. I can see the target and cut through the bull crap," Tom says, smiling.

Margaret stops and grabs Tom's arm, stopping him. She looks into his amber-brown eyes. "So Tom, what is the target, and what is the bull crap right now?" She slowly bats her gemstone-green eyes.

Tom freezes in place, his heart races and his mouth slowly opens. "I can honestly say. I am not sure this time I can tell what the bull crap or the target is."

She stands on her tip-toes and leans to his ear. Tom can feel her breath on his neck. "When you find out what the target is, Thomas Stevenson, you, let me know."

Margaret gracefully steps back, looks at Tom with her green eyes, then turns with a hop to walk home. Tom follows.

Is she flirting with me? Oh my, I don't know what to do. I am attracted to her, but this is not good. Joseph, if you're looking down, man, you have to give me a sign.

"So Tom, do you have a special someone back home in Austin?"

"No, I don't. I broke up with my girlfriend about two months before the draft."

Hoot! Hoot!

An owl calls.

Margaret jumps back and grabs Tom's arm. Tom looks at the sky and thinks, *Is this the sign Joseph?*

The owl flies across the path in front of them.

Margaret shudders. Tom exhales loudly.

Margaret stops as the trail nears its end before it comes out to the yard by her house. She turns to Tom and steps close to him. "So, after all the talking back at the department store tonight, is that all you want to tell me, Thomas Stevenson?"

"We—

Margaret places her fingers over his mouth to stop him from talking. "I think I will call you Thomas Stevenson from now on." She looks at his lips and then back to his eyes. "I like that name. Now, Thomas Stevenson, I want you to look me in the eyes, cut through all the bull crap, and tell me what Thomas Stevenson thinks the target is. From your heart."

Thomas nervously licks his lips. "Margaret, you are a beautiful woman. That is a fact. Joseph used to tell us how mesmerizing you are. As I look into your eyes, I peer into your heart, and that beauty is unmatched. I don't know if this is right or not."

Margaret smiles. "Let me be the judge of that."

"Al—

Margaret cuts him off by swiftly kissing Tom. Their mouths meet, and their tongues intertwine. Tom wraps his arms around her and lifts her off the ground.

Tom's heart is pumping blood through his body at an accelerated pace.

The fire in Margaret is lit, which has been missing for some time and is now raging.

Both are lost in each other's arms. Slowly, Margaret steps back and breaks the embrace. She looks at Tom and hugs him tightly. She whispers in his ear. "Thomas, do me a favor. Always go straight for the target and cut through the bull crap. You understand this?"

Tom kisses her neck by her ear twice. "I understand this. You know this means I will not make my way to Austin any time soon."

She breaks from the embrace and looks him dead in the eye. "Good, you better not." She takes a deep breath. "I need a day or two to break this to William and Henry, but I owe them that. I don't care what the town says of me, but I don't want them hearing of me and you by someone else."

"I agree."

Margaret smiles. "Good, now walk me home."

"Yes Ma'am." Tom proudly extends his arm, and Margaret interlaces her arm in his.

They slowly walk out of the trail and up to the house. Henry lies sleeping on the porch swing.

Margaret looks at Tom and whispers, "He has been my family's protector all this time. I cannot say enough good things about Henry." She holds a finger up for Tom to wait and then discreetly walks into the house.

Tom stands over Henry, looking at him. Margaret walks out with a blanket and places it over Henry as he sleeps. She walks over to Tom and gives him a peck on the cheek. "Come see me after work tomorrow. I get off around 4:30."

"Tomorrow?"

"Oh, yeah, today. Today at 4:30, and I'll let you walk me home."

"I'll be there." Tom winks at her, quickly steps off the porch, and runs down the trail.

Margaret walks into the house and makes her way to Will's room. She peers her head into the room and watches him as he sleeps, looking up at the ceiling. *Joseph, I hope I am doing the right thing and that you're okay with it.*

Will gently stirs. Margaret pulls the blanket up to Will's neck, tucking him in.

Chapter 24 Henry's Revelation

Margaret stirs the eggs in the frying pan. She looks over and picks up a plate. She then places three scrambled eggs on one plate and three more on the other.

"Henry, how is Peggy?"

Henry scoops up a bite of eggs and quickly swallows. "Oh, she is good. She is the best." He pauses for a second and then looks around. "I haven't told anyone this, but we are going to get married. We just haven't set a date yet."

Margaret runs over and wraps her arms around him, kissing him several times on the forehead. "I am so happy for you, Henry. Peggy will make a great wife, and you will be a great husband." Margaret hops around the room in a happy mood.

Will watches on briefly. Henry looks over at him. "Will, is everything okay?"

"No, I am happy for you, Uncle Henry. You will leave, and it will be just Maw and me, is all."

Henry looks at Margaret for a moment. "Hey Will, no, it won't be like that. I will still be here from time to time. I will be down the road."

Margaret looks at Henry and winks at him. Henry wraps his arms around Will. "I promise, if it is in my power, I will be close to you."

Will slowly smiles. "Okay."

"So, would you two gentlemen accompany me to church today?"

"Maw, do we have to?"

"Yes, you do, Will," Henry says sternly.

"Good, then it is settled. Let's all get ready."

Henry opens the door to the church. Margaret walks in, followed by Will. The congregation is seated, and no one greets them.

Will notices Helen and her mom in the back. He notices his friends sitting on the other side.

Margaret looks at Henry and then makes her way to her usual seat. She scoots over two families and sits in the middle. Henry and Will sit on each side of her. As they settle down, Margaret notices people on the row getting up and moving. She nervously looks at Henry.

Henry leans to her and whispers, "This town is full of hypocrites."

The row in front of them gets up and moves. Will looks back as the Pastor stands in front of the podium. The row behind them gets up and moves. Three rows are empty except for Henry, Margaret, and Will.

Margaret grabs Henry and Will's hands and holds them tight.

The Pastor looks across the congregation and says, "It seems the action of some in this town is frowned upon in the House of the Lord."

Joan Bennett stands up from the back. She looks at Helen and nods. They walk up to the row where Margaret sits and scoots in close to them. Joan looks at Henry. "Mr. Wood, would it be alright if I sat by Margaret?"

Henry nods. "Most certainly."

Helen walks to the other side and sits next to Will.

The congregation gasps.

The Pastor's face turns colors in agitation.

Albert, Percy, and Gerald stand up and walk down the aisle to Will. They slide in right next to Helen.

Silence enters the sanctuary, casting its deafening blanket over the congregation. Pastor Phillips' face is red with anger. He slowly opens the bible and looks across the congregation. He loosens his collar and starts to talk but can't get the words out.

Joan stares at him stoically without an ounce of compassion in her eyes.

Henry sits there, trying not to laugh. Margaret sits proudly with her chin lifted. Will and Helen look at each other smirking. Albert, Percy, and Gerald all sit proudly.

"Umm, I do apologize. It seems I have come down with something. Please forgive me," Pastor Phillips says as he steps away.

Everyone in the congregation stares in disbelief.

Joan leans to Margaret. "Now is when all these hypocrites will chatter. Let's leave with our heads held high."

Margaret nods.

Joan looks at Will. "Can you and Helen follow us?"

"Yes Ma'am."

"Mr. Henry Wood, would you do us the honor of leading us out?"

"It is my pleasure, Ma'am."

Everyone gets up and they follow each other out of the church.

They all step out of the church and walk to the parking lot.

Margaret looks at Joan in amazement. "What just happened there?"

"I believe two families finally put the Pastor in his place. A little silent defiance."

Margaret wraps her arm around Joan. "Thank you for standing up for us. So many people in this town have turned their backs on us."

"Margaret, that is a shame," Joan says. "I am truly sorry about your husband, how my soon-to-be ex has treated you, and what you have been through."

"Joan, I know that isn't you. I appreciate it. You have raised a great young lady in Helen."

"And you with Will," Helen replies.

"How about next weekend we have you and Helen over at the house? I will have Henry and his bride-to-be, Peggy, over," Margaret looks at Henry.

"Letting the cat out of the bag, I see," Henry says, smiling.

"You should be proud, Henry," Margaret replies.

"Oh, I am."

"Congratulations, Henry. Peggy is a good woman, and she is getting a good man," Joan replies.

"Thank you again, Helen," Margaret replies. "And think about next weekend."

"Oh, nothing to think about. We will be happy to be there."

"Good," Margaret says as Henry opens the car door for her. Margaret gets in the car.

Henry walks around the car and whistles loudly. "Hey lover boy, you coming with us?"

"Uh, no, I am walking Helen home. Is that okay?"

Henry looks over at Margaret. She nods yes. "Your Maw said yes."

Henry cranks the car, and they drive home.

Margaret steps on the porch, and Henry follows. "Margaret, you are okay with me marrying Peggy, aren't you?"

Margaret gasps and turns around. "Oh, Henry, I am more than pleased about this. You deserve to be happy."

"Well, I worry about you. You deserve to be happy, too."

Margaret walks over to the swing. "You mind me bending your ear for a moment?"

"No Ma'am," Henry replies as he pulls out his harmonica, blows through it once, and then looks at her.

"I love your brother with all my heart. Nothing will ever change that. You know he was the only one for me. There has been no other. He is the only man that I have kissed on the lips with love. I tell you this, Henry because I need you to hear me out. Other men have tried to kiss me, like Earl, but I have never kissed them. Joseph is my heart. I don't want to forget, but I must move on."

Henry starts to stand up. "Mar—

She quickly raises her finger. "Wait, I must be honest. Let me finish. The other morning, I did kiss a man. I kissed Thomas Stevenson, and it was from the heart. He didn't kiss me. I kissed him."

Margaret watches Henry's reaction. He stands up and steps towards her. Then he drops down to his knees in front of her, and he grabs her hands.

"I don't have the best words, so I will say how it makes sense to me if that is okay?"

Margaret nods and takes a deep breath. "You know Margaret, they tell us that history has important lessons. Some say history repeats itself, and we never learn from it."

Margaret looks at Henry, confused.

"Everyone misses this concept and thinks it means something else. Listen to me: how many people on their dying beds regret not truly living life? That is the biggest history lesson that we all overlook. And THAT is what is repeated over and over. So, you only live once, screw everyone else. Joseph would understand. Go for your heart's desire. You are the smartest and strongest woman I know. You have good judgment of character, and Joseph did too. I believe he chose a good friend in Thomas, and I think he would do anything you asked. You do what is good for you and no one else for once."

Tears flow down Margaret's cheeks, and she falls to the ground in Henry's arms as she sobs. "Thank you, Henry. Thank you so much. Your opinion means a lot to me—yours and William's."

She looks around. "Look at me. A blubbering fool."

"Margaret, you are no fool. You have been through a lot and stood solid as a rock. Joseph was always proud of you, and I know why. Don't worry about William. I will set him straight on this."

"Henry, I know, but I must be the one who tells him."

"Margaret, I understand, but I have your back."

Margaret stands up and pulls Henry up slowly.

He chuckles. "What did you think of that ole Pastor today?"

"What I always thought of him. He is nothing more than a bully who isn't used to people standing up to him. Sadly, our church is led by him."

Helen and William step into the front yard from the street. Henry looks over. "Well, it looks like you are about to get your chance now, Margaret." Henry waves with his eyes to the side.

Margaret looks over. "William, I do need a moment of your time."

"Yes Ma'am.'

"Helen, I would like to show you something by the back of the house," Henry says.

"Oh, sure thing, Mr. Wood."

Henry steps off the porch and walks with Helen around the house.

William steps on the porch and looks at Margaret. "Maw, you've been crying. Is everything okay?"

"Oh, your Paw would be so proud of you right now, William. I know I am." Margaret looks to the sky for a moment, then pats the swing. "Come sit with me."

Will sits next to her. Margaret turns to him and grabs his hands. "This is hard, William. Give me a moment."

Will watches her. "Yes Ma'am."

"Your Paw was the only man I have ever kissed. Now Earl kissed me, but I would not kiss him back, and you know what happened there and what almost happened. The only man I have ever wanted to kiss was Joseph Wood." Margaret grins from ear to ear. "Just thinking of him made the butterflies fly fast in my tummy. He was a good man. Even though I was pregnant, your Paw never felt he was fancy enough to marry me." She grabs Will's chin. "That is the real and only reason why we didn't marry until before he went to war."

Will nods with tears in his eyes.

"He adored me and adored you. Now, what I am about to tell you will be rough." Margaret takes a deep breath. "I will never forget him." She clutches Will's hands tightly. "But I must move on, William. He left almost three years ago to go to war."

"Maw, I would expect you to. You are still young and beautiful. You deserve to be happy."

Margaret suddenly wraps her arms around Will. "Thank you for understanding, my precious William. Right now, you and Henry mean the world to me."

Will nods as they separate.

"Now I have two more things to talk about. First, how do you feel about Thomas Stevenson?"

Will tilts his head slightly. "Maw?" Then he smiles. "I think he is a great guy. Paw loved him, and he is genuine."

"Good." Margaret grabs Will's chin. "Now I want you to be brutally honest with me. How far have you and Helen gone?"

"Maw, you would tell me that is none of your business, however we only kissed."

Margaret smirks. "You are right on that one. But keep me informed, young man."

"Yes Ma'am."

"I love you, William."

"I love you, too, Maw."

"Good now go fetch Uncle Henry and your beautiful young friend, Helen."

"Oh, next weekend, we will have a dinner here that will include Helen's Mom as well."

"Yes, Ma'am."

Chapter 25 Courting

Wearing a stunning red pencil dress, Margaret begins to knock on the hotel room door. As her fist rises mid-air, she stops, looks around, and backs away from the door. *This is way too forward. I will go home.* She turns around and starts walking back towards the house. *He does need to chase me, not vice versa.*

She turns down a street and looks at the neighborhood kids running around their yard, having a good time. A baseball bounces into the street in front of her. She picks it up and tosses it back to the kids.

"Good throw," one kid yells.

"Thank you," Margaret says happily.

She heads to the path that leads down to her house. *Wow, just the other night, we kissed. It felt great.* Margaret extends her arms out and spins around, with her head looking at the sky. She turns quickly and then stops. *Oh, Margaret, you're being foolish. He probably went on his way to Austin.* Margaret reaches the trail's end and stops to look at the house.

She watches Helen and Will joyfully chase each other around the yard. *Joseph would have loved to see his son this way. Life goes by fast. I will not miss that history lesson that Henry was talking about.* She walks out of the thicket and into the house. Quickly, she goes to the bedroom and changes into a more comfortable blue and white checkered apron dress with two side pockets. She spins in the dress. "Awe, much better."

Knock! Knock! Knock!

"I'm coming," Margaret yells. She hustles to the door and opens it.

Tom stands outside in grey slacks and a blue long-sleeved button-up shirt. His wavy blond hair seems perfect. He smiles. "I am looking for a Mrs. Margaret Wood."

Margaret smiles. "Well, Mr. Thomas Stevenson, it seems you have found her."

"Might I trouble you for a walk?"

Margaret nods her head. "I think that is doable."

Tom steps to the side, and Margaret walks out the door. They step off the porch together.

Will looks over and waves at them.

Margaret smiles as they step onto the path and walk away from the house. They walk down the trail. "Now, Thomas Stevenson, I want to get one thing straight as we start down this trail."

He turns to her as they walk. "Yes Ma'am."

"I don't want you to think I am fast or easy by any means."

He places his hand over his chest. "That is the furthest thing from my mind."

Margaret looks at him suspiciously. "What is on your mind, Thomas?" She twirls her hair with her hand as she walks.

"I would say that kiss has occupied my mind quite a bit."

"You're not going to be all Doll Dizzy, are you?"

"I don't know. Do you go around kissing every guy you meet?"

Margaret gasps and then hits Thomas on the shoulder.

Thomas laughs.

"I see Thomas, you have a little funny man in you." She points at him. "Remember, I said no impression of me being fast or easy. We may have to start this all over again. Maybe a bit slower."

He stops along the trail and takes a bow. "I will try my best to refrain from such spontaneous jokes." Tom looks up to see her reaction.

She rolls her eyes, with her hand on her hip, and then looks the other way. Tom raises up, and Margaret extends her hand out, still looking the other way. Tom secures her hand, and they walk together.

"Where to?"

"Thomas, I have no idea. We can go to the lake. We can walk the railroad tracks like teenagers. It is Sunday, so nothing is open in Bennett Town. It is supposed to rain today." She turns to him, face to face. A mischievous grin comes over her face. "I figure just being around each other is good enough."

Thomas smiles and starts to lean forward. Margaret ducks out of the way and moves to the side.

"I will not be a fast girl, Thomas," Margaret says, waving her finger at him.

Tom rolls his eyes in frustration. Margaret leans on his arm. "Do you like to dance?"

"Oh, I love to dance. I can dance in a way you have never seen."

Margaret gives him a questioning look.

A light drizzle starts to come down. Thomas looks at Margaret. "Do I need to get you inside somewhere?"

She leans to Thomas. "I won't melt."

Thomas wraps his arm around her waist. Then, with his left hand, he holds her right hand up about head high. He looks into her eyes as the rain comes down. "Are you ready for this?"

Margaret smiles as she nods.

Tom gives her a wink. "One, two, and three." He kicks out with his left foot, an exaggerated kick almost as high as their hands. He looks at Margaret. "You have to kick with me. On three. So one, two, and three." They kick high together.

Margaret laughs hysterically.

"And again, one, two, and three. They lean to Thomas's right and kick high to his left. "One, two, and three." They kick again, and then Thomas changes direction by switching hands, placing his left arm around her waist and his right hand in her left arm. "One, two, three, and kick." They kick together. "One, two, three, and kick higher."

Margaret leans on Thomas, laughing uncontrollably.

The frigid rain pours down on them, soaking their clothes. "I guess that will be our dance."

Thomas pulls her close around the waist. Margaret bites her lower lip as she looks into his eyes. Thomas picks her up and kisses her deeply as the rain pours on them. Both were lost in the moment and couldn't care less about the rain. Thomas slowly sets her down.

"You know a nice lady could catch a cold here in the rain."

Margaret rolls her eyes. "I was pretty warm. I didn't notice the cold." Then, she walks down the trail away from the house and towards town. She looks over her shoulder and motions with her finger for him to follow. Thomas, the obedient one, quickly follows.

He grabs her hand as the rain comes down.

"You got any place in mind?"

"Yep, we are going to the department store. I have the keys. Inside there, I have some towels and blankets. I can change into something there." She looks Thomas up and down. "I'm not sure if there are any men's clothes there," Margaret says with a smile.

The rain pours down as Helen and William run to the front porch. Henry steps onto the porch. He sits in the chair, Helen sits on the swing, and Will runs inside to grab some towels.

"So, how are you and your Maw doing?" Henry asks.

"Oh, we are doing good. Maw cannot stand my Paw anymore."

"What about you?"

"I hate his guts."

Will steps out with a towel and hands it to Helen.

"Will, did your Maw talk to you?"

Will looks at him. "You mean about moving on?"

Henry nods.

"She asked me about Tom also."

"How do you feel about that?"

"Oh, I think he is a good guy. I think he is genuine and will treat Maw right."

Henry nods his head as he watches the rain pour down. "It looks like we may be stuck on the porch for a bit," he says.

"Yes Sir."

Margaret quickly opens the door.

Cling!

She runs inside, followed by Tom. Her chin quivers from the cold, and Tom starts shivering as well.

"Okay, this might not have been such a great idea," Margaret says. She looks at Tom and says, "Lock the door, please."

Then she walks back to the sewing room and grabs a couple of towels. "I know I have a blanket or something here." She looks in Mr. Drum's office only to come up empty-handed. She opens a storage closet behind Mr. Drum's office and pulls out a pillow and blanket. "Ah, here we go." She grabs them and walks over to Tom. "This is what we got: a pillow, two towels, and a blanket."

Tom gives her a suspicious eye as he shakes.

Margaret's chin quivers from the cold clothes. She takes a deep breath and says, "Okay, we are both adults here. We are not teenagers. We are both cold and cannot warm up unless we are out of these wet clothes. We have both seen someone naked before. You have seen a woman naked before?"

"Oh, trust me, I have."

Margaret nods her head, then squints her eyes.

Tom looks at her and places his shaking hand on her shoulder. "I got it. We need body heat."

Margaret stops and looks at Tom. She licks her lips and takes a deep breath. "Yes, but not that type of body heat. No shenanigans."

Tom lifts his chin. "No shenanigans. Deal."

Margaret nods and watches for Tom to do something.

He unfastens his belt and quickly drops his pants.

Margaret's chin drips slightly, and she quickly walks over to the wall where the radiator heater is at and she takes off her dress. Tom removes his wet shirt and shivers in place. He reaches down, grabs a towel, and removes his socks and underwear.

Margaret peeks out of the corner of her eyes. A smirk emerges from the corner of her mouth.

Tom wraps his towel around his waist. Then he rubs his hands together while blowing into them, trying to get warmth. Margaret looks over at him as he does, then grabs the other towel. She smiles and then turns her back to Tom. "Please don't look, Thomas."

Tom smiles and turns around slowly. He notices the mirror behind the mannequin and observes her reflection.

Margaret removes her bra and then removes her panties.

He can see Margaret fully naked. Tom's heart starts pounding. He holds in a gasp, trying not to give away his view.

She places her and Tom's clothes on the radiator. Margaret grabs her towel and dries herself off. She then drops the towel and walks behind Tom. Cautiously, she wraps her arms around his stomach and whispers in his ear. "We can lie down now." She grabs his towel and says, "But this stays on, no shenanigans." She kisses him on the shoulder. Tom turns around and says, "Yes Ma'am."

They curl up in the blanket with Margaret's head snuggled tightly to Tom's chest.

They snuggle for warmth.

Margaret opens her eyes and sees that Tom is missing. She gazes underneath the blanket, and notices she is still naked.

Tom walks back into the sewing room with his clothes on. He smiles and points to the radiator on the wall. "I got the radiator heater a churning for us. I think your dress is dry now. It has stopped raining outside. I will go into the other room while you change."

Margaret holds the blanket back to her chest and extends her arm so Tom can pull her up. He grabs her hand and pulls her up.

"You have color back into your face," Tom says.

Margaret smiles and gives him a peck on the lips. "That is for being a gentleman."

Tom smiles and walks into the other room while she gets dressed.

As she puts her garments on, she says, "What time is it?"

"Oh, it is about 11 at night."

"I think we should dance back tonight."

Tom smiles.

Chapter 26 Redemption

Albert looks around as he leans up against a tree. Albert shakes his head as he sees Percy holding Ruth's hand. "Ruth, are you serious?"

She rubs Percy's chest. "I like your friend Percy. Anything wrong with that?"

Albert takes a deep breath. "I guess not."

Gerald emerges from a trail and walks onto the street in front of Helen's house. He looks at Ruth and then at Percy and smiles. "Are we waiting on Will?"

"Yep," Albert says.

"Does he know?" Gerald asks.

Albert shakes his head. "Remember, Ruth, you got to ditch Loverboy here for a few and be on the lookout."

Percy points in the direction of Will. "There he is. He is walking to Helen's house. He is probably going to walk her to school and all. Are you sure we want to do this? I mean, Will is in the dark on it and all. He probably wants to hang out with Helen. I know I like hanging out with Ruth and all. She is nice."

"Oh, my God! Percy," Albert says, rolling his eyes. "She is still my sister."

"I just do what she wants me to do, that is all."

Gerald laughs as he looks at Albert. "That's part of the problem. If it were just you, no one would worry."

Ruth pulls Percy closer to her and places a hand on his chest. Then, in a baby voice, she says, "Y'all leave my dear Percy alone." She then kisses him on the cheek.

Will walks with Helen down the pathway from Helen's house.

"Okay, fellas, we know the deal. Let's go." Albert directs.

Albert and Gerald walk side by side on the street. Percy and Ruth follow, holding hands. Albert looks at Ruth and nods. Ruth lets go of Percy's hand and scoots up with Albert. Together, they run to catch up with Will and Helen.

Ruth approaches Helen's free side and interlaces her arm with hers. Helen turns to her.

"Tell Will you will see him shortly. You need to come with me," Ruth says.

Albert grabs Will, "Come with me and the boys. We are going a different way to school."

Ruth and Helen continue the usual path.

Albert winks at Will. "Got word that Charles, Ralph, and Walter were going to have a surprise for you this morning on your way to school. So, the fellas and I figured we would outsmart them. The girls are going the normal route. We will circle around them and come in from behind. Those guys were planning on meeting us right before the Ice Plant. Don't worry, Helen is safe with Ruth there. She can fight like a boy."

"Wow, I didn't expect that," Will replies.

"We got to get going," Albert says. He looks over his shoulder and waves at Percy and Gerald to follow. "Let's get going, Will." Albert starts running down a different street with the guys following. They quickly run past Main Street and then hang a right on the back street. They run for about another hundred yards, and Albert lifts his hand for everyone to slowdown. They start walking.

Will moves up next to Albert. "See there. Charles and Walter are at the corner before the Ice Plant. Look, here comes Ralph."

Gerald and Percy walk up behind Will and Albert.

"They never walk this way," Will says.

"Yep, Ruth overheard one of them saying they are going set a trap for the town whore's son this morning." Albert winks at Will. "She is good for more than kissing Percy. They will distract them. When they turn to Ruth and Helen, we will come in from behind them."

Gerald whispers, "Which one do you want, Will?"

"It doesn't matter. I can take any of them one-on-one. Percy, you stay back a little."

"Nope, I owe Charles for a broken arm."

Gerald chuckles. "I will take Ralph."

"I got Charles," Albert says.

"Good Walter was the mouthy one anyway," Will says.

"Look, they are turning. Let's go," Albert says.

All four quietly run out to cross the street.

"Hey Ralph," Ruth yells as she stands next to Helen. She twirls the tip of her hair with her fingertips. You're kind of cute."

Ralph smiles as he walks towards her. "Oh, yeah. I am definitely more of a man than that ole Percy could ever be."

Charles and Walter both walk alongside Ralph.

Ruth smiles. "So what do you mean by that, Ralph?"

Ralph smirks. "I am pretty sure Percy doesn't even know how to—

A fist flies through the air and hits Ralph on the back of the head, completely blindsiding him. He immediately falls to the ground headfirst. Gerald jumps on his back and starts pounding him with his fists.

Albert tackles Charles to the ground, and Percy starts kicking Charles in the legs while Albert punches him in the face.

Will runs, slides, and kicks Walter's legs out from underneath him. He quickly gets up and lunges on top of Walter. His body presses Walter's arm down, suppressing their movement, rendering him defenseless. Will delivers several blows to Walter's face. Will looks at Walter's bloody face. "You got something you want to say?"

Percy quickly moves to Ralph and starts kicking him. Percy screams, "Don't you ever talk to my girlfriend again."

Gerald gets off Ralph, who is lying on the ground in pain. Albert gets off Charles and steps to the middle of the street. Charles lies on the ground, clutching his stomach. Will stands up and pushes Walter away with his foot.

He stands in the middle of the three bodies on the ground, each moaning and in pain. Will extends his arms parallel to the ground. "Here I am. I am here. Who wants some? One on one, right now. Let's end this." He looks down. "I didn't think so. You will listen to me. If you can't fight me now, I better not hear a whisper of you about my Maw, my family, me, or anyone I care about!" He looks around, then screams, "DO YOU HEAR ME?"

Helen watches on with her chin lifted with pride.

Ralph coughs, "Ugh, ugh, I hear you, Will."

"I, I, do too," Walter whispers.

"Charles?"

Charles raises his hand for mercy, "I understand, Will."

"Good, then we are done with this crap! Save it for a football game."

Ruth runs to Percy. "Oh, my Percy was so brave!" She jumps up on him. Percy grabs her legs, staggers back, and struggles to maintain his balance, but somehow does. Ruth kisses him several times on the face.

Helen walks over to Will, looks him in the eyes, gives him a big nod, and then kisses him. As they break from the kiss, Helen looks at the sky and then back to Will. "What time is it, Will?"

Will smiles and looks to the heavens. "Thanks Paw."

"Hey guys, we got to get to school," Albert yells.

Mr. Drum rubs his forehead as he reviews some bills in his office. He looks over the department store mortgage and smiles. "One more payment."

Margaret steps into the doorway. "Mr. Drum, how are you doing?"

Mr. Drum looks up. "Oh, some days better than others. What can I help you with, Margaret?"

"Oh, Saturday, I would like to invite you and Mrs. Drum over to the house. We will have a few people over, eat some food, and play cards."

"That sounds like a good time. We will be there unless I am under the weather. I hope you understand that one."

Margaret nods. "I do. Do you have many bad days?"

"About half the days are good, and half are bad. It seems to be moving faster than I expected. This roller coaster has not been easy, that is for sure," Mr. Drum says while looking down. He looks up and smiles. "But I keep my spirits up."

"If there is anything I can help you with, you let me know, Mr. Drum."

"I will, and I appreciate it. How are you and Will doing?"

"We are doing good. Every day is a blessing."

"Margaret, that is one accurate statement right there."

Henry opens the door to the bank, and he and Peggy walk inside. They walk over to Judith's desk. "Judith, how are you doing?" Henry asks.

Judith smiles. "I am doing good. Don's trial for bringing a gun to the bank and threatening Earl will be sometime next week."

"I see. How are you and Don working out?" Henry asks as Peggy listens on.

"Oh, much better. He's a good man. I never should have been so dumb and gullible."

Judith looks around. "What can I help you two with?"

"Oh, who do we need to talk to about securing a mortgage for a house?" Henry asks.

Judith frowns. "Unfortunately, that will be Earl."

Henry leans on her desk, lowers his head, and then looks up. "Is he in?"

Judith nods. "I'll let him know he has a client."

Henry looks at Peggy and nods.

Judith walks over to Earl's office, says something, then looks at Henry and waves him over.

Henry walks first into Earl's office, and Peggy follows. He leans behind her and shuts the door.

Earl looks up, and his eyes grow angry. "What are you doing here? You can't be within a hundred feet of me."

Henry shrivels his lips. "Earl, I came here to do business. We are looking to purchase a home. I have money to put down, but I will probably need a mortgage of about $2,000."

Earl, as he looks at Henry says, "Why would I do anything for you, Henry? You have been a pain in my ass since you have returned."

Henry looks at Earl and points to him. "Because you will make money off me, is why."

Earl thinks about it momentarily. "True, money is one of my few true loves." He takes a deep breath. "But it gives me great satisfaction to say, ain't no way in hell will I loan you the money. Instead," Earl picks up the phone and says, "Get me the Sheriff, please." He looks back at Henry, "Instead, I will have your ass thrown in jail for violating the distance in the Sheriff's order." Earl looks at Peggy and smiles.

Henry slams his fists on the desk.

"Sheriff, Earl Bennett here. Henry Wood just marched into my office and is here as we speak. I need you to handle this." Earl hangs up the phone, smiling.

"Peggy, let's go," Henry says.

"Oh, Peggy," Earl looks at Henry and then back to her. "I will offer you a solution to this. You can spend the evening at my pleasure tonight, and I will have your Henry out of jail most urgently."

Henry lunges across the table to Earl, but Earl quickly steps to the side. Meanwhile, Judith opens the door. "Henry, you need to go."

Peggy grabs Henry's arm. "Let's go, my love."

Henry stands up and starts to the door. He turns to Earl. "You haven't seen the last of me, Earl. I promise you that."

Earl laughs in their face with no care in the world.

Peggy pulls Henry out of the office, and she looks at Judith. "Thank you, Judith."

"You got to get the Sheriff is on his way."

Henry begrudgingly steps out of the bank.

"We got to go, Henry," Peggy declares.

"No, he will come and arrest me somewhere else. He can arrest me here. If he does, you go and get Margaret. She will know what to do."

Tom pushes the door open at Drum's Department Store.

Cling!

He is wearing his favorite blue suit and, as always, his Fedora. Tom looks around at the dresses on the mannequins inside the store.

Margaret approaches him in a grey cap-sleeve dress with a thick black belt. "May I help you, Mr. Thomas Stevenson?" She smirks as he turns around.

"Well, Mrs. Wood, this store looks vastly different in the day-time."

She licks her lips. "It seems things get interesting here at night."

"Well, if that is a normal evening, I am willing to return tonight." Tom tilts his head and looks at her out of the corner of his eye.

"Hmm, somehow that does sound tempting, Thomas Stevenson."

"Yes, it does."

Cling!

Margaret turns to look at who came into the store.

"Hey, Peggy."

"Ma, Margaret, the Sheriff just arrested Henry," Peggy says frantically.

Margaret grabs her hands. "Oh, my goodness. What happened?"

Peggy shakes from excitement. She takes a deep breath and then exhales. "Henry and I went to the bank to get a loan for a house we want to move into. We went to talk to Earl, and he said, there is no way in hell he will loan us the money. And he called the Sheriff while we were there for breaking the Sheriff's order."

Margaret shakes her head. "Oh, no."

Tom looks at Margaret. "I can handle this."

Margaret looks at Tom. "Are you sure?"

"Yep, I will have him out in a few. You stay here."

He looks over at Peggy. "Peggy, is it?"

She nods.

Tom extends his arm. "Take me to the Sheriff."

Peggy looks at Margaret, then interlaces her arm in his. They walk out the door.

Tom and Peggy step into the Sheriff's office. Inside the jail are six cells surrounded by two desks. Sheriff Welch is sitting behind the big desk overlooking the jail cells.

The sheriff notices Tom and Peggy. "Can I help you?"

"Yes, you have Henry Wood in jail here. Is that correct?"

"It is, and who are you?"

"Oh, my name is Thomas Stevenson. I am here to get Henry out of jail."

The Sheriff chuckles. "That ain't happening. He is here for a good week."

Henry clings to the bars in his cell to listen in.

"Is that so," Thomas asks. "Do you have a phone here?"

Sheriff Welch points to the one on his desk.

"What's the charge?"

Sheriff Welch crosses his arms and rubs his chin. "Oh, let me see here. Violating a restraining order, threatening a person, assault, and whatever else I can think of."

"Gotcha. Who is the operator in the town?"

Thomas walks over to the phone on the Sheriff's desk.

"It is Doris."

Thomas picks up the receiver and holds it to his ear. He grabs the base of the phone and holds the candlestick phone's receiver to his mouth.

"Hello Doris, my name is Thomas Steveson. I am Governor Stevenson's nephew."

Peggy's eyes grow big in surprise.

"I need to call Governor Stevenson's office at 1100 San Jacinto Blvd, Austin, Texas."

Tom watches the Sheriff and Peggy as he waits. He winks at Peggy.

"I know it is a long-distance call. They will accept the call as soon as you say it is from Thomas Stevenson, his nephew."

Tom watches everyone in the room as he waits for someone to answer.

"Oh, Frances, Thomas here. Yep, I need to speak to Uncle Coke." Tom nods and laughs. "Oh yes, I have been back in the States for a few weeks. Yes, it is good to be back in America. Thank you, I will hold."

The Sheriff listens attentively.

Tom smiles. "Uncle Coke, it is good to talk to you." Tom listens for a moment. "Yes, I'm in Bennett Town in Northeast Texas. I came to check in on Joseph Wood's family. You know Joseph Wood, who saved my life. Yes Sir. Wonderful family, Uncle Coke."

Tom's eyes wander around the jail as he listens.

"Well, Uncle Coke, I need a little help here. I got Joseph's brother, Henry. He is a war veteran himself who was wounded overseas. He is an incredible man. He can play the harmonica with the best of them. Well, this town is a bit rough around the edges." Tom looks stoically at the Sheriff. "They just locked him up on some trumped-up charges. I can give you all the details if you would like."

Tom pauses as he listens.

Sheriff Welch's face turns red with anger.

"Well, I will do that over lunch when I return to Austin. Yes, the Sheriff is here. In fact, he is right in front of me."

Peggy rubs her hands together with excitement.

"I sure will, Uncle Coke. I will talk to you soon," Tom says, then removes the earpiece from his ear.

"Sheriff, it seems the Governor would like a word with you."

Sheriff Welch exhales, walks over, and then grabs the phone.

"Sheriff Welch of Bennett Town, Sir." Sheriff Welch tightens his lips as he listens.

Tom walks over to Peggy and leans to her ear as he watches the Sheriff, "Yeah, don't you worry. Henry is about to be released."

Henry listens in, the best he can.

"Yes, Sir, I understand. I will do it immediately. Yes Sir, I will let the Mayor know to give you a call as well. Thank you for your time, Sir."

Sheriff Welch hangs up the phone and looks at Peggy. "It seems the Wood family has more connections than I estimated." He pulls out the jail cell keys, walks over to Henry's cell, and unlocks it. "You are free to go."

Henry grins from ear to ear as he steps out. Peggy runs and hugs him. Henry picks her off her feet and spins around.

"Hmm, I think we need to go and let Margaret know," Tom says.

Henry smiles, "I agree."

Peggy looks at Tom and hugs him. "Thank you, Thomas. Thank you so much."

Chapter 27 Big Gathering

Mr. Drum walks up to Margaret and says. "I hear Henry ran into trouble with Earl again."

"Yep, I don't know all the details yet, but I will tonight."

Cling!

Henry, Peggy, and Thomas step into Drum's Department Store.

Margaret and Mr. Drum both look up as they hear the chime. She smiles. "How did this happen?"

Peggy and Henry look at each other. Henry nods to Peggy. "It seems that Thomas is Governor Stevenson's nephew. He simply made a call to Uncle Coke Stevenson." Peggy motions her fingers in quotations. "Well, the Governor seemed interested in talking to the Sheriff. The Sheriff was very bitter after the call but released him immediately."

Margaret enthusiastically hugs Henry. "Look at our family jail-bird."

"Funny, are we," Henry says, smiling.

She turns to Thomas, wraps her arms around his neck, and kisses him on the lips.

Mr. Drum's jaw drops.

A bit in shock, Henry and Peggy look at each other.

"Hmm," Henry says.

Margaret breaks from the kiss and looks at everyone, their eyes staring her down. She nods. "Okay, so I have some explaining to do." She wraps her arm around Thomas's waist and lifts her chin. "Umm, I am a grown woman old enough to know what I want. Thomas Stevenson and I are courting. If someone has a problem, they can talk to me."

Thomas's eyes light up.

Mr. Drum looks at Margaret and Tom and then extends his hand to Tom. Thomas gladly shakes it. "Mr. Stevenson, Margaret is a good woman. We are kind of protective of her around here. I need you to understand I served in the 4th Division in the Great War."

Thomas smiles. "I fully understand. I also served in the 4th with Joseph."

They break from the handshake. "Then we will get along just fine." Mr. Drum looks at Margaret. "I will bring the cigars on Saturday."

Henry looks at Margaret and gives her a wink. She smiles with pride. Henry looks over at Thomas. "Thomas, I think you will fit in just fine. If not, I would bury you." Henry pats him on the back.

Margaret looks at Peggy. "I hear congratulations are in order for you two. Do we have a wedding date?"

Peggy smiles. "Oh, soon we will have a date. I am excited." She suddenly frowns. "We were trying to get a loan at the bank for a house. Now we will have to figure something else out."

Henry acknowledges Margaret's nod to him.

Henry and Will place a table under the willow tree.

"We got two more tables, Will."

"We got this one from the barn. Where did the other two come from?"

"Oh, I borrowed them from work."

Thomas walks up. "You guys need some help?"

"Yes, Sir," Henry says. "If you and Will can set these tables out. I will go inside and see what else is needed." Henry starts to walk off. "Oh, Will, there are some chairs in the barn and some buckets we can turn upside down for some seats."

"Okay, Uncle Henry."

Henry walks back into the house.

Will looks at Thomas. "So you like my Maw?"

"Yes, Sir, that is true. I do. Your Paw said you like Joe DiMaggio?"

Will smiles. "I do, but you know it is only what we read or hear. I think he is a good ball player. He has a cannon for an arm."

"That is what they say," Tom says, smiling. "Too bad Texas doesn't have a ball club."

"I know. The closest one is in St. Louis. The only player they had that I ever liked was Dizzy Dean."

"Will, do you play baseball?"

"I play baseball and football. I can pitch and play third base. In football, I play linebacker. I like to hit."

Helen walks up with Joan, who is carrying a casserole dish. She looks at Will and says, "Gentlemen, excuse me. Where should I put the casserole?"

"Oh, Mrs. Bennett, you can take it inside."

Joan nods and walks to the house.

Helen stands to the side, and Thomas helps straighten up a table with Will. He leans across the table and whispers to Will, "Now, Will." He rolls his eyes over to Helen and then back to Will. "I would suggest never having a lady waiting on you."

Will smiles. "Oh yeah." He walks over to Helen and hugs her.

Darkness settles in, and Henry grabs a couple of old lanterns and places them on the tables. He lights each one.

Mr. Drum and Mrs. Drum are playing 42 with Margaret and Thomas at one table. Joan, Peggy, and Henry all watch.

Will, Helen, Albert, Percy, Ruth, and Gerald are all running through the woods behind the barn.

Mr. Drum bids. "Pass."

Margaret ,to his left, looks at her dominoes; she nods. "I got 30."

Lucy, across from Mr. Drum, smirks. "31."

Thomas looks at his dominoes and says, "Pass."

"All right, my dear Lucy, it is on us."

Lucy smiles and lays out the double five. "Fives is Trump."

Thomas shakes his head and tosses out the five-one.

Mr. Drum grins, puffs his cigar, and tosses out the five blanks. He gives Lucy a big wink. "That is a 16-point hand right there."

Margaret tosses out the five-two.

Mr. Drum rakes the four dominoes to his side and faces them up and in a row.

Lucy lays out the five-six, then chuckles, "Robert and I are a bit competitive when it comes to 42. I hope you don't mind?"

"Oh, not at all," Margaret says.

"A little healthy competition is not a bad thing," Thomas chimes in.

Robert slams the last domino down, "Bid! I couldn't agree more."

Henry blows into the harmonica softly while Peggy leans on him.

Mr. Drum looks around with a cigar in his hand and points to Joan. "We ain't got no youngsters around. So, let us all talk business here. What are we going to do about your husband?"

Joan takes a sip of the brandy in front of her. "Well, Mr. Drum—

Mr. Drum cuts her off and waves his hands. "Everyone here calls me Robert. You do that, Mr. Drum stuff, when we are at the store."

"Well, Robert, that is soon to be my ex-husband. I filed for a divorce several weeks ago."

Robert takes a sip of his whiskey. "So you going to be one of those de vorce eeys."

Joan squinches her face. "Well, now that you put it that way." She takes a big drink and mimics Robert's voice. "I would rather be a raunchy de vorce eey than Earl's wife."

Peggy and Margaret laugh. Lucy lifts her glass. "Amen to that, Joan. Amen to that."

"Good for you, Joan." Mr. Drum nods.

"So at this table, we have one de vorce eey, one town trollop slash war widow, and a lot of people that can't stand Earl," Margaret declares.

"I'll drink to that," Joan says taking a sip.

Margaret, Peggy, Lucy, Robert, Thomas, and Henry all take a drink.

"You know, I think Peg here is the only one who hasn't had a run-in with him or been burnt by him," Henry says as he looks around. "Or maybe Lucy."

"No, Henry," Lucy says calmly. "Robert and I both had our run-in with Earl. He isn't getting a Christmas card from the Drums." She takes a sip of her drink. "Now Joan, you can come over and open presents with us. You're a strong woman."

Suddenly, a set of headlights shine on the table from the road.

"Who the hell is this?" Henry asks.

The car stops, and the headlights shut off. The door opens, and someone steps out of the vehicle. Everyone adjusts their eyes as a man walks up to the table.

Margaret makes out who it is. "Sheriff Welch, what brings you here tonight? You never stop by here."

He walks up close to the table and looks at everyone around the table. "How is everyone tonight?"

Henry looks at the Sheriff and says, "Oh, we are just having a jolly ole time discussing your benefactor."

"My benefactor?"

"Yep, the one that hands you an envelope full of money, ole Earl," Henry says.

The Sheriff's lips tighten, and he breathes deeply. "Well, I am only here briefly." He looks over at Thomas. "The mayor informed me that he got a phone call from Austin stating that tonight I need to find a war veteran named Henry Wood and apologize to him." He looks at Henry. "I apologize, Henry."

"Well, thank you, Sheriff," Henry says. "Is there anything else?"

"I don't believe so," the Sheriff replies.

"Then leave us to our fun," Henry says.

The Sheriff stomps off, gets in his car, and drives away.

Everyone looks around quietly for a moment, and then Henry laughs out loud, breaking the silence as everyone joins in.

"Okay, Mr. Thomas Stevenson," Margaret says as she squints her eyes at him. She gets up and walks over to where he is sitting. "You joked with me that your uncle was the Governor." She sits in his lap. "Tell us now about this."

"Oh, whenever I tell people my full name," Thomas says as Margaret wraps her arms around his neck. "People will ask if I am related to the Governor. I tell them that he is my uncle. Well, he is. And I will say it like, yeah, he is, and everyone thinks I am joking." Thomas smirks. "But I am just being honest, is all, and they don't realize it."

Margaret kisses him on the lips.

"Ohh, Margaret, you are starting to live up to the town trollop," Joan says.

Margaret breaks from the kiss and looks at Joan. "Coming from the soon-to-be de vorce eey, I will take that as a compliment."

"Touché."

Henry starts blowing into the harmonica.

Peggy smiles. "♪*Danny Boy*♪ Henry."

"I will, but let me play a little upbeat song first. Something with some swing."

Henry blows through the Mississippi saxophone, and out comes a dancing melody.

Margaret jumps up and walks over to Joan. She pulls her to her feet, and they start swing dancing. Lucy puts out her cigarette and nods to Peggy. They get up and dance together, close to Margaret and Joan. All four women are dancing and laughing with no care in the world.

Robert looks at Thomas. "This is a good life right here."

Margaret and Joan are giggling as they dance.

Lucy bites down on her lower lip as her feet kick to the rhythm.

Henry slows the song down and finally finishes.

Peggy grabs her chest as she is almost out of breath.

As they return to the table, Margaret and Joan gasp for air. Margaret puts her arm on Joan's shoulder. "We should have been doing this a long time ago. We could have had a lot of fun."

"Seems to me I found a new friend," Joan says as she sits down.

Margaret walks over and sits in Thomas's lap.

Lucy and Peggy also sit back down.

"There is a rumor around town," Lucy says.

"Oh no, I am the de vorce eey. Margaret is the town trollop."

"I have other names, too," Margaret says.

"Is this rumor about you or Peggy?"

"Peggy picks up her drink and takes a sip."

Lucy looks around. "The rumor is about Henry and Margaret."

"Oh, this is going to be interesting," Joan says.

Peggy looks at Henry while he shrugs his shoulders.

Lucy takes a drink and says, "I hear Henry can play ♪*DannyBoy*♪ on the harmonica, and Margaret has a voice that makes the angels jealous when she sings it."

"Wait!" Joan yells. "That is it?" She looks around, a bit disappointed. Then she looks at Margaret. "Not that I wish anything bad on you, but I was hoping for something a little, hmm, let me think of how to say this." She thinks for a moment. "Oh yeah, disturbing. That's it, more disturbing."

"I am sorry to disappoint you, Joan. I am just a boring war widow and the town trollop."

Lucy walks over and leans on Robert. "So, Henry, can we hear it?"

"Sure," Henry says. He takes a sip of his whiskey. Then, he places his lips on the harmonica. Slowly, he blows into the mouth organ. Margaret's angelic voice softly sings the words in unison of the music.

Lucy lays against Robert's chest, stroking his cheek as they listen.

Joan looks around at Peggy and Thomas, watching Margaret sing and Henry play. Peacefully, she sways her head to the tune.

Thomas watches the gracefulness of Margaret sing, captivated by her beauty.

Peggy's chin lifts with pride as her beau masters the hobo harp.

Henry plays the final tune. Lucy claps loudly. "That was beautiful." She looks around. "Joan, we got to find you a beau. You deserve a good man."

"Oh, I am not in any hurry," Joan says, then smiles while looking at Margaret. "I figure I replace the town trollop for a while."

Joan and Margaret burst out laughing hysterically. Margaret shakes her head. "If I am going to be a trollop, I will only be Thomas's trollop." She kisses Thomas on the cheek.

Robert stands up. "I do apologize, but I am an older man. Lucy and I will have to leave tonight. We need to do this more often. Thank you for the hospitality."

Margaret walks over to Robert and hugs him. "Thank you for always being so good to me, Mr. Drum."

Robert pushes her back and winks at her. Lucy waves at everyone as they walk to the car. Robert holds the door for Lucy as she gets in. He shuts the door, walks around, and gets in the car. He cranks it and pulls away.

Joan looks around. "That's a good man there."

"Yes, he is," Margaret replies.

"Margaret, I am going to run as well," Joan says. "This has been the best time I have had in some time. Oh, I almost forgot. I want to inquire about one of those fancy dresses you make."

"Oh, that is no problem, Joan. Thank you."

Joan gets up, waves at everyone, then walks down the trail.

"We're out of here too," Henry yells as Peggy pulls him up.

"See you at church tomorrow?"

"After last week?"

"Yep and bring your fiancé."

Henry looks at Margaret, "I'll think about it."

Margaret looks at Thomas. "Well, I am going to get Thomas to come to church." She looks at Thomas.

"You are?" Thomas asks.

"Yes, Thomas Stevenson, would you accompany me to church?"

"I guess so."

"See."

"Well, see," Henry says as they leave.

Margaret looks at Thomas. "So, did you have fun?"

"Oh, I did. This was an incredible evening."

"Yes, it was. Let's turn off those lanterns and lay on the blanket looking up at the stars. Maybe even pass out under the stars. What do you think?"

"I like that, Margaret."

"I will have to run to the hotel tonight to get the clothes ready for church and all."

Margaret nods. "I am going to grab a blanket from inside if you can clear off the table."

"Deal."

Margaret walks inside the house.

Will, with all his friends, walks up.

"Hey Tom, where is Maw?"

"Oh, she just went inside. She will be out in a moment."

"Okay, well, I am going to walk Helen home. Everyone else is going their separate ways."

Tom winks at him. "Sounds good, Will. I will tell your Maw."

"Thank you," Will says as they walk away.

Margaret walks out with a blanket and a pillow in her hands.

Thomas is moving things from one table to the next. Margaret places the blanket on the ground. She looks up at the evening sky to get her orientation, then places the pillow and blanket down. She looks at Thomas as he diligently moves things around.

"Thomas, can you put the dominoes and ashtrays on the porch and close the house door?"

"No problem, Margaret." Margaret smiles and walks back into the house while Thomas sorts things out.

Thomas sets two lanterns by the door.

Margaret walks over to the table and looks back to Thomas as he is unaware she is watching him.

She looks up at the stars. "Uh, Thomas, do you want to gaze at the stars with me?"

"On my way," Thomas says as he finishes up. He walks over to her and lays down beside her.

Margaret secures the blanket and scoots to one side. As he lies down, she tosses the blanket on top of him. His hand touches her hand, and she quickly interlocks hers with his. He turns sideways to look at her.

"You are a beautiful woman, Margaret. I can tell you this. I am never going back to Austin. I am making Bennett Town my home. I would love nothing more than to be part of your and Will's life."

"Are you sure?"

Instead of answering Margaret's question, Thomas kisses her passionately.

Earl and Betty Sue lie naked in bed in the old Duncan house.

A stranger walks into the room carrying a flashlight and a pistol. The lights shines on both of them.

Betty and Earl remain asleep.

The stranger walks over to Betty's side and shines the light in her eyes. She squints her eyes, and the person places their hand over her mouth. Then, whispers in her ear, "Leave, and there will be no trouble. Don't get dressed; get your clothes and go." The stranger shines his flashlight on his gun for Betty to see.

She trembles in fear, quickly grabs her clothes, and hurries down the stairs.

The stranger walks over to the window and watches Betty run away.

She runs out the front door, down the porch, and down the road naked with the clothes in her hand.

The stranger smiles, turning its back to Earl, who is still lying asleep on the bed. The stranger sits down in the chair beside a small table, pulling out a deck of cards and a harmonica from a pocket. Meticulously, the stranger lays down five specific cards: the eight of spades, eight of clubs, four of hearts, the ace of clubs, and the ace of spades. The stranger picks up the harmonica and starts to play a bluesy tune.

Earl softly stirs.

The stranger continues playing the harmonica.

Earl feels around next to him for Betty. He gets up slowly. "Betty, why are you playing music in the middle of the night?"

"Hmm, I am not Betty," the stranger says.

Earl's eyes open wide. "Who the hell are you?"

The stranger shines the flashlight in Earl's eyes to disorient him.

"You know, Earl, there is a line of people who would love to be here where I am. You have done a lot of people wrong. Do you have anything to say?"

"Who the hell are you?"

The stranger laughs and then puts the flashlight under their chin.

"You! No, not you."

The stranger turns the flashlight back to Earl, then cocks the pistol as the light shines on Earl.

Earl raises his hands over his head. "Wait! Wait!

Pow! Pow!

Two shots ring out, piercing Earl's skull. He falls to his death on the bed. Blood oozes over the mattress and to the floor.

The stranger leaves as the smoke billows from the stranger's pistol.

Chapter 28 News

Margaret opens her eyes and looks around. She notices she is in her bedroom. Slowly, she lifts the blanket and notices she is nude. A smile comes over her face. *Last night was wonderful. I think I am in love again. Thomas is a wonderful man.* She hears a noise from the kitchen. Margaret carefully listens as she hears footsteps.

Her bedroom door opens, and Thomas walks in with some fresh coffee. He places it on the bedside table.

She sits up. "How did I get here?"

"I carried you in here after you started dozing off," Thomas says, smiling. He kisses her on her forehead.

Margaret pulls him down to her as she falls back to the bed and kisses him passionately. They slowly break from the kiss. She lifts her blanket back, exposing her naked body, batting her eyes, inviting him under the covers.

Thomas shakes his head, leans to her ear, and whispers. "Will and Henry are here. I am not sure you are ready for that."

Margaret smiles and slowly kisses his neck. "Thomas, you get a bye just because you are decked out for church. But next time, that won't be the case."

Thomas smiles and leans back to sit on the edge of the bed.

Margaret pushes the blanket off her and sits up. Her eyes watch his, surveying her body the entire time. She moves next to him and reaches over to grab her coffee. She enjoys the first sip of her coffee. Then, she closes her eyes in satisfaction.

"Oh my goodness, this is good." She leans back over Thomas and places the coffee on the bedside table.

Thomas' eyes survey every inch of her body.

She smiles as his eyes are fixated on her body. She leans to Thomas's ear. "Thomas, what time is it?"

"It is 6:00 in the morning."

She whispers in his ear. "If you think you could be quiet." Her moist lips kiss his neck gently. "I would suggest locking that door over there." Sending goosebumps over his body. Then she whispers again, "But only if you can be quiet."

Thomas shudders and stands up. He walks quietly to her bedroom door and locks it from the inside. He turns as his lady is waiting for him.

Margaret stirs the eggs in the skillet. She looks over her shoulder at the table. Henry, Will, and Thomas are all looking through the paper. While Henry reads the front page, Will and Thomas are mesmerized as they look through the funny papers.

Will looks at Thomas and shakes his head. "We have to wait till next week?"

Thomas smiles and points to the comics, then looks at Will and nods his head to Margaret. Will looks up and laughs.

Margaret watches. "What are you two laughing at?"

Will chuckles, and Thomas smirks.

"Maw, Tom is saying your hair looks like Brenda Starr's."

Margaret walks over. "Oh, really now." She gives Will and Thomas a disappointing look. Then she looks at the comic strip. "Is it the hair he is pointing at for resemblance, or is it her tempting figure that he was pointing at?" Margaret asks.

"Yuck, Maw," Will says as Thomas laughs. "He was pointing to her hair. It looks like yours."

"I am sure he was."

Henry peers over his paper.

"Now Margaret, I may be a soldier boy, but I have decency. I was referring to her hair as red and very similar to yours."

Margaret smiles as she walks back to the stove. "Sure you were. No eggs for you, Thomas."

Henry lowers his paper and shakes his head. "Not starting out on the right foot, Tom." Henry raises his paper.

She grabs a plate and places the eggs on it. "William, can you get three plates and forks out?"

Thomas watches on with curiosity.

Will puts a plate and fork in front of Henry. One in front of Thomas, and a plate in front of where he was sitting. Will sits back down at the table.

Margaret walks over with a plate full of scrambled eggs and places them in the center of the table. "Here you go. Enjoy." She wipes her hands on her apron and straightens up by the stove.

"Margaret, are you not going to eat?" Thomas asks.

"Oh, I am fine, Thomas. If I want some, I will steal some from one of you in a moment."

Will fills his plate and digs in. Henry follows suit. Thomas looks around and fills his plate. Then he gets up and walks over to Margaret with his plate.

"What are you doing?" Margaret asks.

"I figure the lady that prepares us a meal should eat too," Thomas says as he scoops some eggs on the fork.

Henry nudges Will to look. They both look up and see what Thomas and Margaret are doing. Will looks back at Henry and smiles. Henry winks at Will with a smile.

She shakes her head and smiles as Thomas brings the fork to her mouth. She takes a bite, places a hand over her mouth, and mumbles, "Fine, go sit down."

Thomas moves back to the table and pulls a chair next to his. Margaret grabs a fork and sits next to him, sharing his plate.

Henry, Peggy, Will, Margaret, and Thomas congregate outside the church.

Margaret looks to Will. "It's okay, William, go find Helen."

Henry interlaces his arm with Helen's and walks into the church. Margaret interlaces her arm in Thomas' arm and leans to him to whisper, "Don't worry, I won't let the bad people harm you."

Thomas chuckles as they walk in.

Eyes stare relentlessly at them. Margaret walks in with Thomas, and mouths drop. People whisper and stare as they walk into the sanctuary.

Margaret notices the three rows are empty. She proudly walks to the center row and they all sit down. Margaret greets Joan with a hug.

A commotion starts at the church entrance. Albert, Gerald, Ruth, and Percy rush in and run to the pew where Will sits with his family.

"What is going on?" Will asks.

"Well, I don't know how to say it," Percy says as he looks at Helen.

Everyone on the aisle is watching Percy.

"Um, the Sheriff went out to the Duncan house and found Earl shot dead."

Joan gasps and covers her face with her hands. Helen sits in her seat, unable to move. Margaret gasps. Henry nods smugly. Peggy sits there without a change in expression. Thomas sits there calmly, holding Margaret's hand.

"I, I, I am sorry, Helen," Percy says.

Helen doesn't say a word. Tears stream down Joan's face. Margaret switches places with Thomas and holds Joan. "Joan, I don't know what to say."

Joan sobs with her head on Margaret's shoulder, then slowly lifts her head. "I am sobbing because of all the pain I went through. He can't bring pain to me anymore. I have no more tears for him." She wipes her eyes, takes a deep breath, and lifts her chin. She looks at Helen. "Helen, dear, are you okay?"

Helen grabs Joan's hand. "Maw, I am fine. He can't hurt us anymore." She looks over at Will and then back to her Maw. "If I want a man to trust, I have one; that is Will."

Joan looks at Margaret. "After church, can we all go over to my house just to get our heads around this?"

"I will be there," Margaret replies.

"Your whole family, Margaret."

Margaret nods.

Joan steps out of the house and onto her porch. She looks across the yard. She moves to the steps and sits down on them. She thinks to herself, *He is gone. He is finally gone. We can truly move forward from him now. I don't know if I should do cartwheels or sit in peace finally.* She looks up and sees Margaret and her family coming up the walkway.

Joan smiles. "Will, I think all your friends are out back."

Will darts off to the back of the house.

"How is Helen doing?" Margaret asks.

"She is doing fine. She hated him. She saw him beat me," Joan says.

Henry looks down, walks over, pulls out a cigarette, and offers it to Joan. She looks up at him with a smile. "You know you are the first man ever to offer me a cigarette since I met Earl. Men and people were afraid to talk to me. Thank you, Henry." Joan puts it in her mouth and fumbles for a match. Henry pulls one out and lights her cigarette for her.

She takes a puff and blows some smoke out. "Sometimes you just need a damn cigarette."

Margaret sits down on the steps next to her. Joan offers the cigarette to Margaret. She takes it and puffs, then hands it back. "You know what is crazy, and it shows how silly this town is. I was informed by an innocent young man who always knows the town gossip. I did not hear it from the Sheriff or anyone else." She thinks for a moment. "Maybe it is too soon."

Margaret looks at Joan and chuckles. "You know Percy is always on the edge of the gossip. So it may be just coming out."

"Yeah, but we all know the Sheriff was in Earl's pocketbook. It sounds whacky." Joan sits there pondering. "Then again, the whole thing is crazy. I mean, there was not a shortage of enemies for Earl, that is for sure. The whole town wanted him dead."

"What can I help you with, Joan?" Margaret asks.

Joan looks at her. "How crazy is this? I didn't help you one bit when Joseph passed away, the man you loved, and here you are helping me when that womanizer, wife-beater of a husband dies. Life is truly ironic."

Margaret forces a smile. "I just don't want you going through this alone." She hug Joan tightly. "You got help here, even if it is just listening."

Joan smiles. "Or dancing."

Margaret chuckles.

Joan grabs Margaret's hands. "I am good. Thank you, and yes, we will dance again." Joan pats Margaret's hands. "Let's enjoy the day. It is a new beginning." Joan stands up and pulls Margaret up. Joan looks at Thomas. "Besides, you need to tell me all about Thomas. I am happy for you, Margaret."

Margaret smiles as Joan interlaces her arm and walks around the yard.

Chapter 29 The Talk of the Town

Thomas walks down the street towards Drum's Department Store. People stare at him as he walks past them. He approaches the department store's door and turns, facing the street, leaning against the wall. He observes everyone watching and chatting.

From a distance, he notices Margaret gracefully walking up. She grins as she notices Thomas at the store.

Thomas smiles, and his eyes stay on Margaret the whole time. *Wow, she is beautiful. How did I ever get lucky to fall into this predicament where I have a beautiful woman who likes me?*

"Thomas Stevenson," he hears a male voice saying.

Tom turns around. It is the Sheriff.

"Yes, Sheriff?"

The Sheriff has a writing pad in his hand. "I got a few questions for you, Mr. Stevenson."

Tom looks at him. "I see. Should we go down to the station, or is this the right place?"

"Oh, I think this will do," the Sheriff says. "Where were you last night?"

"Oh, I was at Margaret's place. In fact, you saw me there as we were having a good time," Thomas replied.

Margaret walks up and stands next to Thomas.

"Yes, I saw you there, but after that, where were you?" the Sheriff asks.

Margaret grabs Thomas's arm and replies, "He was with me, Sheriff. We were doing things that couples do. Now, if you want more details than that, that is where I will draw the line and say frankly that is none of your business."

The Sheriff looks at Thomas and then back at Margaret. "So, you were also there all night, Mrs. Wood?"

"I just told you that, Sheriff. I was at my house with Thomas."

"I see. What about Henry and Will?"

"Henry left with Peggy, and Will was with Helen," Margaret replies.

"Okay, that is all I need. You two have a good day." The Sheriff closes his notepad and walks away.

Margaret looks at Thomas. "You don't think Will or Henry did anything, do you?"

"I truly hope not."

Margaret unlocks the door and walks in.

Cling!

She turns to Thomas. "You sure you can handle all this small-town drama?"

Thomas wraps his arms around her. "I don't know. It is tasking, but I will probably get by as long as I have evenings under the stars and a willow tree."

Margaret gives him a peck on the lips. "Somehow, I knew you would say that." She turns and walks to the back of the store. "Oh, Henry and Peggy are getting married at the courthouse this weekend. They are coming to the house afterward." She walks into the sewing room, then pokes her head back out. "Oh, and tonight I have to make a dress for Peggy. You can come by. "Margaret stares at Thomas. "Maybe we can go to Rosie's afterward."

"Rosie's the bar?"

Margaret walks back to Thomas and puts her hand on his chest. She looks him in the eyes and says, "Thomas, listen to me. I put my life on hold for three years and lived in the shadows of my husband. I loved Joseph dearly, but I am moving on. I will not hide my love or affection for you."

Thomas grins and hugs Margaret. They slowly separate. She points to Thomas and says, "Now, Thomas, we need to get one thing straight."

"Yes Ma'am, what is it?"

"Do you work? Do you have money? I am not a gold digger or anything, but I need to know that you have means."

Thomas chuckles. "Yep, we have been going so fast. I haven't had a chance to lay all that out."

Margaret puts her hand on her hip and looks at him thoughtfully. "Are you saying I'm fast?"

"Well, after the other morning, um," Thomas says and rolls his eyes. "I'm just saying—

Margaret punches him in the stomach.

"Ohh." Thomas doubles over.

She stands stoically over him as he stands upright, smiling.

"It was an enjoyable and welcoming fast, not a dirty kind of fast."

Margaret holds her chin high and looks down her nose as she listens. She thinks briefly. "I know, you know, that you are the only man besides Joseph who has ever crawled under the blanket with me."

Thomas grabs her shoulders. "I know Margaret, and I respect you for that."

Her chin lowers a little.

"Can we get back to money?"

She smiles and interlaces her arm in his. "Of course."

"So, you are aware my uncle is the Governor."

"Yes, I am."

"Well, most of my army paycheck went to him, and he invested it for me, so I made a good bit on that. We can live comfortably for awhile. Now, I do have banking experience as well."

"Well, it seems a bank might just be on the market here soon," Margaret says, pointing in the air.

Thomas chuckles. "Yep."

She leans to his chest and whispers, "So I don't have to finance my lover?"

"No, Ma'am."

"Good." She kisses him on the neck and steps away. She turns to Tom. "Thomas, you know I would, though."

He tilts his head. "You would what?"

"If it came to it, I would fend for you."

"Oh, Margaret, I have no doubt. But you will never have to do that. My goal is you only work if you want to."

"And my money from Joseph?"

"That is your money. You do with it as you please."

"That's good because if Henry and Peggy can't get a loan, I will give them money for the house. When Will gets old enough, I will do the same for him. Then I will still have a good bit saved."

"Sounds good. Let's talk about what you are having at the bar tonight?"

Margaret's eyes light up. "Oh, I don't know. Maybe a Zombie, a Sidecar, or a Snow White. Hmm, what do you like?"

"Oh, I prefer an Old Fashion. Sometimes I get a Devil's Tail."

Margaret kisses Thomas. "You know I have to get to work."

"That sounds good. I will walk the town and be back when you close up." Thomas gives her a wink and walks out the door.

Henry steps out of the car in front of Peggy's house. She steps out and looks at Henry with a big smile.

Henry yells, "You ready to get started on that dress?"

"I am, but I was hoping for another bicycle ride."

Henry chuckles and grabs his back. "Not sure the ole body can handle that again."

The Sheriff's car pulls up next to Henry's car.

Peggy's smile turns to a frown. Henry turns and looks at the Sheriff exiting the car. He pulls out a pad of paper and a pen.

"Henry Wood and Peggy, I just need a quick word with you."

"Okay, Sheriff," Henry says.

Peggy stands next to Henry.

"Where were you Saturday night?"

"I was with Peggy at Margaret's house. You saw us there, Sheriff."

"Did y'all leave?"

"We did, and we went to the lake."

"So, Peggy was with you all night?"

"That is true," Peggy replies.

The Sheriff exhales. "Okay."

Henry looks at Peggy, then the Sheriff. "Is that it?"

The Sheriff nods, "I believe so." He turns around and walks back to his car.

"Wow! I expected more, to be honest," Henry says.

Peggy shrugs her shoulders and kisses him on the cheek.

The principal enters the classroom and looks at Helen, Will, and Gerald. "I need you three to come with me."

They look at each other and follow quickly. Walking down the hall, they don't say a word but look at each other to see why.

The principal opens the door to his office, and they see the Sheriff sitting in there. Everyone files into the office.

"Okay, I need to know where you were on Saturday night. I already talked to Albert, Percy, and Ruth."

Gerald rolls his eyes and looks at Will.

"Sheriff," Will says. "We were all hanging out by the barn Saturday night."

"What were you doing there?"

Will looks around. "We snuck a bottle from Henry, and we were all taking drinks and playing around."

"Helen, were you there too?" the Sheriff asks.

"I was, and I was with Will afterward."

"Where was this at?"

Helen looks around bashfully, then looks down, "We snuck into my room at my house. Will and I were there until the morning."

"Your Mom didn't know?" the Sheriff asks.

Helen takes a deep breath. "No, she just knows I made it home, is all."

"What do you mean?"

"Well, I went into the house, passed her bedroom, and told her I was home while Will tiptoed upstairs. She was half asleep but awake enough to wave at me."

"So, she was in the house too?"

"Yep, she came home after hanging out at Will's Maw's place."

"What about you, Gerald?"

"I was there with Will and everybody else. When Will and Helen left, I went with Albert to his house and hung out."

"So, you were with Albert?"

"What did you and Albert do?"

Gerald laughs. "We threw rocks at Percy each time he tried to kiss Ruth."

"Thank you, principal, for your time."

"Peggy, turn to the right, just slightly," Margaret says with a pin in her mouth.

Joan grabs the material. "This is going to be just beautiful."

Henry turns to Thomas. "Let's step out of this office, sit in the store, and let the ladies do their thing."

Thomas agrees to that.

Cling!

The front door opens to the department store, and the Sheriff walks in. "Mr. Stevenson and Mr. Wood. Are the ladies here too?"

Henry nods. "Yep, they sure are."

Margaret and Peggy step out of the back sewing room.

He looks at all of them. "You know, there are a lot of people I have talked to today that might be tied to Mr. Bennett's killing. But the ones who stick out most in my mind are in this room. How convenient that you have a party the night of his death. That each of you has a witness."

Joan steps out of the sewing room as well. "Well, Sheriff, you should be glad of that. It helps you narrow it down. So, why are you here if we have a killer on the loose?"

The Sheriff is caught off guard by her comments.

"I mean, Sheriff, you saw each of us together that night. Just some people having fun talking about how a horrible person Earl was. We were simply living our lives. Now, you have a killer on the loose in this community. Why are you here? Not only that, but you have some gall, Sheriff. You have yet to inform me that my husband, although was soon to be ex, was murdered."

"I guess I don't know. I am sorry." He nods, then walks out the door.

Joan looks at everyone. "Why are we talking about depressing things? Margaret, let's get this lady a dress."

Margaret smiles. "Coming right up."

Henry and Peggy walk into Rosie's. Margaret, Thomas, and Joan follow.

Bruce looks up from the bar. "Hey, come on in."

Henry looks around. No one is gambling in the back. He smiles as he approaches the bar. He grabs a couple of bar stools and turns around. "Ladies."

The women sit down on the barstools with their men behind them.

Bruce looks at the women while he wipes the counter. "So, what can we get you?"

"Oh, I want a Ward Eight, my usual," Peggy says.

"I would like a Snow White," Margaret says.

Joan looks at Margaret. "Now that sounds nice. What is in a Snow White?"

Bruce smiles. "Just some good ole Southern Comfort, a bit of vodka and orange juice."

"I see, but I think I will take a Manhattan," Joan replies.

"A Manhattan it is." Bruce looks at the men. "And for the gentlemen?"

"Oh, I will take a French 75," Henry replies.

"I think I will have a simple Old Fashion."

"Oh, Bruce, no one is playing the jukebox tonight. Would you mind if I pulled out the harmonica later?"

"No, not at all."

Margaret looks at Thomas and Joan and says, "The last time I was in here was with Joseph right before he shipped out."

Joan looks at Margaret. "The last time I was here was about ten years ago. I heard Earl was in here all up on some woman. I marched my butt in here, grabbed her by the hair, and punched her."

Margaret's mouth drops.

"Then I told Earl to come home, and he did. Then he beat me black and blue."

"Oh, I am sorry."

"No, not your problem. I just never came back after that."

Bruce slides the drinks down one by one.

"To the future," Joan says as she lifts her drink. In unison, Peggy and Margaret say, "To the future."

Henry leans to Thomas. "Looks like we are along for the ride and money."

"I would say so. It is good for the ladies to let their hair down, though."

"I would agree."

"Joan," Peggy says, "I was thinking. You will no longer be a dee vorce eey. Instead, you're a widow, and since you're not a remorseful one, it's time for you to find a strapping young man. This is where I found my Henry."

Joan takes a drink and then smiles. "Well, I will keep my eyes open, but if you see one, just point that fellow in my direction."

"Now, Joan, you will be the talk of the town before we know it, "Margaret says. "Oh, and soon, you will have every straggler over at your house. They even tracked me to Drum's."

Three gentlemen walk into Rosie's and head over to a table in the corner.

Peggy elbows Margaret and points to the men. Margaret darts her eyes over and catches Joan's attention. She nods towards them. "Okay, ladies, I will need a few more of these Manhattans in me before I get bold enough to talk to anyone."

Margaret turns to Bruce and pats the bar. "Bruce, we will need another Manhattan here soon."

"Coming right up."

Peggy looks at Joan and says, "Joan, make those men pay for your drinks. There's no need for you to buy them."

Joan laughs. "Oh, you are ruthless."

Thomas looks at Henry. "Are you ready for marriage?"

"I don't know if a man is ever ready for marriage, but I will give it my army best."

"Well, I wish you and Peggy the best in this endeavor."

"Thank you, Thomas. How are you and Margaret getting along?"

"Well, how things have turned out was never my intent when I came here. I was coming in to check on your brother's family. Once I got here, things changed quickly. Henry, I want you to know I greatly respect you, Margaret, and Will. I honestly adore Margaret. I have never met a lady as classy or as strong as her. I would do anything for her," Thomas says. "I hope that makes sense to you."

A tall, dark-haired man with a tan complexion and a whiskey glass walks over to the bar where the ladies are. He looks at Margaret and starts to talk. She stops him and points to Joan.

Peggy and Margaret laugh.

"Hi, my name is John. Could I buy you a drink?"

Joan gives Margaret the evil eye. "Sure, John. My name is Joan. I will take a Manhattan."

Peggy turns to Bruce and yells, "Bruce, Joan needs another Manhattan. John is paying."

"So, John, do you come here often?"

"I do, but I've never seen you here before."

"No." she looks down bashfully. "I suppose not. I came here almost ten years ago."

"I see."

Joan looks at John. "So, what are you drinking, John?"

"Oh, a whiskey sour."

Joan grabs his glass and takes a sip. She looks at John and says, "Not bad. Not bad at all."

Margaret and Peggy watch Joan's every move.

"This is the deal, John. I am feeling good right now and am flattered you came over here. But tonight, I am with the ladies. I will comeback one night this week. I don't know when that is, but it will be one night. If you are here," Joan looks into his eyes and touches his arm, "I will let you buy me another drink. Fair enough?"

John taps his glass to her glass. "To another night." He finishes his drink and slides the empty glass towards Bruce. He then puts some money on the bar and walks away. "I will return shortly, Bruce, for another whiskey sour." He winks at Joan with a grin on his face.

Margaret and Peggy look at Joan, smiling. Joan smirks and then jumps off the stool quickly. "I still got it."

They laugh hysterically.

Chapter 30 The Big Day

Peggy and Henry walk into the bank, holding hands.

Henry looks around for a moment and sees Judith sitting at her desk.

"Hey Judith, who do we see now for a loan?"

Judith smiles. "That would be Mr. Melvin Hitchcock. He is the head manager while the bank is in transition."

"Transition?" Henry asks.

"Yes," Judith puts her hands on her hips. "I know you heard Earl died. From our understanding, the bank transitions to Joan, but they are waiting for everything to be filed properly."

"You mean this doesn't go to Butch?" Henry asks, leaning towards her desk.

"Nope, he only did land dealings with Earl. He never had a stake in the business. So, it will go to Joan."

"So, how is Melvin Hitchcock?"

Judith waves her hand at Henry. "He is a good man. Nothing like Earl."

"Good, can we see him?"

"Sure, just give me a minute," Judith says as she walks away. Suddenly, she stops and turns back to them. "Peggy, congratulations on getting married."

"Oh, thank you."

Judith peeks into Mr. Hitchcock's office for a moment. Then she waves Henry and Peggy over.

Henry walks into the office, with Peggy following. Behind the desk is a short, thin man with white hair. He stands up and adjusts his glasses. "Hi, I am Melvin Hitchcock. And who do we have here today?"

"Mr. Hitchcock—

He waves his hands. "Please just call me Melvin."

"Melvin," Henry says. "I am Henry Wood, and this is my fiancé, soon-to-be wife, Peggy Ward. We are coming here because we would like to buy a home."

Melvin adjusts his glasses. "I see. Where do you work, Henry?"

"I work at Trevor's Construction as a manager."

"Really! That is good."

Judith walks in. "Mr. Hitchcock, here is their file."

Melvin takes the file and looks at Judith. "Thank you, Judith. You are on top of it."

She looks over at Peggy and smiles as she leaves.

Melvin looks through the pages. "So, how much do you think you will need?" He looks up for a moment.

"I think close to $2,000," Henry says.

Melvin nods and looks back down at the paperwork.

Henry nervously looks at Peggy and shrugs his shoulders with an unsure look.

"Well, Henry and Peggy, we like to help people's dreams come true here at the bank. I think we can accommodate your loan." Melvin stands up. "When you are ready, you can come see me personally."

Henry and Peggy maintain their composure, and they both stand up. Henry shakes Melvin's hand. "Thank you, Sir."

"You are welcome, Mr. Wood. I look forward to doing business with your family."

Henry and Peggy step outside his office. With tears in Henry's eyes, he scoops Peggy up and carries her outside the bank.

In a dark black suit, Henry stands next to the Justice of the Peace, Kenneth Hester. Will, in his best Sunday suit, is standing next to Henry.

Peggy stands on the opposite side in a white dress and a lace veil that covers her face slightly. Margaret stands next to her in a light pink dress.

Henry looks into Peggy's eyes while holding her hands as the Justice of the Peace talks. As the JP finishes, Henry says confidently, "I do."

Peggy smiles. As the JP finishes, Peggy says, "I do."

"You may now kiss the bride."

Henry wraps his arms around Peggy, kisses her, and dips her as they kiss.

Margaret claps proudly.

Henry stands Peggy upright, and they break from the kiss, huddled together.

The JP holds his arms up. "I hereby give you Mr. and Mrs. Henry Wood."

Henry and Peggy run down the aisle between the spectators.

Margaret stands on top of the table in the yard by the willow tree. She waves her hands. "Okay, everyone. They will be pulling up shortly. I have bags of rice for us to toss at them." Margaret points to a basket. "Then, it is time to present the Bride and Groom with some gifts." She points to two chairs right in front of the porch steps. "Then it is just a fun night together."

Thomas helps Margaret down from the table. Everyone runs to the basket.

The car pulls up, and Henry quickly exits. He waves at everyone, then runs over and opens the door for Peggy. He scoops her up and carries her between two tables.

"Now!" Joan yells as she throws the rice at them.

Everyone follows suit.

Henry continues to carry Peggy up to the chairs. He sits her in her chair, turns around, and thrusts his fists in the air. "YES!"

Everyone claps.

Will walks forward and presents Henry with a pocket-knife and Peggy with a casserole dish.

"Wow, Will, you didn't have to do this," Peggy exclaims.

"Welcome to the family," Will says, smiling.

Joan and Helen walk up carrying a box. They hand the box to Peggy. "Here are some dishes for your home."

Peggy stands up. "Thank you, Joan and Helen."

"The Drums walk up and give Henry and Peggy an envelope. Robert says, "There is money in there which every new couple could use and a gift certificate to our store."

Peggy holds Henry's hand. "Thank you very much."

Margaret and Thomas present Henry and Peggy with an envelope and a bottle of Cognac. Margaret looks at Henry and Peggy and says, "The money is to help with your house." Thomas smiles. "And the Cognac is for later tonight."

Henry stands up and gives Thomas a big hug. "Now, after the honeymoon, I promise to ditch the bottle. Got to clean my act up since I am married."

"Really?" Margaret asks.

"Yes, "Ma'am," Henry says. "Oh, on special occasions, you know."

As Margaret and Thomas step away, he reaches into his pocket and says, "My dear wife Peggy had only one request as we got married. That is for me to play ♪Danny Boy♪ on the harmonica with Margaret singing. Now, I didn't ask Margaret, but I figure on my wedding day, she would surely accommodate."

He pulls out his harmonica and blows through it. He look sat Peggy, and she stands up. She walks behind Henry, leans her head on his back, and wraps her arms around his waist. Henry smiles, then brings the mouth organ to his mouth and blows through it, and the beautiful sounds pass out of the Mississippi Saxophone.

Margaret grabs Thomas's hand as her angelic voice resonates with the lovely words.

Lucy and Robert stand up and slowly sway as they dance to the song.

Percy and Ruth dance together in the back as Helen and Will dance together. Joan watches, smiling.

Gerald and Albert sneak to the back of Henry's car and tie empty cans to it.

Henry slowly finishes the tune. Margaret turns and claps.

Peggy moves in front of Henry. "Thank you all for coming, but Henry and I will be hitting the road for a few days. I am sure Margaret will be happy to keep entertaining everyone, but we are taking a trip."

Henry scoops Peggy up and walks back to the car. He places her in the car, then runs to the driver's seat, cranks it up, and pulls away with the cans rattling down the road.

Chapter 31 Bad News

Thomas and Margaret sit in the swing as the last guest leaves. Margaret's head is resting against Thomas' chest, and he twirls Margaret's hair.

"You know, Thomas, in the last few days, we haven't had a chance to have some you-and-me time lately."

"Oh, that is okay, Margaret. I figure spending the rest of my life with you will give me all that in due time."

Margaret turns around and kisses him passionately. Thomas squeezes her tightly as they kiss. Margaret breaks from the kiss. She smiles. "Good, I just want to make sure we think alike. You want me to get a blanket? You seem to like what's underneath the blanket."

Thomas smirks. "I do, and I will not turn it down. When do you expect Will to return?"

Margaret looks at Thomas. "To be honest, I think he will be home before midnight."

"Let's get a pillow, lay under the willow, and do some stargazing."

"Last time, we didn't get much gazing in," Margaret replies.

"No, no we didn't. But there is always hope," Thomas says.

Margaret stands up and pulls Thomas to his feet. She walks to the door, and Thomas slaps her on the rump.

"Ouch!" Margaret yells, then turns smiling.

Thomas grabs her by the waist, lifting her off her feet as she giggles. "We won't make it to the willow tree if you keep this up," Margaret declares.

"Is that a bad thing?"

"No, I don't think so."

Margaret walks into the bedroom, grabs two blankets, and hands them to Thomas. "Go lay the blanket down for us." He heads outside.

As he walks out, she quickly removes her unmentionables and adjusts her dress. She smiles as she grabs two pillows and walks outside.

Margaret hands him the pillows. He sets them out and pulls the blanket back. Margaret crawls underneath it, and Thomas crawls under the blanket with her.

They look straight up. "I look up at the stars and think how peaceful it is. There is not much going on, just us and the stars. Our eyes are on them, and we are just here, peaceful. Nothing seems to matter."

Margaret snuggles close to him. She slowly unbuttons his shirt's buttons, then tenderly kisses his chest. Thomas rolls over on top of her and rubs his hands along the side of her ribs. He stops.

"Are you missing something," he asks.

Margaret laughs. "Oh yeah, I was just curious how long it would take you to find out." She rolls her eyes, "I know we have your whole life and all, but I figure I would make it easier."

"You are the best, Margaret."

Percy runs up on the porch and knocks on the door.

Knock! Knock! Knock!

Margaret looks at Thomas. "What time is it?"

Thomas looks at his watch. "It is six in the morning."

"Who could be at the door this early?" Margaret asks as she gets up.

"Let me get it, Margaret," Thomas says as he puts his pants on.

Margaret slides into a house dress.

Thomas walks out and opens the front door. He squints his eyes. "Percy, is that you?"

"Yes, Sir. My Maw said I needed to come over and deliver a message. She said it was urgent. I ran faster than I ever ran before. I thought my heart would pop out of my chest. I was panting hard. Not as much as when Ruth and I were kissing and such, but almost—

"Percy!" Margaret shouts. "Get to the point."

"I am sorry, Mrs. Wood, but Mr. Drum passed away late last night."

Margaret drops to her knees. "Oh my, Percy. Oh my."

Thomas looks at Percy. "Thank you, Percy. Tell your Maw we appreciate it."

"I will, Mr. Stevenson."

Margaret's hands rest on her cheeks in disbelief. "He, he had cancer and knew his time was short but wasn't sure how much time he had left."

"Margaret, can I get you anything?"

"No, I am good."

Thomas helps her to her feet.

"When no one in this town cared, he was there for us. He was a good man. We have to go and make sure Lucy is alright."

Margaret, in a black pencil dress, stands on the porch of the Drums' house with Thomas in his blue suit and Will in grey slacks and a white shirt. She is holding a casserole.

Will knocks on the door.

Knock! Knock! Knock!

Lucy opens the front door, and she nods as she looks at Margaret. Margaret hands the casserole to Will and then hugs Lucy.

"I am sorry, Lucy."

Lucy sniffles as they embrace. As they separate, she says, "You know Margaret, he thought of you as his daughter. He adored you."

Margaret nods, fighting back the tears. "I want you to know, Lucy. If there is anything you need, we are here for you. Oh, I brought you a casserole."

Will hands the dish to Lucy. "Thank you, Will."

"Mrs. Drum, I am so sorry for your loss. Your husband seemed like a great man."

Lucy squinches her lips together. "Thank you, Thomas."

Margaret looks at Lucy. "I will keep the store closed next week if that is what you want."

Lucy sniffles. "Oh, heaven's no. Robert laid everything out that he wanted done when he passed away. He wants the store to remain open except on the day of the funeral. He told me to make you the manager and let you run it." Lucy chuckles. "His exact words, she runs it anyway."

Margaret suppresses a smile.

"But we can talk about that later," Lucy says, placing her hand on her chest. "It means the world to me, that you all came by."

Margaret nods, steps back, and Lucy walks back into the house.

"Hey, I'm going into the store to check things out. I'll have to open it up tomorrow, and I just want to make sure everything is straight."

"You want me to stop by later, Margaret?"

"Yeah, that will be fine. I need an hour alone."

"Okay, Will and I will stop by the diner and get a shake. I will meet you there, afterwards."

Margaret walks towards the department store. *Oh my goodness, Mr. Drum always tried to protect me and the family when others wouldn't. I cannot believe we just laid him to rest today. Lucy is a strongwoman. This last year has been rough, with a lot of tragedy thrown in.* She stops in front of the department store.

Margaret pulls the keys out and opens the door.

Cling!

She grins as she walks in and hears the door chime. She looks around, then walks to the office and just peers in. *He would be sitting there working through paperwork.* Margaret takes a deep breath and walks over to the sewing room.

"Well, if I am going to be the manager, I better straighten this room up," Margaret says out loud as she walks behind the sewing machine. On the sewing machine table lies a note attached to an envelope. She looks at the note and reads it.

Margaret,

Robert wanted you to have this letter.

Love Lucy.

Margaret opens the envelope and pulls out a letter. She unfolds it slowly and then reads it.

Dear Margaret,

I know this letter will seem odd, but please bear with me. I tossed and turned about this for a long time.

When Joseph went to war. I found out he was in the 4th Division. I, too, was in the 4th in the Great War. I sent him a note, promising that I, a fellow Ivy Division soldier, would do everything in my power to look after you until he came home.

Well, as we know, he didn't come home. Then another 4th Division soldier came into your life, Thomas. We had a conversation that you may not know about, and it was simply about how 4th soldiers look out for each other.

My cancer has been unforgiving, and it would take me away from my promise of looking after you. So, I figured I would do the next best thing. That was to take the problem in your life out of the equation. I just wasn't sure how. But as everyone knows, Earl is dead. I found a way to ensure that. So, if *anyone comes around accusing people who did it. Just pull out this letter from me.*

I hope you and Thomas find a happy life together. May it be a peaceful one.

All my love,

RD The Widow's Savior

Margaret gasps. "Oh, my goodness. He took care of me. He looked after me."

Cling!

Margaret tries to catch her breath as tears flow down her cheeks.

"Are you okay, Margaret?"

She looks across the sewing machine to Thomas and hands the letter to him. He walks over and reads it slowly.

Suddenly, he gasps, "Wow!" Thomas looks at Margaret. "I agree he was truly A Widow's Savior."

"Thomas dear. We can't tell anyone this."

"I agree, but Margaret, this needs to be some place secure."

She points to Thomas. "I have an idea. Follow me."

Thomas and Margaret walk into the bank together and stop at Judith's desk.

"Can I help you, Margaret?"

"Yes, we need access to my safety deposit box."

"Okay, not a problem. Do you have your key?"

"I do," Margaret replies.

"Follow me," Judith says as she pulls her ring of keys with her. "Which box is it?"

"Box 74," Margaret says.

Judith leads them to the vault, and they walk in. She walks over to box 74, opens the door, and removes the box. Judith places it on the table. "You have your key, right?"

Margaret shows her key 74.

"Good. I will be outside the vault. Take your time. When you're done, come get me, and I will secure it."

"Sounds good."

Judith steps out.

Margaret opens the box and pulls the letter out of her purse. She looks at Thomas. Margaret nods, and he returns the nod. She places the letter in the safety deposit box. She then closes the lid and locks the box. Margaret and Thomas walk out of the safe and look at Judith. "We are done, Judith."

"Okay, I will secure it," Judith says as they leave the bank.

Chapter 32 New Beginnings

Margaret and Joan look at each other and smile.

"Time to set things right," Margaret says as she flashes a folder.

Joan smiles at her.

They walk into the church and head to the Pastor's office.

Joan knocks on the door.

"Come in," Pastor Phillips says as he stands up from behind his desk.

Joan walks in, and Margaret follows. "Yes, Pastor, you called this meeting."

"Please have a seat," the Pastor says, pointing to the two chairs across from his desk.

Joan sits down with her stoic eyes on the Pastor. Margaret sits down gracefully.

"It seems we may have crossed each other and are off on the wrong foot," Pastor Phillips suggests.

Margaret tightens her lips and nods.

Joan raises a finger. "Pastor, before we begin, let's get something out of the way first."

Pastor Phillips nods hesitantly. "Sure."

"You see, Pastor Phillips, this church has 230 members. We have a letter signed by 225 members asking for your dismal," Joan says and points to Margaret.

Margaret pulls a couple of pages from the folder, stands up, and places them on the desk.

Pastor Phillips is speechless. He rests his head on one hand and shuffles through the pages.

"Oh, Pastor Phillips, that is not all. We also have the signatures of another 150 people from this town who would be glad to be members of our church, with one stipulation. You are not the Pastor anymore."

Margaret gracefully places those pages on his desk.

"Now, with all that said, Pastor. The true matter at hand." Joan points to Margaret.

Margaret places a single page before him on the desk and hands him a pen.

"Your resignation is effective immediately," Joan says. "Let's not make a spectacle out of this, Clyde. Margaret and I are all about this community growing. For that to happen, you are not in the equation."

Pastor Phillips looks up at Margaret.

Margaret's green eyes burn with intensity. "Clyde Phillips, I lost my husband, and you made it a point to not even consider Henry's grief. I would suggest finding another occupation."

Clyde Phillips takes a deep breath and looks back at the paper. He quickly scribbles his name on it. Margaret snatches it up, turns to Joan, and grins.

"Clyde you can leave the keys to the church at Lucy Drum's house. You know the grieving widow you never visited," Joan declares as she stands up.

Margaret puts the resignation letter in her purse and walks out the door with Joan. They walk down the halls of the church as if they own the place. Joan looks at Margaret and says, "You know, we have three widows in this town from this last year who are cleaning this town up slowly."

Margaret lifts her finger. "Awe but we have one more."

Joan chuckles. "Yes we do."

Henry pulls on his suspenders as he looks at Peggy. "You ready?"

"I am my handsome husband."

Henry looks at Margaret and Thomas. "Y'all ready?"

"I think we are," Thomas says as Margaret smiles back at him.

"Henry, you got this," Lucy yells amongst a large crowd. "Go do it, Henry."

"Good, this will be a good show," Henry says. He turns to Will. "Will, Albert, Percy, Helen, and Gerald y'all ready?"

They all nod yes.

"Thomas, is your cavalry ready?" Henry asks.

"Oh yes, this is going to be good," Thomas says.

"Good, let's do it." Henry turns and pushes the door open to the Sheriff's office. Everyone follows behind him. "What is everyone doing here? What do you y'all want?" The Sheriff asks as he rises from behind his desk and walks closer to the center of the room.

Henry smiles as he walks close to the Sheriff. "It's a funny thing, Sheriff. You seem to have the whole world in your hands," Henry says as he watches the Sheriff.

The Sheriff looks around as everyone circles him in a safe distance except for Henry.

"I am not sure what you are saying, Henry."

Henry nods and reaches into his pocket. He pulls out his harmonica and then walks around the Sheriff's desk. Sheriff Welch, a bit intimidated, doesn't do anything. Henry sits in the Sheriff's chair and blows into his harmonica to clear it. Then he looks at the Sheriff.

Henry reaches into his left sleeve and pulls out a playing card. "You know what this is, Sheriff?"

"Looks like a playing card to me."

Henry holds the card, standing it on the desk by the corner of the card while he holds the other corner with his finger. He smiles and looks up at the Sheriff. "This is the ace of spades." Henry shows it to the Sheriff. "You know we would give the ace of spades to the enemy after we conquered them. You can go ahead and take it."

The Sheriff doesn't move and squints his eyes.

Henry laughs at him, saying, "I'll just leave it here for you so you know you have been conquered."

Henry leans back in the chair.

"So, I hear that you are running for re-election, Sheriff. The election will be held in four weeks, Sheriff. Is that correct?"

With a confused look, the Sheriff replies, "That's true."

"I also heard that today is the last day for anyone to enter the race and that you are running unopposed as of this morning. Is that correct?"

The Sheriff looks around for a second, trying to piece this puzzle together. "Yes, that is true."

Henry smiles. "Well, Sheriff. I am here to let you know that you have an opponent as of 9:00 am this morning."

The Sheriff is a bit surprised. "Who is that?"

Henry pulls out his cigarettes. He strikes a match from the bottom of his shoe and lights the cigarette. Slowly, he takes a puff and then blows out the smoke. "Well, that would be me, Sheriff. I figured I would try out my desk today since today is not only the last day to enter the race but also the last day for you to withdraw from the race."

"Why would I withdraw from the race?"

"Oh, something tells me that won't be a choice you get to make, Milton," Henry says. "It's about to be done for you."

Henry turns his head to Will. "Will, go open the door."

"Yes, Sir," Will says and walks to the door of the Sheriff's office. Judith and Don Ross walk in. Joan and Helen Bennett, Bruce, and Lucy Drum follow.

"I think you know everyone here, Sheriff," Henry says. "So, to start with. We have witnesses that saw you take a paid bribe from Earl Bennett to keep Don Ross in jail while Earl kept Judith distracted to sneak their house from underneath them."

"You have no proof," the Sheriff says.

"We have four witnesses to you accepting money during that conversation right outside the Duncan house. It seems you didn't check your surroundings. Not only that, but Judith was also smart enough to pull the written calendar that Earl was using to mark down the days for this to happen. I mean, you kept Don in jail for weeks."

"Could have been a debt he owed me," The Sheriff says.

Judith steps forward in anger but Don grabs her.

"That's okay. We have two other witnesses of you accepting bribes from Earl Bennett."

"Who is that?" the Sheriff asks.

"Helen and Joan both have witnessed you being paid by Earl," Henry says.

Milton looks around at everyone. "This is bullshit, everyone in here is a murder suspect to Earl Bennett, and you are just trying to cover it up."

Henry snubs out his cigarette in the ashtray on the desk and stands up. He walks over to the Sheriff. "Then there is little matter that lacked all human decency. The attempted rape on Margaret Wood, and you swept it under the carpet." Henry leans close to Milton. Henry waves his hands as he talks. "You know that was the one that did it. I knew right then I would take you down."

Henry looks at the three widows. "Three widows asked me how we clean this town up. This was after Earl's murder, but that was definitely a key domino falling. But after that, two people needed to be removed from power. The first of the two fell this morning. Is that right, Lucy?"

"It is. I got the keys to the church and the resignation letter before coming here," Lucy says proudly.

Milton looks at everyone awkwardly. "You think I am resigning? You are fools."

Henry walks back to the desk. "No, Milton. After the deal with Margaret, resigning was out of the question." Henry sits down.

"Thomas, do your magic," Henry commands.

"Most definitely," Thomas says.

Margaret's chin lifts proudly. Joan nods with pride. Lucy smiles.

Thomas walks to the front door and opens it. "Fellas, I believe who you are looking for is in here."

Two Texas Rangers walk directly to Milton.

Thomas waves everyone else in. The towns people flood into the Sheriff's office.

One Ranger looks at Milton while the other walks behind him. The Ranger facing Milton says, "You are under arrest by the State of Texas."

The second Ranger secures his hands behind his back and cuffs him.

Peggy runs over to Henry and hugs him. Margaret, Thomas, Joan, and Lucy all move over to Henry.

Margaret says, "Not bad for three widows."

"Nope," Joan says, "It sure isn't."

"We took back our town, "Lucy says. "Just like Robert would have wanted."

The End!

Also by

Rick & Katja Series

The Birth of a Spy Couple, Rick & Katja Book 1, award-winning
book
33 or 9, Rick & Katja Book 2, a multiple award-winning book
Betrayal from Within, Rick & Katja Book 3, a multiple
award-winning book

Other Works

The Story of Briar, Coming of Age in Rural East Texas, the
multiple award-winning book
Trash Can Terry, a multiple award-winning book

About the author

Ian Griffin is a multiple award-winning author who served in the United States Army for 31 years and was stationed in Germany for nine years, which gave him a perspective of living in Europe. His time in the military, woven with his upbringing in East Texas, has given him unique experiences and observations. He has been able to manifest these experiences into spinning a yarn. Ian relishes writing about the complexities of life.

Webpage: iangriffinbooks.com

Facebook: @iangriffinbooks

Instagram: iangriffinbooks

Tik Tok: ian_griffin_books

YouTube: @iangriffinbooks

email: contact@iangriffinbooks.com or iangriffinbooks@gmail.com

Milton Keynes UK
Ingram Content Group UK Ltd.
UKHW010822131024
449535UK00017B/734